Four exceptional authors, four enticing stories. Wrap yourself up in the heat of the best in erotic romance from Changeling Press.

Angela Knight -- Blood Service
Ann Jacobs -- Branded
Dakota Cassidy -- Slave School Dropout
Kate Hill -- Tainted Kisses

The hunter and the hunted... **Best selling author Angela Knight brings you vampire bounty hunters that sizzle.**

Adiva Mayhew is a spy -- and a damn good one. But now she's running for her life from a deadly bounty hunter -- who's also a Vampire. General Borian Tang has offered a high reward for her capture, and the man known only as Vigilante apparently means to collect. When Vigilante catches up to her, she soon finds all he wants to do is take her -- over and over again. And as she yields to his seductive domination, Adiva finds she wouldn't have it any other way. Trouble is, Tang is still determined to capture her, and there are other bounty hunters eager to claim the reward...

A distant planet, a man on a path of discovery and a tortured woman. **Author Ann Jacobs explores sexual healing.**

Cole Callender -- an entrepreneur with an eye to the future. Branded a sexual deviant under Earth laws, Cole adopts Obsidion as his future. Here he will build more than just a safe haven for Doms and subs practicing BDSM -- Cole thinks in terms of community, and the future of Obsidion as a world.

Amber -- a sub with a death wish. She's barely escaped a cruel Dom with her life. The scars she's left with, both inside and out, may be permanent. Now she wants nothing more than to be Cole's loving slave. Cole sees beyond her scars, but is his love enough to help Amber learn to live again?

***Two shapeshifting cats* -- one kinky cupboard equals author Dakota Cassidy's humorous slant on BDSM.**

Nyla is a cat. So is Lucas. Nyla is an Egyptian Mau, descendant of the Goddess Bast. Lucas… isn't. In fact, he's a Tom cat. Unlikely lifemates at best.

Lucas is also a sexual Dominant who enjoys just a smidge of rocky road with his bedroom pleasures. But Nyla's never considered herself submissive. No one is the boss of her. Oh, and it never hurts to mention that Nyla's family is a snobbish, upper crust bunch of shifters who will probably want nothing more than to see to it that Lucas and Nyla's newly acquired lifemate status is revoked by the lifemate council!

***A primeval vampire,* a woman intent in saving her village at all costs and a bargain. Author Kate Hill journeys into the ultimate surrender.**

Dancing with the devil…

Pure Evil. Stolen from his mother's womb by the very creature responsible for her death, Etlu was raised to destroy without mercy and sate his lust like an animal. Yet, peering through villagers' windows in the dark of night, he sees men and women sharing unfamiliar pleasures and longs to understand…

Meets pure good. Niabi uses her powers in defense of the weak. When Etlu's army of Viking warriors devastates a village she's sworn to protect, Niabi's only choice is to strike a bargain with Etlu – the humans' lives in exchange for her complete surrender to his desires.

Can she find anything in him worth saving?

www.ChangelingPress.com

All Wrapped Up

Angela Knight, Blood Service
Ann Jacobs, Branded
Dakota Cassidy, Slave School Dropout
Kate Hill, Tainted Kisses

ISBN (10) 1-59596-284-0
ISBN (13) 978-1-59596-284-3

Publisher:
Changeling Press LLC
PO Box 1561
Shepherdstown, WV 25443-1561
www.ChangelingPress.com

Printed in the U.S.A.
Lightning Source, Inc.
1246 Heil Quaker Blvd
La Vergne TN 37086
www.lightningsource.com

Anthology Editors: Margaret Riley, Sheri Ross Fogarty
Cover Artist: Bryan Keller

All Wrapped Up: Blood Service
Angela Knight

Chapter One

Close. She was so damn close. Eyes burning, Adiva stared at the airlock, willing it to open. She was fifth in line to board the warpship, and her heart was pounding. If only she had five more minutes, she'd be in the clear. Beyond the bounty hunter's reach.

The Vigilante himself had come to Adorev to collect the reward of two million credits General Borian Tang had put on Adiva's head. If she didn't get offworld before he found her, she was finished.

The Vigilante. If he had another name, she'd been unable to find it. The legendary bounty hunter specialized in capturing the most wanted criminals in human stellar territory. He went wherever his prey was, kidnapped them, and brought them back to whoever offered the bounty. Not always in one piece, either. There were very ugly stories of what he'd done to captives who pissed him off.

It was so fucking unfair. Adiva was nothing like his usual prey -- rapists, pedophiles, and murderers of every stripe. She was on the side of the angels. The rebel Alliance had been locked in battle with Tang and his gang of thugs for the past five years, and they were winning. In a few more months at most, Tang's government would collapse and the people of Adorev would finally be free.

She regretted nothing she'd done. It was infuriating to find herself somehow classed with the kind of psychopath Vigilante normally hunted. What the hell was his problem, anyway? Tang deserved to be overthrown -- the man was psychotic, a racist megalomaniac who had terrorized his people for decades, murdering thousands because he didn't find their bloodlines acceptable. That was why she and Jorge had come to Adorev to begin with. It had never been about a mercenary's paycheck to either of them. Otherwise she wouldn't have stayed and fought on after Jorge's death.

With a huff of impatience, Adiva swung her duffle onto the opposite shoulder and shifted from foot to foot. "Hurry it up, damn it," she murmured under her breath. "I feel like I've got a great big target printed on my back." If the Vigilante caught up to her, she was dead. Even if he didn't kill her, Tang would. Probably after days of torture.

She'd fight to the death to avoid a trip to Tang's Red Palace. Unfortunately, she doubted the battle would do her much good. Despite her well-developed combat skills, she was no match for a vampire. Particularly one with Vigilante's reputation.

If the bounty hunter caught her, Adiva figured her only chance was to goad him into killing her quickly. Better that than entertaining Tang's torturers. Her will was strong, but everyone had a breaking point. And Adiva was damned if she'd betray the Allies.

The hair rose on the back of her neck. For a moment she thought it was merely her imagination reacting to the memory of the Vigilante's dossier. Then finely honed instincts began to hum so insistently, she threw a quick glance over her shoulder. Her heart stopped beating for one long, endless instant.

A tall, broad-shouldered man stood a bare twenty meters away, his hair a dark gold under the harsh spaceport lights, his vivid green eyes stabbing into hers. She knew that face. She'd spent the morning staring at his dossier as her stomach twisted itself in knots.

It was him. The Vigilante.

Adiva didn't think twice. She threw aside her heavy duffle and ran. Ducking around the ship's massive gray bulk, she sprinted for the nearest corridor, pouring on the speed. If she didn't get away from him now, he'd run her down like a rabbit.

A deep voice shouted, "Adiva Mayhew! Stop!" Boots rang on the deck as he pounded after her.

Spotting a branching corridor off to the left, Adiva shot down it, then took another, then a third, choosing turns at random. Fear filled her mouth with a bitter, metallic taste.

The ring of boot steps grew louder.

Her heart lunged in her chest so hard it literally hurt, but Adiva ignored both the pain and the cold bloom of fear. She had to keep moving, keep thinking. Keep fighting. She rounded a corner and shot down a darkened corridor… And skidded to a halt, sick with terror and despair. In front of her loomed a blank wall.

Dead end.

Frantic, Adiva spun. The vampire stood ten meters away, watching her, his expression dispassionate. Sucking in a breath, she looked for another door, another corridor, a way out.

Nothing. There was nothing there but him.

As all the blood drained from her face, her gaze returned helplessly to his. The Vigilante was almost two meters tall, as broad-shouldered and brawny as any genetically engineered Space Marine. The gleaming black battlesuit he wore emphasized every ridge and hollow. She bit back a moan of fear, imagining how strong he must be, with all that sheer muscle amplified by a vampire's powers.

Under other circumstances, Adiva might have found him handsome. There was a sculpted beauty to his face, with its knife-blade cheekbones and square jaw. His nose was narrow, widening to flared nostrils that gave him a wolfish expression, an effect enhanced when he inhaled as if trying to catch her scent. There was a certain cruel sensuality about his mouth, even held in that tight, grim line. His thick blond hair gleamed like a coin in the muted light.

"You played this well, at least until now." Vigilante's voice was deep, almost hypnotic, with a note of sensuality in its rumble. "You almost lost me completely in Charon."

Adiva had boarded a shuttle in that flea speck of a town this morning and flown up to the orbital space port here, intent on catching the first outbound ship she could find. She'd hated to leave the fight on Adorev, but she had no choice. Allied Command agreed -- she knew too much they didn't want Tang's torturers to discover.

"Unfortunately, 'almost' losing you isn't good enough," Adiva said bitterly, falling into a crouch. She bared her teeth at him. "But I'm still not going to let you hand me over to the Red Palace."

"Do you seriously think you can stop me?" He stalked toward her, his gaze unblinking, his big body gliding like oil over glass. "*If* that's what I decide to do."

For just a moment, Adiva felt the warm breath of hope before common sense kicked in. "You saying I could buy you off? Offer you money, or maybe just pussy?" She curled a contemptuous lip. "Don't try to play me. I've seen your dossier. You don't bribe."

"I don't lie either." He was only three meters away now. Much, much too close.

Adiva backed away, eyes flicking as she scanned for an escape route. "Let me guess -- this is where I offer you anything and let you fuck me, after which you take me in anyway. Sorry, I'm not that big an…"

With a low growl, he lunged for her.

She blocked a grab from one of his big hands with a thrust of her palm. Pivoting, Adiva drove a punch at his face, but he ducked aside, grabbed her wrist, and whirled her around. A brawny arm snapped across her waist like a trap springing closed. She drove an elbow back into the vampire's muscled gut, but he didn't even flinch as he pinned her against his rock hard body. "Now, you'll…"

She didn't let him get the rest out of his mouth. Desperate and terrified, Adiva went wild, punching, kicking, clawing any part of him she could reach. Her nails drew blood from his wrist as her booted heels drummed his shins.

"That's enough, vixen." He caught one flailing wrist with that infuriating vampire strength and twisted, cranking her double. The hot pain ripped a gasp from her mouth. Before she could even think about trying to wrench away, he smoothly shifted his grip.

Suddenly Adiva was unable to move at all. Frantic, she wrenched, trying to pull free, but she was caught fast, one arm twisted behind her, the other dragged up into a half nelson over his arm, held in place by the fist he had buried in her hair. She flung her weight forward, fighting to throw him...

Vigilante turned and smashed her into the bulkhead so hard she saw stars. For a minute she couldn't even breathe. The vampire used the opportunity to pin her between the unyielding steel and his equally unyielding body.

"As I was saying, we have two alternatives." He didn't even sound winded, the bastard -- just icily pissed off. Shifting his grip, he caught her beneath the chin, wrapping his long, blunt fingers around her jaw. "I can put you in restraints and cart you off to the Red Palace, where they'll no doubt torture you for every scrap of information you ever had. Or..."

Involuntary tears stung her eyes, and she blinked them fiercely away. She had to make him lose his temper and kill her. "Quit playing with me, you son of a bitch. How does it feel, playing hunting hound for a psycho like Tang?" She tried to kick back at him again, but he had her pinned too well. All she could do was curse him in every language she knew.

Fingers tightened around her jaw with such force, she broke off, gasping. "That's no way to talk to a man who's about to offer you a deal."

Another sickly burst of hope. It was probably a trick, but... "What kind of deal?"

"I've decided to acquire a bloodthrall." He rolled his hips against her backside in a slow, suggestive grind. "I'm considering you for the position."

"And right after I fuck you, you'll deliver me to the Red Palace."

"Only if you disappoint me."

She fell silent, breathing hard. Despite her common sense, that flicker of hope strengthened, mixed with calculation. "What exactly are you proposing?"

"It strikes me that it would be a waste to hand a high-level bloodthrall over to an ignorant thug like Tang." The vampire lowered his head next to her ear. His breath felt seductively warm. "On the other hand, I could always use two million credits. Convince me to keep you."

Adiva swallowed. Before coming to this world with Jorge, she'd undergone the surgical procedure that had made her a "bloodthrall" -- a perfect donor for her new vampire partner. Vamps coveted relationships with willing bloodthralls, preferring them over drinking synthetic blood. Still… "You'd violate a contract with General Tang?"

"I have no contract with Tang. He put a bounty out on you, but I don't have to collect it. If, that is, you prove sufficiently convincing."

"What guarantee do I have that you won't turn me in anyway?"

"None, of course." His tone was blandly matter-of-fact. "May I remind you, I don't have to give you any guarantees, Adiva. You're the one who has to convince me."

She licked her dry lips. "How do you propose I do that?"

A long silence ticked by as he let her sweat. "According to your dossier, you're a seventeenth level submissive. Quite high, and relatively rare. I'm a twenty-first level dominant. That means I've got a nasty streak I rarely have the opportunity to indulge -- sexually, at least."

"Meaning that those you pursue are fair game for whatever sadism you care to practice." And he cared to practice quite a bit, according to his file.

She felt him shrug against her. "Given that my typical prey runs toward pedophiles and serial murderers, I don't lose much sleep over what I do to them."

"Yeah, well, I'm neither of those things. So why the fuck are you tormenting me?"

"Darling, you managed to piss the wrong people off during a war. What did you expect?"

"Tang is psychotic! The Adorevians have a right to overthrow…" She broke off, reining in her outrage and reaching for calm. "Never mind. Spell it out for me, Vigilante, or whatever the hell you call yourself. How do I 'convince' you?"

His smile was slow and dark. "Why, by submitting, darling."

"To what?"

"Isn't it obvious? Whatever I want."

She swallowed, all too aware of him -- his hard, hot body crowding her much smaller one. He was just so damn big. So damn male. With every breath, her senses filled with his scent, masculine and dark and more than a little wild. "So what *do* you want?"

The Vigilante laughed softly. "That's the question, isn't it?" He leaned into her. She realized that the thick ridge pressing against her ass was an impressive erection. "Choose, Adiva. Convince me. Or don't."

She licked her dry lips, intrigued despite herself by that promising cock. Jorge had not been a small man by any means, but Vigilante felt massive. How would he feel thrusting hard into her cunt, stretching her, tormenting her? She'd dreamed of a lover like that. And she didn't want to die without experiencing one.

"I think you'll find me very convincing…" Adiva had to swallow before she could give him the title she knew he'd demand. "… Master."

He laughed. The sound was rich with satisfaction and triumph. "Then why don't we get started?" He released her throat and found the seal on her jacket. "Let's see what you have to offer."

"Here?" she protested instinctively. "But anybody could come along!"

"And you assume that matters to me?" His tone was coolly pleasant, but she heard the steel beneath.

Adiva swallowed. "No, I imagine you'd strip me naked in front of half the station if it suited you."

He laughed softly. "You assume right. In fact..."

Breath caught, she looked down as he started sliding open the seal of her armored jacket, baring the mounds of her cleavage.

"Very promising." Big hands caught the edges of her jacket and jerked. Her breasts sprang free, naked and pale in the dim light, their tips a blushing pink. And tightly erect. Adiva wasn't surprised. She could already feel herself starting to cream.

"Mmm," he rumbled. "I was right -- you *were* hiding a bloodthrall's tits beneath all that leather. Very pretty."

His big, long-fingered hands closed over the full globes to gently pluck both taut nipples. The hot bloom of pleasure made her close her eyes and swallow.

"Sensitive?" the vampire purred.

"Yeah." She tried to moderate her rough breathing.

"Good." He tugged both tips, twisting them until she gasped at the hot pleasure. "I look forward to putting them in clamps. Just until the circulation starts to go. Then I'll take them off." He leaned down and traced his tongue over her earlobe in a wet, seductive swirl. "When the blood comes rushing back, that's when I like to bite."

Adiva couldn't help it. She gasped.

Vigilante laughed, a deep masculine rumble. "Oh, come on! You mean Jorge never sank his fangs in these?" He gave her nipples another teasing tug.

"No." She closed her eyes, feeling the hot trickle of wetness between her thighs. Her voice rasped when she spoke. "Only my neck."

"But they're so pink and perfect." Another seductive tug. She didn't quite suppress the groan. "You know what we call nipples like these?" He grinned again, flashing fang. "Vampire candy."

Five minutes ago, I wanted to beat his head in, Adiva thought wildly. *How the hell did he get me this hot, this fast*?

She knew the answer, of course. Her captor was the kind of dominant she'd secretly dreamed of. Unfortunately, Jorge had been an innately kind man who couldn't bring himself to hurt her, even knowing what she instinctively craved.

"I'm nothing like that," the Vigilante said.

"What?" She'd lost the thread of the conversation.

"You were thinking that Jorge couldn't bring himself to hurt you even though it's what you wanted."

Adiva felt her face heat. "Shit."

"You know vampires are telepaths." He laughed and raked a ruthless thumbnail across her nipple. She inhaled at the tiny pain. "Among other things." There was a universe of velvet threat in that last sentence.

She moaned, unable to help herself. God help her, he really did know exactly how to get to her.

"Yes, as a matter of fact -- I do. Exactly." The vampire released her breasts and caught her by the back of the neck, turning her toward the back wall of the corridor. "Brace your hands on the wall." His cold bark contrasted starkly with the warm, seductive whisper of a moment ago.

Helplessly turned on, Adiva obeyed. Her arms shook.

"Spread your legs and lean in." He kicked her booted feet apart, almost knocking her into the wall. "I want a look at that ass."

Quivering, she obeyed and waited. She was so wet, she could literally smell it. And his senses were even more acute than hers...

Reaching around her hip, he found the seal on her pants and opened it, pushing them out of the way, then tugged her snugs down to her thighs. Adiva felt the cool touch of air on her bare butt as he stepped back, appraising. *Anybody could come along and see me like this.* She closed her eyes again, shuddering with the force of her arousal.

"Very pretty. Like a ripe peach." One warm palm came to rest on her left cheek, big and arousing. "I'm going to enjoy taking a stimwhip to this ass."

The swat he gave her bounced her up on her toes. Startled by the sharp pain, Adiva let her tongue get the better of her. "Fucker!"

"That," Vigilante said, "is not the way a bloodthrall talks to her master." Grabbing her hair, he shoved her into the wall. She grunted as he leaned his weight into her back, mashing her against the cool metal bulkhead. From the corner of her eye, she saw him step away and lift his free hand. Closing her eyes, she braced herself.

Chapter Two

The ten blazing swats that followed heated her ass until Adiva yelped, "I'm sorry, Master!"

The vampire grinned, cool and just slightly vicious. "I seriously doubt that. I smell wet pussy."

He leaned in until she could feel his erection against her naked hip. Adiva caught her breath in anticipation as he slid a hand over her belly and between her thighs. The first thrust of his big finger into her cunt made her shudder.

"You are wet, aren't you?" Dark male anticipation put a rumble in his voice. "Tight, slick, ready to be fucked. Eager for your new master's dick?"

Her mouth was so dry, she couldn't answer.

Another swat jolted her forward onto his impaling finger. "I asked you a question!"

"Yes!" she gasped. "God, yes!"

"Well, you're not going to get it. Not yet. I'm not through exploring my new acquisition." He withdrew the finger from her twat and stepped back. "Bend over and spread your cheeks. I want a look at your asshole."

Helpless blood heated her face. "Here?"

He lifted a brow. "You're on thin ice, Adiva."

Shit. "Yes, Master."

Her heart hammering, she bent over and grabbed her cheeks in both hands, spreading them apart. *God, what if someone walks by?*

"They'll see your master exploring your anus." But as he moved in behind her, she realized he was so damn big, he'd block the view of anyone who happened by. She wondered if he did it on purpose…

Probably not.

Then the blunt finger tracing the seam of her ass made her forget everything else.

Jorge had fingered her butt before, but his hands were smaller than Vigilante's. The sensation of that big fingertip working its way up her anus was both painful and deliciously arousing.

"God, you're tight. I'm going to enjoy grinding my…" He broke off. When he spoke again, there was surprise in his voice. "Jorge never took you here?"

She didn't want to talk about Jorge. His finger felt delicious. "He was… umm… well endowed. He didn't want to hurt me."

"I don't give a shit." Vigilante's voice was icy with disapproval. "If he accepted the responsibility of being your master, it was his duty to give you what you needed, regardless of his own tastes."

Startled, she frowned at him over her shoulder. Why did he care? "Jorge was a good man."

"What he was," the vampire growled, withdrawing his hand, "is lucky I didn't run into you two. I'd have called him out and taken you."

"He didn't neglect me badly enough to…" She broke off, realizing suddenly that if they *had* encountered Vigilante, Jorge probably would have simply handed her over.

Vivid green eyes scanned her face. "He knew he wasn't enough, didn't he? And it bothered him."

Adiva frowned, not comfortable with this conversation. "He was a good friend." He just hadn't been dominant enough for her. Not that she had any intention of telling her captor that.

The Vigilante's sensual mouth curled into a sneer. "Well, I have no interest in being your *friend*." He dragged her backward, thrusting two fingers ruthlessly deep up her ass. She groaned at the fiery sensation. "I'm going to fuck this little hole the way you've always wanted it fucked. After, that is, I whip your sweet ass until I'm rock hard." He wrapped the fingers of his other hand into her dark hair, pulling her away from the wall and onto those impaling fingers. "It's going to be a delicious ride, Adiva. You're going to love every minute of it, even when you're begging for mercy."

Still screwing her asshole with his fingers, he used the hand in her hair to pull her head back. Panting, impossibly aroused, she saw his fangs flash as he bent toward her hammering pulse. The sensation of those sharp teeth sinking into the vein made her cry out in pain and startled hunger. She shuddered as she heard him swallow the first deep mouthful.

Jorge had drunk from her too many times to count, but it had never been like this -- a stark, ruthless possession. The Vigilante's fingers pumped her ass, stretching and tormenting the delicate flesh as he drank her blood. Pleasure and pain twined up Adiva's spine in a bright, breathtaking braid. She shivered, feeling stunned and helpless.

And she loved every hot, pulsing moment of it.

This. This was why she'd become a bloodthrall. It had nothing to do with gaining fantastic strength and near immortality, and everything to do with a man like this -- predatory in his dominance, willing to give her exactly what she hungered for. Even though she hated to admit it, she craved this edgy, ruthless sex, the sensation of being at the mercy of a man who had no mercy at all.

And yet, though the Vigilante stepped right to the edge of brutality, somehow she sensed he wouldn't really hurt her.

At least, not sexually.

Yes. The thought pierced her consciousness, driven by his telepathy. *That's exactly how it's going to be. See what I'll do to you…*

Images flashed through her mind: herself, bound on her back across some kind of restraint device as he tormented her nipples. Tied hand and foot in a helpless ball, jerking under the stimwhip he laid across her ass in ruthless strokes. Cuffed spread eagle as he pumped his thick cock into her wet cunt, driving her to yowling orgasm. Kneeling at his feet, submissively sucking him despite the clamps biting into her nipples. His fangs sinking into her -- neck, breasts, inner thighs. Providing a hot, willing feast for his lust, moaning as he took her.

Mine, his mind growled into hers, as his fingers stabbed deep in her asshole, fucking it in long digs that pleasured and punished. *Every inch of you is mine now. I could fuck you right here… But I think I'll make you wait for it.*

The climax took her by surprise, a sudden jet of burning delight that streamed from her violated ass to her violated throat and back again. She screamed hoarsely, arching against him. "Vigilante!"

Through the hot, white fire, she heard his thought: *I own you, Adiva.*

And then she was aware of nothing except the pulsing pleasure of his pumping fingers. And his mouth, working against her flesh as he fed in those long, deep swallows.

* * *

At last Vigilante released her throat and looked down at her. She felt weak, lightheaded from more than blood loss, but she forced her legs to stiffen and gave him a cheeky smile. "Enjoy yourself?"

He lifted a blond brow. "Not bad -- for an appetizer." Reaching into a back pocket of his battlesuit, he pulled out a pair of gold wrist restraints. Her cocky mood instantly fled as she felt the blood draining from her face.

His face went cool, professionally blank, as though he hadn't driven her to a savage orgasm a moment ago. "Give me your wrists."

She licked her lips as her heart began to pound again. "You don't need those."

Green eyes narrowed in silent warning. "No, but I'm going to use them anyway."

"As a vampire binding his bloodthrall, or a bounty hunter restraining a captive?"

"What do you think?"

I think my life would be a lot simpler if I were telepathic. She stared at him, unmoving, as her palms began to sweat.

He gave her a long, assessing look. "Just how submissive are you, Adiva?"

Snarling a mental curse she didn't dare voice, she thrust her hands out in front of her. With an offhand skill that suggested just how many times he'd done this, the Vigilante snapped the restraints onto each wrist, grabbed her shoulders, and turned her around. Positioning her bound wrists across one another, he pulled them down against her ass. A flick of his thumb activated the cuffs, paralyzing her muscles so they no longer responded to her brain's commands.

Glancing down, she realized her jacket was still open. The pose thrust her bare breasts out in a brazen offering. The station air blew cool across her naked nipples. They tightened, drawing into tight little pink peaks.

"Mmmmm," Vigilante purred, as he stepped around in front of her. His eyes were no longer cold, but hot and hungry as they stared down at the hard tips. "Like I said, vampire candy. And me with a sweet tooth…" He crouched and leaned in to take one stiff nipple into his mouth. Adiva caught her breath, wondering if he was going to sink those fangs into her tender flesh.

Instead, he swirled his tongue across the puckered tip. Pleasure spilled through her in warm streamers that intensified as he suckled her with surprising tenderness. She let her head fall back with a moan of arousal.

"Sweet," he rumbled. "And sensitive. I'm going to have a lot of fun with these."

Sitting back on his heels, he grabbed the waistband of her pants and drew them back up over her hips, then sealed the closure. Hooking an arm around her hips, he stood, spilling her across his shoulder to hang head down.

"My jacket!" Adiva protested. "You left my jacket open!"

He chuckled and gave one cheek a light slap. "So I did."

Cheeks burning in humiliation, Adiva could only hang there as he carried her down the corridor.

* * *

Galen Vordire steadied Adiva's warm weight on his shoulder, enjoying his euphoric triumph. His dick was hard as a tachyon cannon behind his fly, and his balls were tight with anticipation.

She was his at last.

He'd been making do with synthetic blood for months now, just as he'd made do with the women he'd picked up in bars. Both had barely taken the edge off his considerable hungers. But pretty little Adiva was an erotic feast, with those long legs, full, luscious breasts, and big, anxious honey eyes.

And he intended to enjoy every bite.

As soon as Galen had downloaded her bounty file, he'd known he'd have to move fast before some other hunter got to her. Two million credits was a reward tempting enough to attract even Melusinde's attention. He'd have hated to fight his bloodmother over Adiva -- he owed his vampire creator far too much. On the other hand, he had no intention of letting the bloodthrall fall into Tang's vicious hands either. The thought of what the bastard would do to her fragile beauty was enough to turn his stomach.

Luckily, Galen had gotten to the girl first. All he had to do now was reinforce her impression that he was a stone-hearted killer who'd do damn near anything.

In other words, the dominant of her submissive dreams.

Far from being the doormats the public believed, most submissives were actually adrenaline junkies who craved the excitement of sexual risk. For them, the epitome of that risk was an affair with a sadistic dominant skilled in inflicting both pleasure and pain -- the kind of man who would stop at nothing to achieve his own erotic satisfaction.

In reality, someone like that was too carelessly brutal to see to his sub's needs. A good Dom had to be utterly focused on his partner's well-being and sexual gratification, even to the exclusion of his own. He might play at being a sadist, but he had to do so very, very carefully.

Galen was an extremely good dominant.

His cock twitched behind his fly at the thought of everything he intended to do to Adiva. Judging by what he'd seen so far, her reaction should be delicious.

He turned down the next passageway with his captive, planning the next step in her sexual conquest. The corridor was virtually empty at this point in the station's day cycle, except for one grim-faced cyborg Space Marine striding toward him.

The man's gray eyes fell on Adiva's shapely backside and widened with interest. His gaze flicking to meet Galen's, he sent a silent com message: *Lucky bastard.*

Galen grinned as his internal computer relayed the message. The grin broadened as he got a very wicked idea.

He gave the firm curve of Adiva's ass a vicious pinch just as the Marine started to step around them. She kicked out with a startled curse of pain, catching the cyborg right in the face with the toe of her boot. The Marine yelped in outraged pain, grabbing his nose. "What the fuck?"

"Adiva!" Dumping his captive off his shoulder and onto her feet, Galen gestured at the Marine in mock rage. "Look what you did!"

"What are you -- oh." Meeting the cyborg's glare as he clutched his injured nose, she flushed. "I'm sorry, but he..."

The Marine snarled, two meters of pissed-off muscle. "You little..."

"Don't worry, Lieutenant, I'm going to punish her for that." Galen pulled his stimwhip from his belt pouch and activated it with a flick of his thumb. Instantly, the long glowing lash uncoiled with a sibilant hiss. The sound was pure effect, since the lash wasn't physical, though programmed to act as if it was. A tightly focused neuro-stimulant field, it could inflict either pain or pleasure at the whim of its user.

Adiva knew exactly what it was capable of, because her eyes widened and she took a wary step back. Catching sight of her naked breasts, the Marine lost his angry glower and lifted an intrigued dark brow.

Galen sent a quick mental order to Adiva's cuffs, and her wrists sprang free. "Take down your pants and assume the position," he growled.

"What?" Honey brown eyes widened even more. "No!"

He flicked his wrist. The whip responded with the threatening pop he'd programmed into it. "You heard me. Or maybe you'd rather I collect that bounty?"

Adiva hesitated, glancing from him to the towering Marine. Galen didn't blame her for looking intimidated; the cyborg was almost half a meter taller than she was, a brawny blond who looked strong enough to juggle tachyon cannons. Given the cybernetic enhancements Galen sensed, he could probably do just that. Which, considering Adiva's obvious taste for big men, made him perfect for the role of voyeur.

"You heard me," Galen growled, and flicked the whip again. It cracked threateningly.

Reluctantly, Adiva's delicate hands dropped to the closure of her pants. A flick of her fingers opened the seal, exposing an arrow of skin-tight white snugs beneath. A glower of defiance on her face, she pushed the pants down her long thighs.

"The snugs too," Galen growled.

"This is ridiculous!" Adiva glowered, her full lower lip drawing into an adorable pout. A combination of anger, embarrassment, and excitement lit those big brown eyes.

"Hey, you kicked me in the nose, lady," the Marine said, folding his massive arms and rocking back on his heels. The attempt at self-righteousness was marred by the huge erection growing behind his fly.

Adiva's gaze flicked down to it. She swallowed.

"The man wants his pound of flesh, Adiva," Galen said. "And we're going to give it to him. Take off the pants." He gave her his best tone of icy menace. "I won't tell you again." The whip popped so loudly she jumped.

Snarling something uncomplimentary, she kicked off her boots, whirled around and jerked her snugs and pants down to her ankles, then stepped clear from them.

"About time," Galen said in his best sadistic dominant snarl. "Brace your hands on the wall. You're getting fifteen for insubordination."

She obeyed, simultaneously spreading her feet apart without having to be told. Galen and the Marine exchanged a significant glance at that telling gesture.

Apparently, she wasn't all that averse to being whipped.

With a flick of his wrist, Galen laid the glowing stimwhip across her ass. Adiva bounced onto her toes with a startled yelp. The pretty muscles of her cheeks flexed at the sharp pain.

From the corner of his eye, Galen saw the Marine swallow. The bulge behind the cyborg's fly swelled even more.

Galen didn't blame him. Adiva had one of the most gorgeous asses he'd ever seen -- round and firm as a peach, with a tuft of toffee curls showing between her spread legs.

He sent the lash cracking across her butt again, making her bounce on her toes. Another flick, this one cutting from the other direction. Another delicious yelp and jiggle.

Then he sent a mental command to the whip, changing its settings before sending the tip popping right at the joining of her spread legs. Adiva threw back her head with a startled shout.

It wasn't a cry of pain. He'd set the whip to stimulate her pleasure receptors.

The next crack caught her between the cheeks, right on her asshole. She tossed her head, sending dark curls dancing along her spine. "Shit!"

"Oh, yeah," the Marine rumbled. "Do that again."

Galen grinned and obliged him, cracking the tiny pink rosebud twice in succession until she writhed deliciously.

"She's got a pretty little asshole," the Marine said, licking his lips.

"Yeah," Galen said, giving it another ruthless whip-crack, this time with a bit more sting. "And I'm looking forward to stretching it with my dick."

The Marine shook his head. "I was right -- you *are* a lucky bastard."

Adiva looked back at them, wild-eyed. Meeting her gaze, the cyborg opened his fly and pulled out his massive cock. "I hope you don't mind," he said to Galen. "This isn't the kind of sight I get to enjoy very often."

"Go right ahead." Galen sent another order to the whip and laid it hard across her cheek.

She yelped. "Dammit, that hurt!"

He grinned. "That's the idea."

"New slave?" The Marine stroked his cock in long pulls.

"That asshole wouldn't be virgin otherwise." The next flick landed right between her vaginal lips, delivering a burst of pleasure so strong, Galen felt it through his telepathy. She gasped.

The Marine echoed the sound, yanking his prick hard and rising on his toes. "Oh, shit, I hope you fuck it hard."

"I'm going to grind my dick in until she begs for mercy."

"She loves it." The cyborg was gasping now as he worked his cock with one hand and his balls with the other. "Smell that wet pussy."

"Yeah." Galen gave her another stinging crack across the cheeks. "She knows what we want to do to her. And she knows where my cock is going the minute I get her back to the ship."

Another crack. Adiva whimpered.

Galen smiled.

She didn't think she'd ever been so hot in her life.

Each snap of the whip alternated unpredictably between liquid pleasure and stinging pain until the blended sensation set her nervous system ablaze like a torch.

Meanwhile the two big men stood watching her as she writhed and danced, their eyes glittering with hot excitement. The Marine's cock was huge, and he jacked off without shame, his gaze locked on her ass. Vigilante's erection was every bit as big behind his fly as he plied his whip in a searing assault on her self-control.

Anybody could come around the corner, she thought helplessly, shuddering as blow after blow rained across her ass. *This shouldn't be turning me on this way.*

But it was. God help her, it was.

Suddenly the Marine's back arched. He bellowed as come shot from his cock in a long white stream.

The next time the whip struck her, the pain it inflicted almost tipped her over into her own orgasm. She leaned into the wall, groaning helplessly.

And the whip stopped flying.

What? Don't stop now!

The Marine sagged against the nearest wall as if unable to stand. "Shit. My comp is picking up the boarding call for my ship. Doesn't that just figure?"

Vigilante gave him a crooked smile. "Hey, at least you got a good show out of it."

"That's putting it mildly." He tucked himself away and gave them both a taunting salute. "Fuck her hard, you lucky bastard."

With a sigh, he sealed his pants and walked off.

Adiva wanted to scream. She'd been so close. Another stroke or two, and…

"Get over here."

Her eyes widened as she met Vigilante's narrow stare. His hand dropped to the seal of his ship suit and slowly opened it, revealing his muscled chest and liberating his cock. It jutted at her, a thick length of rosy meat.

"You heard me," he rumbled. "Get over here and suck."

Adiva hesitated only a moment before hurrying over and dropping to her knees so that the flushed head bobbed demandingly before her eyes.

"Take it in your mouth."

Licking her lips, Adiva wrapped one hand around the thick shaft and obeyed.

He tasted salty and clean, flavored with the tang she'd learned to associate with vampires. Eagerly, she swirled her tongue over his cock, exploring the big, smooth head. At the same time, she stroked the shaft, enjoying the silken skin and the thick vein she could feel running up its length. With her other hand, she cupped his furry balls, teasing and stroking.

"More," he rasped. "Take it all. Right down that pretty throat."

Widening her jaws, she swallowed, sucking him deep in one long swoop. To her satisfaction, she felt him dip against her, as if his knees had gone weak for an instant.

Oh, yeah, Adiva thought. *I've got you now.*

And then she started to suck.

It was hardly the first time Galen had received a blow job, but Adiva was stunningly good even by his standards. Her cheeks hollowed as she suckled, bobbing her head up and down the length of his shaft. With every bob, her lips and tongue caressed his aching cock, milking him in long, luscious pulls.

Feeling heat gathering in a demanding knot between his thighs, he knew he couldn't take much more of this. As if sensing how close he was, she slowed her oral worship, pulling him back from the brink, teasing and suckling in a sweet, mind-blowing assault on his self-control.

Until she suddenly swooped down over him, taking him right to the root in a breath-stealing wet satin rush. His balls seemed to detonate, blowing hot pulse after pulse of come up his shaft. He locked his fists in her hair and threw his head back. "Drink it!" Galen gritted. "Drink it all!"

He felt the muscles of her throat ripple as she did just that.

That was when he realized there might be more to his new slave than he'd anticipated.

Chapter Three

Vigilante's vessel was no luxury star yacht, but it wasn't a tub either. By its long, graceful lines, it was a decommissioned military Raider Class warp ship -- gleaming black and one hundred meters long, bristling with tachyon cannons and sensor arrays. The painted image of a chained, naked blonde was stretched across its bow, languidly draped over the name *Vigilante's Pet*.

"Tacky, Vigilante," Adiva said.

"Not as tacky as sucking your master off in a space station corridor. That Marine really loved watching you get your ass whipped, didn't he?" Their boots clattered on the metal ramp as he hauled her after him toward the *Pet*'s airlock. Though Galen had been tempted to force her to go naked, he'd reluctantly allowed her to dress after she'd given him that stunning blow job.

And she was still fretting about it, too. "What if there had been kids around?"

"This part of the station's strictly for military, law enforcement or paramilitary. And it was late in the cycle. Anybody who saw you either had the same equipment or enjoyed the view. That cyborg certainly did."

She gave him a honey-eyed pout. "You enjoy humiliating me, don't you?"

"Don't lie to the telepath, Adiva. You loved watching that Marine jerk off while he watched you get your ass whipped. I could smell you creaming."

"I know," she snapped back. "Why do you think I was humiliated?"

He shouted in laughter as the airlock doors slid open.

Adiva followed him down a long corridor and into the master's cabin. While he went to work unlocking her cuffs, she scanned the room. Most of the area was taken up by a sprawling bed. Off to one side stood a sensory chair -- among other things, he'd be able to interface with the ship's computer from it in an emergency. The walls were lined with the usual drawers and compartments for his clothing and equipment.

There were also a couple of wall niches. She wasn't surprised that they held figurines of women, bound in suggestive positions.

"Bed," Vigilante said, "bondage configuration D-4." The mattress instantly drew into a long, narrow ridge.

She turned to stare at him. "You programmed it for bondage?"

"Of course. Strip." He stepped back and leaned a broad shoulder against the wall.

Curious, Adiva eyed him. "Just how many configurations did you program it with, anyway?" She shrugged off her jacket and handed it to him, then sat down to drag off her boots.

"Enough." Vigilante watched her with the intent hunger of a cat staring at a mouse hole. His eyes kindled to a green blaze as she started wiggling out of her tight trousers. "I add new ones as I go along."

Naked, she folded her pants and underwear, mostly for something to do with her hands. "My duffle," she said, remembering it. "I threw it down back at the *Star Tripper*."

"I know. They passed it off to station security before they took off. I've made arrangements to have it delivered."

Adiva looked up at him, startled. "When did you do that? I didn't hear you use a com unit."

Vigilante shrugged. "I have a computer implant."

"A battlefield model?"

"Yeah. A Cybercore 5000."

Which was a top of the line unit. Great. On top of everything else, he was a cyborg. If he ever shot at her, she was dead; with the targeting capability the implant gave him, he'd never miss.

His eyes glittered. "So don't give me a reason to shoot you. Lie back on the bed, arms spread. On top of the hump."

Licking her lips, Adiva obeyed. The bed shifted beneath her as she lay down, supporting and lifting her as if in offering as she positioned herself.

The Vigilante pulled another set of cuffs from a pocket. She felt the warm brush of his fingers, then the cool metal slapping around first one ankle, then the other. He spread her legs wide and arranged her arms to his satisfaction. As he stepped back from the bed, she felt the field click in, locking her limbs helplessly in place. She could move her torso, but the rest of her body was paralyzed. Available for anything he wanted to do to her.

"You're creaming again." His voice was a low, dark rumble as he reached for the seal of his suit. Mouth dry, she watched as he stripped.

She'd assumed at least some of his size was due to the armor he wore, but it was pure Vigilante. The chest he bared for her was broad and sculpted with slabs and ridges of muscle. A neat cloud of golden hair stretched from one nipple to the other, then snaked down over his abdomen to his waistband. As Adiva watched in fascination, he pulled off the suit. When he finally stripped it down his brawny thighs, she caught her breath.

Despite the blow job she'd just given him, his cock was hard again, massive and ruddy above a pair of thickly furred balls. Jorge hadn't exactly been under-endowed, but Vigilante made him look tiny.

"God," he rumbled as he put his suit down the cleaning shaft, "I love the look on your face. Your eyes are the size of dinner plates." He took his rod in hand and gave it a slow, taunting stroke. "And yes, this *is* going in every orifice you've got, just as deep as I can stuff it."

She grinned despite the common sense that warned her not to taunt the vampire. "You don't do subtle well, do you?"

Vigilante snorted. "I've never been a subtle man." He studied her sprawled nudity, and his eyes kindled. "Especially not when I'm hungry."

Her heart kicked into high gear as he moved around the bed with a long, lazy stride, a dark smile growing on his face as he studied her. Adiva's gaze slid helplessly from the anticipation in those green eyes to the lustful jut of his cock. It jerked upward under her stare, lengthening as she watched.

"You're even more exquisite than I expected," he said in that low, masculine rumble that made her inner muscles clench. "Those long pretty legs, those absolutely delicious breasts. And the way your dark hair curls around your anxious little face..." He gave his cock a slow stroke, as if unable to resist his own hunger. "Not that I blame you for being worried." Another teasing stroke as he licked his fangs. "Maybe you should be grateful you're not telepathic, sweet. I don't think you'd find my thoughts particularly reassuring."

Adiva swallowed. "You're good at that."

Vigilante lifted a brow in wordless question.

"The whole menacing dominant routine."

"Oh, darling, it's not a routine. As you're about to discover." He walked to one of the wall panels beside the bed, which slid silently open at his approach. Adiva watched with a combination of fear and anticipation as he contemplated its contents. After a nerve-wracking pause, he collected several objects and arranged them on the bed.

Her heart pounded as he sat down beside her bound body. Selecting a small tube from the collection, he popped the top off it and started smearing the contents of it over a short, stubby object. Shaped something like an elongated top, the object was studded with dozens of soft little projections. After a moment, she realized it was a butt plug.

"I'd tell you that you need the stretching," he said, slicking the gel more thickly over the plug, "but we'd both know that would be a lie. Bloodthralls retain their tightness no matter how many times you fuck them -- even with a dick like mine." His grin suggested he intended to enjoy that fact on a regular basis.

Adiva swallowed, watching nervously as the Vigilante rose and moved around between her widespread legs. When she inhaled sharply in fearful anticipation, she could smell her own musk.

But instead of simply driving the plug home, he thumbed her clit and slipped a long forefinger into her sex. Adiva moaned at the delicious sensation.

"You are wet, aren't you?" His hooded gaze watched her face. "I'm tempted to forget about the games and just shove my cock in here for a good, hard fuck. But..." He shrugged. "I don't want this session over that fast, so I'll just have to control myself." He added a second finger in a slow pump. She rolled her hips upward with a helpless groan.

Which promptly became a gasp as he inserted the plug in the mouth of her anus and forced it home. "God, Vigilante!" She clenched her teeth as he rotated his wrist, screwing it in. "That hurts!"

"I'm not surprised, as tight as you are." His smile was downright nasty. "I'll have to remember to gag you before I use your ass. Virgins tend to get so noisy when I settle in for a good, hard reaming."

He drew the plug out a bit and pushed it back in. To Adiva's surprise, it started to vibrate, the soft little studs tormenting and pleasuring by turns. She whimpered. His smile broadened.

Still easing the butt plug in, Vigilante settled down between her thighs and lowered his head. The first pass of his tongue over her wet and aching flesh tore a desperate gasp from her mouth.

The gasp became a startled shout as he twisted the plug hard and swirled his tongue over her clit. The combination of sensations was so savage, she instinctively tried to pull back. But bound as she was, there was no escape.

He went right on licking and suckling as he fingered her cunt and plunged the butt plug in and out of her ass. Plug and finger rubbed past each other through the thin flesh between her channels, creating a maddening friction.

The ecstasy he created with his tongue was just as ferocious. As the long, hot moments spun past, she realized the pain of his anal probing actually enhanced her enjoyment. Her inner muscles drew tighter and tighter as each thrust built her burning pleasure.

Climax!

Adiva screamed, her orgasm tearing up her spine like a fountain of fire as he worked ass, cunt, and clit simultaneously. Despite the probing plug, she found herself grinding into his thrusts as she yowled.

She'd never felt so fucked. So taken. And she loved it.

Endless burning moments past before she collapsed at last, panting and dazed.

"Mmmm," he purred, pushing himself off the bed. "I'm definitely looking forward to reaming that sensitive little ass. Your reaction should be interesting, to say the least."

Breathing hard, Adiva looked down her bound body at him, taking in the massive jut of his cock. It was a hell of a lot bigger than the plug. "You're going to kill me."

He laughed. "Not quite, but you'll definitely need that gag."

Adiva eyed him. "You're not a nice man, are you?"

Another flash of fang. "No." His attention fell on her nipples, and the dark smile widened. "But since you seem in some doubt, why don't I provide another demonstration?"

Her eyes widened. "That's not necessary!" To her embarrassment, her voice actually squeaked.

"I think it is." He picked up one of the remaining objects he'd left beside her hip. She recognized it with a little thrill of fear and anticipation.

It was a nipple clamp.

Chapter Four

The Vigilante dropped the tiny device on Adiva's chest, then stretched out on the bed beside her. As he rolled onto his elbow, she stared at the clamp with burning eyes. To her relief, it didn't have teeth -- its jaws seemed to be padded. And the clamp wasn't all that big, so maybe it didn't have much of a...

"Oh, don't worry," he murmured in her ear, "it's going to hurt."

One big, warm hand settled on her right breast for a slow squeeze. "You do have the prettiest tits." His thumb brushed over her nipple, stroking it to aching hardness. "No wonder that Marine was drooling."

"Ummm -- thanks." Despite her anxiety, she had to admit he knew what to do with his hands. His fingers felt delicious, kneading and flicking, each tiny caress sending sweet jolts of pleasure through her body.

Her captor grinned. "Don't thank me. I have a feeling you won't consider my admiration a compliment once I get started." He lowered his head toward her nipple.

She tensed, anticipating the sting of his fangs.

Green eyes flicked up toward her face. "Don't worry, darling. I'm not going to bite you." He swirled his tongue over the peak. "Yet."

Adiva groaned. "You *are* a sadist."

"They didn't give me that twenty-first level rating because of my sunny personality." Another delicate lick.

"Guess not. Jesus, Vigilante!"

"I like to make sure they're nice and hard first." Brushing his hand across her chest, he found her left breast and started gently teasing it as he tenderly licked her right.

This is going to hurt. Adiva swallowed the saliva that flooded her mouth, just like the cream she could feel pooling inside her. *Why the hell is it turning me on*?

"Because you're a seventeenth level submissive, darling." Vigilante scooped up one of the clamps.

Before she could brace herself, he closed its tiny jaws over her left nipple. The sharp pain made Adiva yelp. "Bastard!"

"Yep." He tauntingly swirled his tongue over her other nip. The luscious sensation contrasted sharply against the sting of the clamp. Her pleasure-pain intensified even more as he started suckling, simultaneously flicking the clamp with his thumb.

Adiva writhed against the mattress, tried to pull in her arms, but her cuffed hands wouldn't obey. It was maddening.

She'd never been more turned on in her life.

"Because you've always been in control," Vigilante murmured, apparently reading her mind again. "As a spy, you had to stay one jump ahead of everyone else, or you were dead." He gave her nipple another delicious swirl of his tongue. "But now, I'm in control. I can do anything I want to you."

He picked up the second clamp and let it close on her nipple. Pain bit into the little peak, as intense as the pleasure had been.

"Shit!" Adiva tried to jerk free of her bonds, but her muscles refused to obey.

"You're mine now. All mine. Utterly mine." Vigilante rolled on top of her, bracing his muscled forearms on either side of her chest. "Go ahead -- lie to yourself. Tell yourself I won't really hurt you."

She felt the thick, hard knob of his cockhead brush her wet pubic hair. He reached down, aimed himself, and entered her.

Wet as she was, it should have been an easy stroke, but he was thick, and she hadn't had a man since Jorge died. The vampire had to bear down, forcing his massive cock deeper and deeper yet, stretching her inner walls. Stuffing her one luscious centimeter at a time.

God, it felt good. So good she was barely even aware of the dull throb from the clamps.

"Mmmm," he purred. "Oh, yeah, you are wet." Shoving another inch, he added, "And tight."

Dazed, she stared up into his handsome face as he kept working his way inside her. Centimeter by centimeter, every one of them making her body blaze with heat and need. Until he was finally in up to the balls.

"Jesus," the Vigilante growled. "I've been looking forward to this moment since I read your file." He drew out slightly and pumped in. "I took one look at your picture and knew you were going to be..." deeper thrust "... just like this."

Abruptly the bed began to move under her, lifting her hips upward, dropping her chest, apparently reacting to some command he sent through his computer implant. Dazed, she stirred. "What?"

"Just getting you into position." He kept pumping, lengthening his strokes.

"God, you feel so good!" Adiva tossed her head on the pillow.

"So do you." He plucked one of the clamps off her nipples. She gasped at the burn of returning blood.

Vigilante lowered his head.

Adiva stiffened, expecting him to bite. Instead his mouth closed over the aching peak, suckling her sweetly as he ground his cock in and out of her sex. She shuddered, mindless with the pleasure storming through her body. Pleasure that grew stronger with every hard thrust of cock into helpless cunt.

He flicked the clamp off the other nipple, then transferred his mouth to it. The sharp rake of his fangs jerked her into a startled bow. "Shit! Vigilante, that hurts!"

His only response was a growl as he sucked hard, drinking from the cuts he'd inflicted. Feeding as he fucked her.

"Ohhhhhhh!" Adiva yelped, writhing against his grinding hips, his cock pumping deep, feeling so damned incredible every time it teased and twisted her slick inner walls. At the same time, he suckled her aching nipple, drinking her blood in hungry swallows. Pleasure competing with hot throbs of pain until it became impossible to tell where one ended and the other began. As, somehow, each intensified the other in a fiery feedback loop.

Which abruptly snapped, flinging her into her orgasm with a scream. She bucked, mindless in the grip of his hard, muscled body as he rode her, still feeding, milking pleasure and blood from her tormented breast.

"Vigilante!" she screamed. She'd never felt so utterly possessed.

He released her nipple to roar his climax at the ceiling. "Adiva!"

Deep inside her, she could feel his cock jerking, pumping her full of his come.

Chapter Five

When Adiva woke the next morning, her body stung and ached in a dozen places. She stretched, suspecting her smile was more than a little smug. The dream of nights like last night was the reason she'd become a bloodthrall to begin with, but reality had never quite measured up.

Until the Vigilante. Her vampire captor did a very thorough job of measuring up, in every conceivable dimension.

Where was he, anyway? She lifted her head, frowning.

"You fuck." His voice came from the next compartment, low and vicious with such rage, every hair stood on the back of her neck. "You're a dead man." She knew by his tone he meant every word.

Alarmed, Adiva rolled out of bed. Were they being attacked?

Ignoring her nakedness -- she didn't want to take the time to get dressed -- she made for the door. It slid open at her approach, and she darted a glance around the corner, ready to attack if he needed help.

Instead he sat rigidly at a computer console, his face a mask of rage, a set of trid images floating in the air in front of him. Images so horrific that even combat veteran Adiva wasn't entirely sure what she was seeing.

For a moment, she thought the women had been the victims of some kind of bomb blast, but as she stepped into the room, she saw their injuries were more surgical than that.

"What the hell is this?" Revolted, she covered her mouth with her hand and swallowed against her rising gorge.

"Richard Corvile at work. Erstwhile duke of Eron Three and sadistic serial murderer. You can see why they want him dead or alive." A muscle flexed in his jaw. "It's going to be dead."

"My God." She couldn't stand seeing the images any more, so she looked at the Vigilante instead. His face was pale, almost gray, except for two flags of rage burning on his high cheekbones and the hectic green glitter of his eyes. "You're hunting him now?"

"Yeah." The word was flat. He slapped a hand on the console, and the images blessedly winked out, to be replaced by a shot of a man's face. Considering how horrific his crimes were, the killer looked almost shockingly ordinary, with pleasantly handsome features and a muscular build. Yet there was something flat and reptilian in his eyes that belied his cheerful smile. Looking into those eyes, she could believe he was responsible for the atrocities she'd just seen.

The Vigilante's expression as he stared at the image was so nakedly murderous, a chill skated Adiva's spine. She was suddenly very, very glad he hadn't thought she deserved killing.

She cleared her throat with a rasp. "So this Corvile kills women."

"At least twenty-five that we know of. Fifteen of them back on Eron Three by the time they caught him." A muscle flexed in the vampire's strong jaw. "A jury found him not guilty on all counts. The fact that the jury foreman was shot down the day before the verdict might have had something to do with it. The judge should have declared a mistrial, but…"

"Mysteriously, he didn't."

The vampire leaned back in his seat, his expression brooding. "Exactly. Corvile then emigrated to Saris Eight, taking his fortune with him. Of course, he proceeded to start killing again. Unfortunately, he'd gotten better at it, and the planetary authorities couldn't tie him to any of the deaths. At least, until he killed the pretty young wife of a man even richer than he."

Adiva eased into a seat next to Vigilante, hypnotized by his feral intensity. "And that's the man who hired you," she guessed.

The Vigilante nodded. "Unfortunately, Corvile has gotten wind that there's a bounty on his head. He's disappeared." Burning green eyes narrowed. "Fortunately, it's very, very hard to hide from a telepath who can pull the truth from the mind of anyone who might know anything about where you went." He bared his fangs. "I'm going to find him. And when I do, he'll be as dead as his victims."

The Vigilante was as good as his word. They left the station an hour later, shortly after a runner dropped off Adiva's duffle and got a generous tip for his pains.

Once they were into C-space -- underway at faster-than-light speeds -- Adiva found herself naked on her knees in front of his pilot's chair, suckling her new master's cock. Afterward, he hauled her into his lap and fed from her throat while driving her to orgasm with skillful fingers.

* * *

The hunt for Corvile took more than a month as the Vigilante tracked his new prey to planet after planet. At every stop, he left her wearing the force restraints while he was gone. Though he didn't activate them, she was well aware the *Pet*'s computer would use them to stop her if she tried to leave the ship.

Each night, the vampire returned to her for another mind-blowing sexual encounter. At times she suspected he was taking his frustration out on her with his whips and clamps, but she found she didn't mind.

Adiva had known she was a submissive, of course, but she'd had no idea exactly how much she would love submitting to a man like the Vigilante. Sometimes he could be brutal in his demands, while on other occasions he was almost tender. Whichever mood he was in, it always precisely matched hers, as if he sensed when she wasn't up to satisfying his more ferocious tastes. Telepath that he was, he probably did sense exactly what she needed, but she was surprised he'd care enough to let her needs affect his behavior.

The only thing he didn't do was take her ass. He told her he was saving her backside for after he captured Corvile. Adiva had to admit, she was beginning to look forward to his victory celebration.

She probably wouldn't be able to walk for a week.

Finally the Vigilante got the lead he was looking for when he learned Corvile had taken a transport to Sebasa, a true backwater of a planet on the edge of human stellar space. Better yet, the bastard had left for the colony barely the week before.

"I've got the son of a bitch," the Vigilante told Adiva as he charted a course for Sebasa on the *Pet*'s bridge. "He's a dead man."

She fidgeted, frowning. It had become harder and harder to cool her heels on the *Pet* while Vigilante went off to hunt the killer. "Why don't you let me go with you this time? You could use some backup."

The vampire's green eyes flickered. "I think not."

Adiva contemplated him, one brow lifted. "You don't trust me."

"I have many positive characteristics --"

"You do?" She gave him a mock-astonished blink.

"-- but a trusting nature is not one of them." He shrugged. "Besides, considering Corvile's tastes, I'd prefer you stayed as far from him as possible."

"Why, Vigilante, I didn't know you cared."

His eyes cooled. "I don't. But considering all the trouble I went to in acquiring you, it would be a waste to lose you to that vile little prick."

* * *

They docked at Sebasa's one space station port. The Vigilante donned his body armor and armed himself with his usual assortment of beamers, jammers, and neural-stun poppers, then disappeared out the *Pet*'s airlock.

Exhausted from another of his dominance fucks, Adiva tried to sleep. Unfortunately, a nagging sense of worry wouldn't permit it. She dressed in one of the filmy gowns he'd bought her, ignoring the restraints he'd again left deactivated around her wrists and ankles, then headed for the galley to get something to eat.

Like the rest of the ship, the galley was roomy enough to keep a spacer from going nuts from cabin fever. There was also a wall-length viddie screen for use with games and all manner of entertainments; at the moment it showed only Sebasa, shimmering blue and green in the glow of its sun.

Adiva ordered up a meal from the synther -- Vigilante had stocked his ship with food in the correct assumption that she'd accept his deal -- and sat down to eat. She was just ripping the cover off a plate of m'shili noodles when she heard the hiss of the airlock. She rose from her galley chair and walked into the corridor. "Vigilante? I didn't expect you back this..."

Richard Corvile stepped out of the airlock, a beamblade in his hand and a vicious grin on his face. "Well, well! Hello, there. When I heard Vigilante had been seen with a woman, I hoped it was a lover. And here you are."

Adiva eyed the blade warily. "How the fuck did you get past the ship's security locks?"

He lifted his left hand, displaying the electronic overrider he held. Adiva had used similar lockpicks herself during her espionage career. "All things are possible to a man with enough money. But I doubt we have much time, so let's get busy." Corvile took a menacing step forward. "I want to have you nicely gutted by the time the vampire gets..."

He lunged with a long vicious slash aimed right at Adiva's throat. She sidestepped with a bloodthrall's speed, settling into a combat crouch.

Corvile smirked, eyeing her nipples through the filmy gown. "Oh, so you want to play? I'm very good at playing."

She sneered. "I seriously doubt that."

Just as she'd intended, her taunt ignited his fury. He leaped at her, the blade lifted for a vicious downward slash. Coolly, Adiva stepped in, grabbed his knife wrist, and pivoted around behind him, cranking his arm up and back. "I'm not your average helpless victim, you stupid shit. I'm a *bloodthrall*." She twisted his wrist brutally until she heard something crack with a wet snap. "That means I'm as strong as a vampire my size." The killer roared in startled agony. "Which makes me more than a match for psychopathic little fucks like you." Grabbing him by the back of the head, she slammed him face-first into the bulkhead. His howl cut off with a crunch as his skull shattered.

Stepping back, she let the body fall and contemplated it with a grim smile. "God, I love being underestimated."

Behind her, the airlock thumped into its cycle. She turned as Vigilante barreled through, white-faced. "Adiva!"

"It's okay, I've already killed him." She gestured at the corpse as the vampire stopped short in astonishment. "Son of a bitch used an overrider to get past…"

The Vigilante jerked her into his arms before she could get the rest of the sentence out of her mouth. "I sensed him," he said, his voice gruff. "I sensed what he meant to do. I was afraid I wouldn't make it back in time."

Oddly touched, she slid her arms up his shoulders and met his relieved gaze. "He was just a human. A really nasty human, but still, I've got five times his strength. And since he assumed I'd be as easy to kill as all those other women, I was in no real danger."

"Of course not." Blond lashes veiled Vigilante's eyes, and the concern vanished from his face, leaving him coolly expressionless. He dropped his arms from around her and stepped back. "I should have realized you were more than capable of defending yourself." Looking down at the body, he grimaced. "You made quite a mess here, didn't you? Go clean up while I get the body into stasis for the trip back to Saris Eight. I want to collect that bounty."

Adiva eyed him, feeling strangely cheated by his mood shift. "Whatever you say -- Master."

He grunted as she started down the corridor toward the ship's head.

Adiva had done a very thorough job on Corvile. Galen's only regret was that he hadn't had a chance to give the bastard the kind of slow death he so richly deserved. Still, it was a good thing she'd been able to take the killer out so fast. She was obviously every bit as good as her enemies insisted.

Galen frowned as he loaded the corpse into its stasis crate for the trip to Saris Eight, remembering all too clearly the icy terror that had seized him when he'd realized the killer's intentions. He'd have been concerned for anyone in Corvile's sadistic hands, but this fear had been far more intense than that, something perilously close to panic.

And he knew exactly what it meant.

He'd only known Adiva a month, but she was already getting to him. He wasn't really surprised, given her intelligence, cheeky sense of humor, and lush sensuality. Add in that truly outrageous beauty and the sweet taste of her blood, and any vampire would find himself falling for her. Particularly considering the gnawing loneliness that had driven Galen to hunt her to begin with.

The trouble was, he couldn't afford to let Adiva realize he was starting to care. She wanted an ice-cold dream dominant, not another lovesick vampire like that wretched Jorge. Which meant he'd damn well better convince her she'd imagined any weakness she'd seen.

And he knew just how to do it.

Adiva stood under the pulsing spray of the *Pet*'s real-water shower -- a bit of sybaritic luxury if ever she'd encountered one. Even as the spray sluiced over her skin, she kept seeing the fear and rage on Vigilante's face when he'd burst out of that airlock, all set to kill Corvile. True, he'd been intent on doing away with the prick all along, but what she'd seen in his eyes had been more than that. He'd been terrified.

For her.

She'd never have expected that kind of protectiveness from her big, stone-hearted vampire master. It also made her feel a little better about her nagging suspicion she was beginning to fall for him. The Vigilante was so damned sexy, so skilled, so intelligent and darkly seductive, it was impossible to resist him.

But he was also such a bastard ninety percent of the time, she felt like an idiot for feeling anything for him at all. What kind of moronic dishrag would fall in love with a man who considered her a combination sex object and blood supply?

But if he saw her as more than that…

"Get out of there, Adiva." His growl rumbled over the hiss of the shower.

She whirled to peer through the shower tube's frosted shield. An unmistakable broad-shouldered silhouette loomed on the other side, arms crossed, blatantly naked. And from the sound of his voice, in one of his Big Bad Dom moods.

Her nipples hardened in anticipation.

"Adiva!" he barked.

"I'm coming!" She ordered the water off.

The shield slid open. The vampire stood waiting, every inch of that brawny body on glorious display, his green eyes glittering with hot lust, his cock a ruddy, hungry jut. He grinned, flashing his fangs. "Brace yourself, darling. It's time for my victory celebration."

Adiva hung helplessly in mid-air, bent over a thick, cylindrical field generator. A set of force fields held her hands up and back over her head as her hips lay across the cylinder. Her legs were spread wide, toes not even touching the floor, held apart by yet another set of fields. She was stretched almost upright, but her ass was thrust out. It stung savagely. The Vigilante had already given her a good working over with his stimwhip.

And that, she knew, was only the appetizer for the night's entertainment, because her anus was precisely at the height of Vigilante's dick. He'd greased it generously and inserted a thick butt plug that made the tight little opening ache.

Now, as she watched, panting, the vampire paced in front of her, a wicked grin on his face, his cock bobbing with every stride. In one hand he held the stimwhip he'd been using, this one in the form of a cat-o'-nine-tails. Its nine short glowing lashes hissed as he eyed her.

Suddenly he sent the whip flicking out to strike right across her bare breasts, thrust outward by her position across the cylinder. Some of the lashes stung, but others, perversely, stimulated her pleasure centers. The combined effect was enough to make her writhe, torn between begging him to stop and pleading with him to keep going.

Gasping, Adiva watched the thick muscles of his torso ripple as he snapped the whip again. This time the lashes felt as if phantom mouths licked and suckled her while clamps simultaneously bit into her flesh.

"God," he growled, "I adore those nipples. They're flushed as fat and red as cherries." Stepping up to her, he set the whip on the shelf and dropped to one knee. "I always did love cherries."

She caught her breath in anticipation as he sucked one of the tight crowns into his mouth. His tongue stroked and swirled around it. Eyes shuttered in helpless lust, she could only hang there. Even as he suckled her, she was intently aware of the plug burning her ass.

Soon he was going to replace it with that massive cock of his. And God help her, she couldn't wait. By the time he rose from her aching nipples, she was panting, on the verge of begging for anything he wanted to do to her. "Vigilante, God, please..."

"Give me that mouth." He grabbed the back of her head and swooped in, sucking and licking at her lips until she opened for him. His tongue swirled inside her mouth in long mating thrusts. His free hand cupped one breast, thumbing the swollen point until she gasped. Unable to do anything else, she kissed him back, chasing his tongue with hers, silently begging for mercy -- or perhaps for more. She wasn't sure which.

Finally he drew back a bare fraction and breathed against her mouth, "How's your ass, Adiva? Ready for my cock?"

She had to pant for breath before she could speak. "You don't care whether I'm ready or not."

His fingers tightened on her nipple, tugging it deliciously. "Not really, no." His lips quirked up. "Let's have a look at that little hole, shall we?"

She shuddered as he released her and walked around behind her helpless backside. When one of those big, warm hands landed on her butt, she flinched with a combination of dread and desire. He'd spent ten minutes flogging her ass with that damn cat before starting work on her tits.

"Lovely color," Vigilante purred. "Nice and rosy." A finger traced between her spread cheeks right down to her labia, then slid smoothly through them to circle her clit. She jerked and moaned. "You're wet too. Enjoying yourself, dove?"

She laughed, unable to help herself. "Yes, you bastard."

One broad palm landed on her cheek in a stinging slap. "That's Master Bastard to you, darling."

Something cool and cylindrical touched her labia, then began to slowly work its way inside her cunt. "Is that the… Oh God!… whip?"

"The butt makes a nice dildo, don't you think?" He forced another inch deep, rotating his wrist to screw it inside.

Then the fingers of his other hand brushed her ass and caught the butt plug, easing it out of her stinging, violated rectum. She caught her breath, then moaned as he flicked on the whip. Its lashes began broadcasting a pleasure field that seemed to wrap around her clit in burning pulses. Maddened by growing lust, Adiva rolled her hips, fucking the whip.

"Feels good, doesn't it?" He slid the butt in deep. The lashes swayed between her thighs, sending waves of ecstasy into her sex.

"Yessss," she groaned. "Oh, yes!"

"Yes, what?" Something hit the deck with a rattle. She suspected it was the butt plug.

"Yes, Master!"

He slid a forefinger deep into her ass as he simultaneously withdrew the whip. "You've got a really tight little asshole, slave. You know what I want to do with it?"

The muscles of her thighs were twitching. "Fuck it." She licked her dry lips and shuttered her lids. "Grind your big cock into it."

"That's right." The whip butt clattered to the floor. She groaned in disappointment, wanting more of that hot, wicked ecstasy. "And how's it going to feel when I grind my cock up this tight little ass?" A second finger joined the one stretching her rectum.

"It's going to hurt." She was panting.

"But you want it anyway."

"God, yes!"

"That's what I thought." He pulled his fingers from her and stepped in close. Something broad and smooth brushed her sensitive anus. Adiva caught her breath in a combination of fear and consuming lust.

Slowly, he leaned into her, forcing the massive crown into her ass. She felt herself stretching painfully around the knob and whimpered.

"Push out," he gritted.

With a helpless moan, she obeyed. Centimeter by centimeter, the big shaft sank deep. "Shit, that hurts!" she gasped.

He laughed, a short, savage bark. "Funny, it feels delicious to me." Another burning fraction. And another.

Vigilante reached around her hip and found her clit with a forefinger, circling it. And kept impaling her in a slow, relentless drive until finally she felt his hips plastered against hers, the entire flaming length of his cock buried deep.

He leaned in until he could breathe in her ear. "How does it feel to have your master's cock jammed up your virgin ass?"

She'd never felt so helpless, so utterly *taken* in her entire life. "Hotter than hell."

Vigilante laughed, a deep rumble. "That's my bloodthrall. Hold on, sweet. You're about to get reamed."

He started pulling out. In contrast to the pain of entry, there was a dark, perverse pleasure in the sensation of that thick rod sliding endlessly out of her ass. He enhanced it with a finger circling her clit, making her writhe again.

Then he pushed deep in another long, agonizing thrust, followed by a sweet, kinky withdrawal. Adiva felt the climax she'd been chasing all night begin to gather and pulse. She whimpered in helpless ecstasy.

With a rumble of satisfaction, Vigilante began fucking her ass. "God," he growled, "I love breaking in a virgin."

She felt incredibly tight, the muscled ring of her rectum gripping his cock fiercely as he sawed in and out. Galen had to fight to keep his pace slow. He wanted to take his time conquering Adiva's ass.

But it wasn't easy, not with her sheath milking his dick as she hung helplessly in her bonds. He cupped her breast in one hand and fingered her clit with the other, all the while slowly working his cock in and out of that snug anus. With his telepathy, he could feel her orgasm gathering with every ruthless stroke. All he had to do was hang on a little longer…

In. Slick and tight. Out, muscles massaging his shaft. In again, silken heat rippling around him, his balls tightening between his thighs. The tight knot of pleasure swelling in her belly. In. And out. In and out…

And…

She screamed, bucking against him as she climaxed. With a triumphant growl, he let go, fucking hard, grinding deep until his hips slapped hers, her anus milking his dick in sweet pulses with every thrust.

His own climax detonated in a shower of psychic sparks, long rolling pulses of it. He stiffened, feeling his come jet up that tight ass. Releasing her breast, he grabbed her hair, pulled her head back, and buried his fangs into her straining neck. Her blood filled his mouth as his seed filled her violated rectum.

Mine, he thought. *Mine*!

She wouldn't forget that now.

Chapter Six

One Month Later

Adiva ghosted along behind the woman, staying far enough back to keep her from realizing she was being followed. Somewhere up ahead, Vigilante strolled along as though he didn't have a care in the world. With any luck the woman's lover, an escaped pirate, would soon show his face. The minute he did, they'd have him.

After Adiva had dealt so successfully with Corvile, Vigilante decided to let her assist on his missions. Despite the vampire's powers, there were times it was useful to have backup, and he had to admit her espionage experience had given her the skills for the job.

Of course, as soon as they took care of whatever prey they hunted, she always ended up bound in some deliciously erotic position while he fucked and fed on her, with a little flogging and nipple torture thrown in for spice.

She didn't think she'd ever been happier, though she was still haunted by the nagging question of whether she was anything more than a meal to him.

Up ahead, the pirate's woman turned down an alley between a nightclub and a triddie palace. Adiva's heart began to beat faster. *Heading for a little rendezvous, dear*? She lengthened her stride, wary of losing her prey, and rounded the corner just short of a run…

Light exploded in her skull with a burst of blinding pain. She dropped to one knee, stunned, blood rolling hot down her chin. Hard hands grabbed her by her collar and hauled her to her feet.

A cold female voice snapped, "Adiva Mayhew, you are under arrest by order of General Borian Tang for espionage against the Tangian government." Her captor slammed her face first against the plastocrete wall so hard, she swallowed blood.

What the fuck?

With a snarl, Adiva twisted and slammed her elbow into her attacker's face. The woman staggered back, cursing, and she tore free, falling into a battle crouch. "Are you insane? Tang's going to fall to the Allies any day now!"

The woman wiped the blood from her split lip and sneered. "Well, he's not down yet, and the bounty on your head is up to three million."

She had fangs.

Oh, great -- just what Adiva needed, another vampire bounty hunter. Luckily, the woman was a head shorter than she was, a petite redheaded doll. With her bloodthrall strength, Adiva should be able to…

A hand wrapped in her hair and jerked her off her feet, dragging her into a big, rock hard body. Before she could even think of twisting free, a muscular forearm snapped around her throat, threatening to choke her into submission. "Don't give us any trouble, and you won't get hurt -- any more than you have to be," the man growled.

Inhaling, she realized his wasn't a human's scent. Bloody hell, yet another vamp -- and from the feel of him, one almost as big as the Vigilante. There was no way she'd be able to fight off both of them.

Unfortunately, she had no choice except to try. She sure as hell wasn't going back to the Red Palace.

Adiva raked her sharp nails across the vamp's bare hand, simultaneously stomping her booted foot on his instep. His grip loosened, but before she could slip free, the redhead stepped in and punched her so hard, her legs gave and her vision grayed.

Distantly, Adiva heard a male voice roar in fury. The arms around her vanished, and she hit the ground on her knees. Something slammed into her back and she fell on her face.

Stunned, she lay there a moment, distantly aware of male curses and grunts over the thud of blows and the scrape of boots. A woman shouted in fury.

Then, quite clearly, she heard Vigilante's snarl. "She's *mine,* Melusinde. And by God, I'm keeping her."

Blinking, Adiva lifted her throbbing head. Her lover stood over the dark-haired male vampire, who was shaking his head as if trying to recover from a blow. The redheaded female vamp faced him, obviously boiling with fury.

"Are you insane?" she raged. "That little bitch is worth three million creds. I'm turning her in!"

Vigilante balled his big fists. "Tang is a psychotic murderer who'd torture her to death! Assuming he even pays you, since he's going to need every credivo he's got to flee his own fucking planet when his government collapses!"

"He'll pay me, or I'll kill him myself. The bitch goes back, Galen."

Galen?

He curled his lip, and Adiva's eyes widened. It was a deadly insult to show fangs to another vampire. "Over my dead body."

"How dare you?" The redhead's face was bright with fury. "I'm your bloodmother, you ungrateful bastard. I freed you!"

"And I paid back every credivo you spent," the Vigilante growled. "As to your siring me, my gratitude does not extend to letting you deliver my woman to Borian Tang."

The redhead had made the Vigilante a vampire?

Adiva's heart sank. Traditionally, vamps owed complicated debts of gratitude and honor to their creators. If this Melusinde insisted, he'd have to surrender Adiva whether he liked it or not.

"*Your* woman?" Melusinde's ice blue eyes narrowed in what looked a lot like jealousy to Adiva. "She's just a bloodthrall, Galen. You speak as if you're in..." The redhead broke off, her jaw dropping. "You *are*! You're in love with the little slut! I can feel it there in your mind!"

"*You're not taking her*!"

"You fickle prick!"

Adiva barely heard the venom that followed.

She was far too stunned by the revelation that Vigilante loved her to care about anything else.

An incredulous joy welled in her mind, so intense she forgot her throbbing skull and rose to her feet. She took a step toward him…

Melusinde whirled and grabbed her, iron fingers closing over her shoulder. Wild eyes glared into hers. "He's not who you think, girl. Your 'Master' was a slave and a whore when I found him. He specialized in playing the dominant in a gigolo bordello on Gaow. I thought he was the master I wanted, so I freed him and made him a vampire." The vampire curled a lip. "I found out too late how weak he is."

Adiva blinked in stunned surprise. The redhead was a submissive? And the Vigilante had been a *slave*?

Obviously reading her mind, Melusinde shot Galen a vicious, triumphant look. "He's very good at pretending to be cold and merciless, but I knew his thoughts. He fell in love with me. Underneath that icy shell, he's *soft*. So I threw him out." She turned that nasty sneer on Adiva. "He'll never be the master you want. *He's a pussy.*"

"Lady, you're a fucking moron." Adiva drove her fist right into Melusinde's face with every ounce of her strength. The redhead hit the ferocrete on her back, stunned. "One, because you think Vi… Galen is weak, and two, because he *loved* you and you threw it away."

Melusinde glared up at her, rage and jealousy in her eyes. "I see now. You think you're in love with him too!"

"No shit, genius." Adiva looked around to meet Galen's wary emerald gaze. "What did you ever see in this twit?"

Relief flooded his eyes. She realized he'd expected Melusinde's revelations to matter. "I thought she was something she wasn't."

With a screech of fury, the redhead sprang at her throat. As she ducked the vamp's wild lunge, Adiva saw the dark-haired male climb to his feet, sigh, and go after Galen.

Then she lost track of her lover, too busy dodging punches and kicks while getting in her own. Galen was more than a match for the other vamp anyway.

It took ten minutes of sweaty effort, but she finally managed to land a kick to the jaw that put Melusinde down and out. As the vampire slumped to the ground, Adiva looked around, bleeding and exhausted.

The two men circled one another further up the alley, each obviously searching for an opening. The dark man glanced past Galen's shoulder and saw that Melusinde was down. Straightening, he threw up his hands. "This is stupid. I'm done."

Galen arrested the punch he was about to throw and eyed him. "What about the three million?"

He shrugged. "You're right -- Tang's government will fall long before we get a chance to collect it. Not that Melusinde will admit it." He sighed in resignation and started toward his mistress, Galen following warily at his heels. "I'd better get her back to the ship. She'll probably kick me out when she comes to."

Galen shrugged and wiped the blood from his mouth. "You won't be the first. Come to think of it, neither was I. She's looking for somebody who'll give her what she thinks she deserves, and she's not going to be happy until she finds him."

The vamp bent and picked Melusinde up, then slung her across his shoulder. "You were right," he told Adiva with a faint, dry smile. "She is an idiot." He hesitated a moment, staring at her as if arrested by something he saw in her mind. Then he grinned at Galen. "And *you* are a lucky bastard. Don't screw it up."

Galen stepped protectively close to her, as if silently warning off the other vampire. "I don't plan to."

"Jesus." Adiva blew out a breath and winced, suddenly aware of every scrape and bruise she'd collected in the fight. "I feel as if I've been worked through a grinder. Damn, that little bitch fights like a rabid rat."

"Tell me about it." Turning her to face him, he cupped her chin, lifting her head until their eyes met. "My name is Galen Vordire."

Then his lips covered hers. She kissed him back hungrily in a fierce mating of lips and tongues, joy swelling in her mind. *He loves me.*

He lifted his head. "Yeah, I do."

For a moment, her heart seemed to just stop. She'd hoped, but somehow she hadn't expected him to admit it. "Why didn't you tell me?"

Green eyes searched hers, the love in them now undisguised. "After meeting Melusinde, you have to ask?"

Adiva punched him lightly in the shoulder. "Idiot. You read minds. You should have known I'm nothing like her."

"You didn't seem to be," he admitted, cupping her face. "But I couldn't be sure how you'd react when you found out how I felt. It seemed safer to hide it."

She gave him a look. "Since when have you ever played it safe, Galen Vordire?"

He let her see the vulnerability in his green eyes. "Since I started loving you this much."

"I love you too. Idiot."

Then Adiva was in his arms again in another kiss just as sweet and hot and luscious as the one that had gone before.

* * *

They decided hunting the pirate could wait a few hours, so they returned to the orbital station where the *Pet* was docked. On the way, Galen explained he'd been barely sixteen when his mother died and left him homeless.

At the time, he'd been a bit too pretty for his own good, and a Gaowian slaver spotted him. The man kidnapped him and took him to Gaow, where sexual slavery was legal.

Galen hadn't made a good slave -- "No kidding," Adiva drawled -- and he'd changed masters six times over the next two years. Though he glossed over most of it, she got the impression he'd suffered horrendous abuse at the hands of his owners before he was bought by a woman who ran a submissives' brothel. Recognizing his temperament, she trained him to be a professional dominant.

"I loved it," Galen told Adiva as they walked through the station's winding corridors toward the *Pet*'s dock. "I was still a slave, but the submissives, who were free women, treated me as if I were master. I learned how to please them even as I played at dominating them." His gaze turned brooding. "It was the first time I ever knew pleasure."

"And then you met Melusinde, and she thought you were the Dom of her dreams," Adiva guessed.

He nodded. "I didn't care for her at first --"

"I wonder why." Adiva curled her lip.

"She was always a little difficult," Galen continued, ignoring the quip, "so at first it was easy to be the hardass she wanted. But she'd freed me, and when she made me a vampire, she gave me the power I'd always dreamed of. I was grateful, and I mistook that for love."

And given his life since his mother's death, he'd desperately needed to love someone, Adiva realized. What's more, Galen had needed someone to love him. But something had damaged Melusinde a bit too much, and she thought the last thing she needed was anyone's love.

"You're a bit too perceptive," Galen told her, lifting a brow.

"Yeah, I'm annoying like that. If you don't want to hear it, don't read my mind."

"You're getting cocky. Maybe you need another session with the whip to put you in your place."

Adiva snorted, trying to ignore the little thrill that crept up her spine at the chill menace in his tone. "I know exactly where my place is."

He dropped his voice to a deadly whisper that carried no further than her bloodthrall ears. "Yes -- bent over, taking my dick up your ass."

She swallowed. "That -- sounds about right."

Galen boomed out a laugh. Adiva found herself joining in, amused at her own reaction to his extravagant sexuality. They continued the length of the corridor before she took up the story again. "So you two became bounty hunters?"

"Melusinde was always a bounty hunter. I learned the job from her. I created the Vigilante identity because I thought if people knew my name, they'd connect me with my past as a slave." He bared his teeth. "I didn't want the scum I was hunting to think they'd found a weakness."

She nodded thoughtfully, realizing there was probably an element of crusade to his hunts too, since he was no stranger to abusive bastards from his life on Gaow. Being a bounty hunter allowed him to take revenge on men like his former masters.

"You're assuming I didn't take *direct* revenge." He bared his fangs. "Don't underestimate me."

Adiva glowered at him. "You really need to stop reading my mind."

"Not likely. I need every advantage I can get with you."

"Don't you have enough advantages as it is? I mean, really."

His smile was slow and sensual. "But I like having you at my mercy."

"I wasn't aware you *had* any."

Galen pretended to consider the question. "You know, you're right. I don't." As she laughed, he caught her by the waist and swung her into his arms for another of those long, delicious kisses.

Adiva was panting by the time she came up for air, only to squeal in surprise as he ducked, scooped her over his shoulder, and carried her around the corner and into the cavernous space dock where the *Pet* stood waiting.

"You've got to quit doing this," she told him, thumping him on the back of the head. "Let me have a little dignity!"

"What dignity?" He gave her backside a stinging slap that made her laugh and kick at him.

Then those long fingers began tracing the seam of her leather pants, pressing between her labia. Adiva caught her breath, knowing she was starting to cream.

Galen teased her all the way across the dock, through the *Pet*'s airlock, and down the corridor to their quarters before tossing her on the bed. She landed, laughing and flushed, and watched as he promptly began stripping off the civvies he'd worn on their pirate hunt.

"You're overdressed," he growled, peeling off his skin-tight synthleather vest and tossing it onto a chair.

"Can't have that." Heart pounding, Adiva went to work on her own clothing, watching breathlessly as he revealed that tall, powerful body in all its splendid nudity.

She paused to admire his muscular ass as he strolled toward the panel that concealed his extensive collection of toys. But as he started to pull out a set of restraints, she said, "I don't have to be bound to make love to you, Galen."

He stopped and gave her a long look. "You're a seventeenth level bloodthrall..."

"And you're a twenty-first level vampire dominant. But that doesn't mean we can't make love." Adiva smiled slightly. "Sweet love."

Leaving the restraints where they were and closing the panel, Galen turned to face her. "You think we're ready for sweet?"

"Why not?" Her smile became a grin. "I'm in the mood for something kinky."

He grinned back. "Meaning that for us, sweet *is* kinky."

Suddenly unsure, Adiva studied Galen, feeling abruptly vulnerable. Maybe he wouldn't be comfortable showing how he really felt.

"Hey, I can do sweet." He moved toward her in a slow, delicious stalk. His thick cock bobbed, eliminating any worry that he didn't find the idea arousing.

"You certainly can. That looks yummy." She crawled to the edge of the bed to watch him and his impressive erection approach. "Let me have a bite."

Galen laughed and stopped in front of her. "Oh, darling, I have every intention of giving you a bite."

"I'm sure you do, you wicked vampire." Adiva wrapped her fingers around the long shaft and leaned in to lick away the drop of pre-come beading on its head. With a moan, she swirled her tongue over it, then sucked him into her mouth for a slow, gentle pull. He groaned and threaded his fingers through her hair, letting his head fall back as she suckled him. Several luxuriant moments ticked by as she stroked and tasted.

Finally big hands came to rest on her shoulders, tipping her gently backward. Galen moved onto the bed, covering her body with his, letting his warm weight settle over her. His mouth found one nipple, and it was her turn to groan as he licked. Softly, slowly, he raked his teeth over the tight bud, teasing it until it was almost as hard as the cock she could feel against her thigh.

Adiva sighed and caressed his shoulders, loving the feeling of his skin, so like velvet over the cabled steel of his muscles. One hand came to rest on the tight rise of his ass and gave it a gentle squeeze. He responded with a mock growl and kneaded the breast he wasn't suckling. Her need rose in a long, lazy spiral. "You feel so damn good," she whispered.

Galen lifted his head. "So do you." Shifting his weight, he reached between her spread legs with his free hand, teasing his fingers between her labia. She caught her breath as he entered in a long, luscious glide. "You're wet." His green gaze searched hers, oddly surprised.

"You have that effect on me." She grinned impishly. "Even without the whips and the chains."

Heat flared in his eyes, and he reared off her, grabbed her under the hips, and tossed her lightly up the bed. Then he spread her knees wide, flung himself between her thighs, and lowered his head. Adiva gasped and fisted her hands in his blond hair as he lapped his tongue through the seam of her labia. A skillful flick and swirl circled her clit, making her moan.

The moan became a strangled shout as an index finger found her vagina and slid deep, followed by a middle finger up her ass. She spread herself wider as he gently forked his fingers in and out, teasing her with deep thrusts while licking her wet button.

Lifting his head at last, Galen rested it on her inner thigh and met her dazed gaze. "Like that?"

"God, yes." She rolled her hips desperately. "More!"

He withdrew his fingers until they were barely in her openings, then paused. "Are you sure? Could be too much for you..."

Adiva threw her head back and ground her teeth in frustration. "Sadist!"

"And don't you ever forget it." Galen plunged his fingers deep and attacked her clit with ruthless strokes of his tongue. She writhed, on the verge of an orgasm so intense, she suspected it would blow the top off her skull.

Suddenly he snatched his fingers from her and sat up between her legs.

"Galen!" she wailed.

"Patience." He aimed his cock for her creamy core, grabbed her knees, lifted them high, and thrust, driving to her depths in one ruthless plunge.

The sensation of all that massive cock spearing her was enough to kick Adiva right over the edge. She yowled, blinded by her own ferocious climax. He growled and started lunging, each pumping penetration adding another sweet pulse to her orgasm. The long ripples went on and on as he fucked her, a rolling sexual blaze fiercer than anything she'd ever felt.

Until he abruptly drove to the balls and stiffened, coming with a passionate roar. "Adiva! I love you!" Deep within her, she could feel the hot, wet pulses.

At last he collapsed over her, sweat-damp and shaken. Still quivering with the force of her climax, she wrapped her arms and legs around him and whispered in his ear, "I love you too, Galen Vordire."

"Marry me."

She froze at his hoarse whisper as astonished joy added itself to the emotion flooding her mind. "God, yes!"

With a growl of triumph, he pulled back her head and sank his fangs into her pulse. Adiva jolted at the startling pleasure-pain, then moaned helplessly as he began to feed.

Claiming her.

She wrapped her fingers in his hair and tightened her grip on his strong body.

Claiming him.

* * *

They were lying together, mutually drained and deliciously sated, when Galen suddenly broke into deep-throated laughter. Adiva opened one annoyed eye. She'd almost dropped off to sleep. "What?"

He rose on one elbow to grin down at her in satisfaction. "I told my comp to monitor news broadcasts from Adorev. It just notified me that Tang's government has fallen. Seems one of his bodyguards put a beamer blast through his skull."

Adiva grinned. "Bye-bye, bounty."

Galen pulled her into his arms. "Too bad, too."

She lifted her head, outraged. "I beg your pardon? Were you planning to collect?"

He raised a brow and drawled, "Actually, I intended to go to Adorev and kill him myself."

"You don't have time." Adiva grinned wickedly. "We've got a wedding to plan. So, are we inviting Melusinde?"

He snatched up his pillow and hit her across the head. She collapsed, giggling, and grabbed her own to defend herself.

"Wench!" Galen fended her pillow off. "You do realize I'm going to tie you up and ream that little ass?"

Adiva smiled smugly. "Darling, I'm looking forward to it."

The End

Angela Knight

Angela Knight's career as a professional writer has taken many turns. She's been a comic book writer, a newspaper reporter, and a novelist. Her work has won several awards, including a number of South Carolina Press Association awards for her newspaper reporting.

Still, her first writing love has always been romance. In 1996, her first romance novella, "Roarke's Prisoner," was published in Red Sage's *Secrets* 2 anthology.

Angela is now multi-published, as both an author and a cover artist, and her titles have held spots on the *USA Today* and the *New York Times* Best Seller's Lists. But her success would be hollow without the love and support of her friends and family.

You're welcome to visit her website at www.angelasknights.com or contact her through her blog at http://angelasknights.blogspot.com.

All Wrapped Up: Branded
Ann Jacobs

Prologue

The year 2150, Federation of Earth

The sub met him at the side door of the underground club and practically jerked him inside. "I'm sorry to have dragged you here, Master Cole. I know you don't come to the clubs any more, but I saw Mistress Ciel here with Amber. When Master Dax came in, I figured there was going to be trouble."

"Not your fault, Ellen. How long have they been here?"

"About two hours." Ellen sounded apologetic as she hurried them down the stairs to the underground levels. "Master Dax only got here about an hour ago. That was when I called you. When he joined them in one of the chambers."

Oh, shit. This club occupied the basement and sub-basements of an old garment factory. Only two exits, the one at ground level through which he'd entered, and an emergency escape route through a hollowed-out tunnel from one of the lower tiers. Bouncers manned the main door, always on the lookout for cops, so with luck the patrons could escape through the tunnel in case of a raid. That is, unless the cops discovered both exits and capture them all like rats in a trap.

The place reminded Cole of a dungeon, but not the kind he preferred, set up for the type of pleasure a certain amount of pain might bring to submissives. This dungeon was more like those used centuries ago, during the Inquisition, where pain was all about pain. Fear. Sweat and blood.

He quickened his pace as the sounds of flogging and the cries of submissives grew louder. "How much farther?"

"All the way down, Master." Ellen started taking steps two at the time, as though the noises were getting to her too.

Cole wanted to strangle his crazy sister. Why the hell had she gotten it into her head she could top Master Dax. Idiot! The vicious Dom was a known psychopath, a fine example of the type of BDSM practitioners that had gotten the lifestyle outlawed. Stupid! The laws now allowed Doms like Dax free rein, since dungeons were all illegal, and thus unregulated.

A high-pitched scream pierced the fetid air of the stairway. Cole charged toward the sound. An image of Amber's sweet face, her large eyes and soft pink lips, flashed in his mind. Nausea rose in him. Anxiety. More for Amber than for Ciel, who'd brought this on herself. If she had a death wish, that was one thing. But Amber would go down with her because that was what a good submissive would do.

He pictured her, bloodied and bruised. "Fuck!" He'd kill the bastard. "Which room?"

"That one, Master Cole."

Kicking the door in, the first thing Cole saw was Amber, bound to a St. Andrew's Cross. A cane whistled through the air, hit her breasts with a sickening thud. Blood dripped from other cuts on her shoulders, her belly, her thighs. Tears stained her cheeks, mingled with blood where the cane had struck.

Dax raised the cane again, and Cole charged in. "I'm gonna kill you, you sadistic sonofabitch."

Amber blinked through her tears. He'd come. She could hardly believe it. For the past year Cole had apparently wanted little to do with her and Ciel. Before, he'd always smiled at her when they crossed paths. He'd even taken time to do a little casual flirting when he'd run into them.

What would he do if he knew how many times she'd replayed those moments in her mind, pretending she'd read more than casual affection for his sister's friend in his smiling eyes? How she'd hoped he'd invite her and Ciel to one of his parties? In the old days when his preferred club had been open, she'd often watched him, wished she'd been the sub he'd had on her knees, lovingly servicing his cock.

The two men crashed into the wall, sending equipment clattering to the floor. Cole seized a flogger, caught the cane Dax swung at his face. If she could get free, she could help him. She could…

Cole had the bastard now. Would flog him within an inch of his worthless life. Foot planted in the center of Dax's chest, Cole raised the flogger and laid it across Dax's thighs. Dax screamed. "You don't much like it when it's being done to you, do you, you sadistic prick?" Cole raised the flogger again, but Ciel came out of the shadows like a madwoman.

"Leave him alone," she yelled, struggling to get control of the flogger, just as the door flew open and the chamber filled with cops.

"Back off, Ciel." Cole dropped the flogger. "And try to act like a victim." No chance to save himself, but with luck he'd be able to keep the cops from taking his sister as well as Amber. "Oh, shit, here come the reporters."

He whipped around, faced Amber, tried to block her so they couldn't get a shot of her naked, bleeding body. Dax and Ciel both wore concealing masks. His own face, however, would be out there on the six o'clock news for everyone to see.

As a cop clamped the cuffs on him and dragged him away with Master Dax, Cole tried to imagine a scenario where he'd come out of this smelling like anything but leftovers from last week's fish dinner.

Nothing came immediately to mind.

* * *

Eight hours later Cole sat on the hot seat -- a leather chair in front of Federation Commissioner Alan Callender's desk -- having just been bailed out of the county lockup by his powerful father to the tune of ten thousand credits. Cole made himself focus on a spot beyond his disappointed parent's left ear.

He'd tried, worked hard with Alan at his various businesses since graduating from college. In that way, at least, Cole was certain he'd made his father proud. He'd taken several startup concerns and turned them into successful businesses, as well as reviving some older endeavors and making them yield profits again. There was only one thing -- his lifestyle -- that had always given his father reason for concern.

Cole didn't kid himself. Alan knew he was into BDSM, probably even knew why he'd been at the illegal club: Ciel, who made no effort to hide her disdain for the law and who'd gotten herself into scrapes before, situations from which Alan himself had found it necessary to extricate her.

Alan looked him in the eye. "This is a difficult situation, son. I'm thinking there's only one choice here, other than imprisonment."

Cole attempted a smile. "I didn't realize there was a choice." He attempted a smile, failed. "I thought I was destined for a prison job for the next five years."

"Not if I have to collect on every bit of political capital I've accumulated, son." Alan paused, then continued. "You know, you've amassed a impressive portfolio yourself while running my companies the past few years. And earned every credit. You're a sharp businessman."

Right now Cole didn't feel very proud. "I'm afraid tonight doesn't reflect well on me. Or you."

Alan shook his head. "Treating the women as helpless victims was a clever stroke. You knew their identities wouldn't be revealed that way, and only your name and that of the other man would be involved. I'm not such a fool, though, that I don't realize all this was about Ciel."

Ciel? In his mind, Cole saw Amber, felt the pain that had radiated from her, from every bleeding welt caused by Dax's cane. She'd been a helpless victim, victim of Ciel as well as Dax. Not for the first time, Cole wondered what motivated Amber to allow such extremes to be done to her without availing herself of safe words.

"What are my choices, Father? What will help you the most?"

"It's not about me. It's about you. And exile is the choice. Permanent transportation off Planet Earth."

"What?"

"You could go to Obsidion. There's been talk of letting private investors turn it into an off-world pleasure resort."

Excitement caught Cole up for the first time since his arrest. "I could open a club there."

"That's what I was thinking -- you could capitalize on the fact there are many Earthlings who espouse a lifestyle unacceptable here. I imagine a man with your business acumen could capitalize on that, create a resort that would allow aficionados of BDSM to indulge those desires safely. A place that might allow fathers like me not to worry quite so much."

"A resort." Cole pictured not just the upscale club that first had crossed his mind, but a full-fledged vacation paradise. Hotel, restaurants, casinos, night clubs with imported talent from Earth. All the draws of Las Vegas, but with the added attraction of open, guilt-free practice of the BDSM lifestyle. "I like the idea."

It certainly beat spending the next five years in prison. "I believe I'll start out building the kind of club that will attract the more desirable elements of the lifestyle, then start on the resort."

His father nodded, sad resignation in his expression. "I'll miss you, but Obsidion is the best place for you now. I hope you'll find the happiness there that has eluded you lately. Perhaps I will send Ceil there too. You managed to save her from arrest this time, but if she stays, sooner or later she'll be caught."

"If you send her to me, I'll do my best to take care of her. Father, I am sorry."

"You will not be sorry. I will, for I will miss my youngest and dearest child." Rising, Alan circled his massive desk and drew Cole to his feet. "Perhaps someday I will visit, try to comprehend what it is about BDSM that makes people risk their freedom in order to practice it."

Cole hugged his father, hard. "And perhaps one day I will return here."

Chapter One

A year later, on the planet Obsidion

Everything was shaping up for an opening of *No Bounds* two weeks from Tuesday. Cole stood in his office, shrugging into a fresh shirt. They'd finished installing the equipment in the dungeon rooms, and he and the dozen men and women he'd hired to serve as club Doms and subs had been putting the equipment through its paces the past couple of days.

Fuck, but that hot Domme from Warsaw -- Magda Something Unpronounceable -- knew how to give a blow job. Cole's cock still gave an occasional twitch, and it had been half an hour since she'd gone down on him. While Magda was a natural Domme, she'd filled in as a sub when needed at her former place of employment. She'd shown him how a Dom could tie her up to the shiny rotating St. Andrew's cross and she could still make him come and come and come. Yeah, Magda would be a prime attraction for all the male subs who'd be flocking to the club. She'd be a hit with some of the other Doms as well, he imagined.

But even after a year away from Earth, Cole couldn't look down at the crown of Magda's head and not fantasize about Amber -- her soft blonde hair curling around her angel face, her delicate ears and slender throat. He couldn't help imagining how silky her skin would feel if he grazed his fingertips over her shoulders and arms while she serviced him -- a scene he'd never experienced except in occasional dreams.

He'd imagined a lot of things about Amber these past months.

And worried about her. It made Cole's gut tighten, thinking about Amber being in a place like the one where they'd been caught. Unfortunately, he had no doubt his sister had taken her right back into that maelstrom.

He'd known Amber since they were kids. She'd moved into his neighborhood to live with elderly relatives after her parents' deaths. Although she was Cole's age, Amber had let the older, more sophisticated Ciel take her under her wing. Many a time Cole had lusted after Amber but quashed his feelings because of his sister's obvious claim.

Truth was, as his attraction toward Amber had grown, he'd distanced himself more from Ciel's social pursuits -- and not only because he'd tried to keep his lifestyle under wraps once BDSM was outlawed, although that's what he'd told himself. He'd avoided Ciel because seeing Amber with her had fueled feelings he'd convinced himself were wrong.

Now it seemed Ciel was avoiding him.

His father had looked worried yesterday when they'd had their weekly conversation on the vid-phone.

"Ciel's just as uncontrolled as ever, and she still refuses to join you on Obsidion," Alan had told him after they'd exhausted the topic of progress Cole was making on *No Bounds*. Ciel's decision made Cole uneasy, because he knew whatever trouble his sister got into back on Earth, Amber would be right there with her.

The vid-phone's com link lit up just then, and Cole pushed the connect button when he saw his father's ID on the screen. "Is something wrong?" He'd talked to Alan only yesterday, and interplanetary vid-phone calls weren't cheap.

"Your sister was caught in a raid last night with her friend Amber -- you may know her. She has no choice now but to accept exile. I'm putting them both onto the next transporter leaving for Obsidion. It is due to leave here day after tomorrow."

Cole wanted to strangle Ciel for having put Amber at risk again. He couldn't deny the part of him that wanted to hug her, too, because now Amber would be coming to Obsidion.

* * *

Finally. Ten days later Cole had practically finished training his staff. Only one had not worked out so far, a Dom whose tactics reminded him of a Dax-in-training. No problem, because Cole could fill in as the fourth club Dom until he could find a suitable replacement. If he'd been into black leather and tattoos, he could have picked as many as a dozen Doms from the applicants he'd turned away, but he wanted to keep the atmosphere here more upscale so as not to scare away the women who wanted to dabble in the world of BDSM while on vacation but who weren't deeply into the lifestyle.

After all, it took a good many credits to hop on a transporter and blast off-planet for a taste of the pleasure-pain Cole would be selling at *No Bounds*. In his experience, affluence and conventionality went hand in hand, at least as far as what people expected Doms and subs to look like.

He'd leave the heavy metal and the leather to the two sleazy clubs that had beaten him into business here on the Pleasure Planet, and any that might follow. If *No Bounds* became the hit with customers that Cole expected, he'd soon be able to open the resort hotel he'd had designed, where discriminating customers might indulge their every sexual fantasy in an atmosphere of sybaritic luxury.

"Master Cole?"

His assistant stood inside his office door gawking at him, apparently enjoying the view as he began to button his shirt. Not surprising since she was also one of the subs he'd hired. "Yes, Kara?"

She held up a note. "Your father just sent you this message on the secure line. He said it was urgent and I should give it to you right away."

Frowning, for drama was not Alan's forte, Cole took the message, cursing as he read the first few lines:

Cole, I just learned Dax Petrone was shipped out on the same transporter as your sister. Even though she has her friend Amber with her, I am concerned as this man has caused Ciel so much trouble. Please do what you can.

Cole dropped the note on his desk and bolted out the door, not bothering to finish buttoning his shirt, hoping he wasn't too late. Apparently whatever arrangements Dax had made to avoid either prison or transportation had fallen through, and if so Dax was going to be furious, ready to take out his frustration on everyone around him -- particularly Ciel and Amber.

Fuck. The transporter ships that brought exiles here had nothing in the way of security for anyone but the pilots. Cade gunned the hovercraft and made for the transporter docks.

* * *

Amber lay, bound hand and foot, on the cold hard metal floor of the transporter's austere rear cabin, alone except for Master Dax. When she saw the sizzling branding iron, she understood what he meant to do, why he'd dragged her away from the main cabin and the rest of the exiles. The iron glowed an eerie blue-red before her eyes, held steady by the smiling satyr who had it in his grasp. "You will pay for having gotten me exiled, slave."

"No. Please, Master Dax, do not." Amber struggled through the haze of a stupor induced by too much pain, too much fucking. If Ciel were here, she'd have kept Master Dax from hurting her this way, but she wasn't. Her friend had been sleeping in the main cabin when Dax dragged her in here. As Dax brought the iron closer, Amber tried to recall the safe word. Slowly the iron descended, then disappeared from her range of vision.

"Noooooo." The stench of her own skin burning practically blotted out the agony of being branded, the sound of sizzling flesh on her left ass cheek as Dax held it there.

Dax put pressure on the red-hot brand as though he intended to burn all her flesh away. "This is but the first of many. Learn to love it. I won't stop until I've marked every inch of you for your treachery." He raised the branding iron, watched as it regained the heat it had poured into Amber's flesh.

The transporter shuddered, then lurched forward. "*Turbulence*!" Amber screamed, suddenly remembering the safe word Dax had given her long ago.

"You have no safe word now. None. You have, however, earned a brief reprieve, for it seems we're about to land on

Obsidion." He unplugged the branding iron and set it in its cradle.

Where was Ciel? Dax had to have done something to her, knocked her out. Ciel would never have stood still and let him brand her. Amber forced her eyes open as soon as they'd docked, but she could barely see through her tears.

Something crashed into the metal door, the noise making Amber cringe even before someone burst in, his accompaniment a string of curses. "You sadistic son of a bitch!" It sounded like Cole, Ciel's brother. Amber held her breath, hoping…

"Fuck you, rich boy." Dax said more, but the sounds coming from his lips morphed into a scream. Cole's meaty fist hit Dax's open mouth with enough force to make him stagger backward, spitting teeth, blood spurting from his lips.

Amber saw Cole now, standing over Dax's prone body like an avenging angel. Spots of blood dotted Cole's fists, and she saw murder in his dark expression. Amber strained against the cuffs and belts that held her on her belly, unable to move more than a few inches in any direction. Despite the burning in her butt she took solace in the knowledge Dax was feeling pain as well.

Guilt swamped her for feeling that way about a master. A submissive wasn't supposed to harbor such thoughts. But she'd used the safe word. Why hadn't he listened? How come he never listened?

Instinctively she knew Master Cole would never have ignored her plea to stop. Ever. Now, even though she was in excruciating pain, Amber felt the first sense of real happiness she'd experienced since learning Cole had been exiled more than a year earlier. A sense of joy spread over her as she looked at him, the hard-muscled chest framed in the two sides of his open shirt, the powerful thighs encased in snug denim that drew her gaze there and higher, at the outline of his cock and balls. His taut expression she imagined would soften when he was being pleasured by his slave. Amazingly, arousal stirred in her despite her burning ass cheek, her shock…

Ciel! What had Dax done to her? Amber opened her mouth, managed to croak out her friend's name… but nothing more. Her throat constricted, and she had to gasp for breath.

"I sent for the medics to take care of Ciel," Cole said. "Be thankful I'm a rational man, or I'd also be summoning a mortician if there were one here on Obsidion. For this piece of shit."

"But Ciel's not dead --"

"No. If she were, I'd have killed Dax without a second thought. She's in bad shape though." Cole stripped the belt from around his narrow waist, used it to bind Dax's limp arms behind his back. Then he came to Amber, removed the cuffs and shackles that bound her. "I'll take you home and have the medics see to you too. Did you allow him to do this to you?"

"I told him no. Didn't want… I used the safe word." Amber hated the look of revulsion on Cole's handsome face. As a Dom, Cole took care never to damage his subs. Besides, she *had* used the safe word, never mind that she'd done so after Dax had pressed that red-hot brand into her tender flesh.

"I'll kill him."

The tender way Cole lifted her in his arms surprised her, considering the fierce tone of his voice. "Please do not," she said as he carried her off the transporter and settled her on her belly next to Ciel, in the cargo area of a large hovercraft marked *No Bounds*. "I couldn't bear to see you imprisoned because of me."

* * *

Amber's worry for him moved Cole, bolstered him and kept him going through the next few hours. He brought in Ulrica, one of the most highly recommended Obsidion medics, and had her give Amber something for her pain before watching the woman spend almost six intense hours working on Ciel.

Ulrica pumped Ciel's stomach of the drugs Dax had forced on her, then monitored her until it appeared she'd pull through without lasting damage to her brain or other vital organs.

During that time, Amber lay in the room across the hall, and Cole peered in on her every few minutes, seeing her pain subside -- and return far too soon despite the drugs. He couldn't bear watching her suffer. As soon as Ulrica backed away from Ciel, he asked for something stronger to give Amber.

Ten hours later, Ciel had stabilized, though she still was unconscious. Cole needed the time he took to pull a chair up beside Amber's bed and watch her sleep, reach out and stroke her hair back from her face. She'd taken the sedative, watched him with her innocent-looking blue eyes as she drank the water he held to her lips. She could have held it herself, but he hadn't let her, hadn't questioned why he insisted on making her take the pill from his hand, insisting she slake her thirst the same way.

But he knew why. He wanted her. But she was Ciel's. He had to get a grip.

"How is Ciel?" Those blue eyes were on him now as he raised his weary head from his hands and focused on her. Pale and shaken yet in no apparent pain, she managed a smile, then repeated, "What did he do to Ciel?"

"She'll survive. Barely. The bastard force-fed her enough drugs to choke a horse." He stood and pulled back the covers, grimacing when he looked at the angry wound that covered Amber's left ass cheek. "The medic told me when this heals it will be the bastard's initials. Then it can be removed with a series of skin grafts. She also mentioned it could be modified now, turned into something more attractive before your skin begins to heal."

Amber shuddered, as though the idea of enduring more of the excruciating pain Dax had inflicted terrified her. Stepping back, Cole pulled the sheet back up over a sort of platform the medic had erected to keep the covers from touching her wound and causing more discomfort.

"It would be done with a laser tool and you'd be sedated," he said, even as ire built in him for her having thought he'd countenance her going through a branding in his home.

"How would she modify the design?" Obviously Amber wasn't thrilled at having the sadistic master's initial branded on her ass even for the length of time required to do corrective surgery, and that pleased Cole immeasurably.

"The medic said it could be turned into a simple flower. A lily, maybe. Or a rose. Would you like that?"

"I believe I would like it if it were done on your order, Master Cole."

Amber, calling him Master? They'd been playmates, friends… equals. He'd tried never to let himself fantasize about the beautiful, sexy Amber as a potential slave. In fact he'd often had to remind himself he considered her more the property of his sister, not so much in a sexual way as in the manner of a companion, a submissive follower Ciel could dangle like a carrot in the faces of other Dommes and Doms she wanted to impress.

But the wanting had been there, Cole knew, buried deeply under the veneer of friendship. He recalled many nights he'd dreamed of tasting Amber's soft, pink lips, feeling those lips stretched around his cock… of claiming her cunt and ass until she came as she'd never come before… Cole grew dizzy as blood rushed to his cock, making it rock-hard and turning his brain to mush. "My order? Are you saying you wish to be my slave?"

The look in Amber's golden eyes when she raised her gaze to his slammed into Cole's gut. "If that would please you, Master," she said, her honeyed words seducing him, making him wild to take her, mark her as his in every way he knew.

Except with a brand. And he'd have to do that or wait months for the signs of Dax's abuse to be obliterated. Once again Cole wished he'd killed Petrone when he had the opportunity. He pictured that bastard holding her, ignoring her pleas to stop, cooking the tender flesh of her ass with red-hot metal. Had the pervert come while he'd been making her flesh sizzle?

Cole traced the faint blue line that marked Amber's jugular vein, realizing how small, how fragile she really was. "It would please me to take you, to control you, to care for you. But what about Ciel? What is your relationship with her?"

"I love her as a sister. We have never been lovers, except when it pleased her to use me in order to torture her slave of the moment. She will recover fully?"

Cole shook his head. "I hope so. The medics are not so sure. I know that if -- when -- Ciel comes back to us in spirit as well as fact, I will insist she get some therapy. This baiting of Dominants like Dax will be the death of her. If not now, then soon."

"Master, I believe Ciel is not a true Domme."

"You think she's a switch?" Cole doubted that, but it certainly was a possibility he was willing to consider.

"No, a submissive determined to resist those yearnings." Amber turned her head toward Cole, gave him a smile that brought out every protective instinct he'd ever had. "Unlike me. I want nothing more than to be enslaved by a master like you."

Cole wanted nothing more than he wanted to take Amber, make her his in every way. But not yet. What she needed now was tenderness, time to heal. "And I want nothing more than to claim you. For now, though, I'm going to watch over you, take care of you... make sure you heal properly." He paused, bent, and brushed his lips across hers. "I've waited years for you, you know."

"You need not wait, Master."

"Yes. I do. Loving you the way I want to would only make this hurt more." He laid a hand on the opposite ass cheek from the raw wound of the brand, caressed her gently.

"Will you have your medic change the brand, Master?"

"Yes, sweetheart. I'll find the tattoo artist now." When he reached the door, he paused. Damn it, he hated the thought of burning her. "Are you sure?"

She turned her head, met his gaze with sober blue eyes. "I want to wear no man's brand but yours."

Chapter Two

He couldn't watch, yet he couldn't leave. Cole paced in front of a window that looked out on Obsidion's rugged terrain, trying to imagine it a year from now, once the straggly trees and shrubs grew up to lend some green to a setting now mostly rock and hard, red clay. Every time the smell of burning flesh began to gag him, he reminded himself Ulrica had sedated Amber, that she felt nothing the tattoo artist was doing to transform Petrone's initial.

She'd assured them it would look like a graceful lily once she was done. But Cole was getting impatient. He wanted her finished before the anesthetic wore off. "How much longer?" he asked, steeling himself to see what was going on and moving toward the bed.

"Would you care to see?" The artist straightened and set the white-hot laser tool in its cradle.

The first thing Cole saw were tears streaming from Amber's eyes, staining her cheeks and dampening the pillow. "You hurt her." Anger bubbled up, threatened to spill over into action. Cole took a step forward, surprised at how much Amber's tears affected him.

"Your slave was completely numbed. I would not have caused her further distress," the artist said, shooting Cole a look of disdain as she assembled her tools, fast, as though she thought it prudent to beat a quick retreat.

Amber reached out and took Cole's hand, spoke softly to him. "She didn't hurt me, Master. I cry when I am happy, and I'm very happy I will be wearing your mark and not Master Dax's."

Cole wasn't happy. He wanted to storm the jail, find Petrone, and kill him. But what he wanted wasn't nearly as important as caring for Amber. Numb now, she'd be suffering agonizing pain before long -- pain she'd endured mostly because of Petrone, but partially because of him as well.

The door opened, and Ulrica stepped inside. "Good. I see that the work is done. If you wish, I can leave some medicine that will dull the pain once the anesthetic wears off."

"Of course I wish it. I have no desire for Amber to suffer." From the expression on Ulrica's face, Cole doubted she believed him.

"Sir..." Ulrica spoke hesitantly, as though she wasn't sure he wanted to hear what she had to say. "You will need to keep the wound covered with an antibiotic ointment while it heals. If you'd like, I can return every day to tend it."

"I will tend her myself." A labor of love, touching her so intimately yet not taking his pleasure of her while she healed -- Cole wanted to care for her, not just sexually but in every way.

"All right. Give her one of these every four hours for the pain." Ulrica handed over a bottle of capsules -- the same painkiller Dax had used to try to kill Ciel, he realized when he glanced at the label. "And you might put her on one of those swing contraptions downstairs if she gets tired of lying here on her side or belly. Don't let her move around much for at least three or four days, or the brand might break open and start to bleed."

Downstairs? Was the woman crazy? Cole wasn't about to hang Amber out for everybody who walked in *No Bounds* to gawk at. "Don't worry, I'll take good care of Amber," he said, not ready to explore the sudden sense of possessiveness his new slave evoked. "Has my sister shown any sign of coming around?"

"No, sir. As I told you, I don't expect Mistress Ciel to wake up until sometime tomorrow. She's lucky to be alive, considering the level of drugs we found in her bloodstream." Ulrica pursed her lips disapprovingly.

Apparently she thought Ciel had overdosed herself. "You've got it wrong if you think Ciel would take that stuff on her own. Petrone forced it down her, probably to get her out of the way while he tortured Amber."

Ulrica shook her head. "I hadn't thought of that possibility. In any case, I have my rounds to make at *The Leather Gallery* and

Pierced Princes. When you get *No Bounds* opened up, I imagine I'll be needing to find a partner. Never understood it, not at all, folks like her" -- she nodded toward Amber -- "getting off by getting hurt. It's human nature, though, to lord it over another human, the way you masters do. Still, BDSM keeps us medics in business."

Cole barely managed to rein in his temper. "I don't imagine you'll be getting much, if any, business from *No Bounds.* I won't allow my employees or patrons to inflict injuries that might necessitate your services." Now, though, Cole was beginning to understand the look of fear and revulsion he'd seen in the medic's cool blue eyes when she'd first arrived in answer to his call for help. She'd obviously gotten a warped impression of the lifestyle he'd chosen, probably back on Earth -- although from what he'd seen on Obsidion, what went on at his competition had definitely reinforced her view. "I appreciate your taking care of Amber and Ciel though."

"It's my job." Ulrica picked up her bag and headed out, but when she paused downstairs at the door, Cole saw tears glistening in her eyes. "Once it heals, your slave's brand will be a thing of beauty. Unlike mine. I will never again show myself unclothed."

There had to be a story there, Cole thought as he watched Ulrica make her way down the street, past the businesses between *No Bounds* and *The Leather Gallery.* There was something about the woman, something that made him want to know her secrets, keep her from harm. Although, from her attitude, it seemed clear she wanted no protector. He couldn't help thinking she'd been hurt as Amber had, and in healing she'd lost much of herself.

Cole wouldn't let that happen to his beautiful Amber. He did have a problem now, however, because there was no way in hell he'd put her to work as a club sub the way she apparently expected him to, no possibility he'd stand by and watch customers maul what belonged to him. Exclusively.

When he went back upstairs, he paused at the closed door to Ciel's room. Amber insisted his sister had no claim on her, that they were only friends and sometimes participants in the same D/s scenes. But Cole wasn't so sure. Not that he doubted Amber, for he trusted her implicitly, but he had a feeling Ciel might harbor more proprietary feelings toward her friend.

* * *

Amber woke slowly, focusing first on a mural opposite the bed. Excellent art work, it depicted lovers… a master on his knees, pleasuring his ecstatic slave. The drapes that covered her breasts and belly were dark blue, like the midnight sky back home on Earth. Like the incredibly soft covers beneath Amber's seeking fingers. Everything about the room bespoke luxury… privilege… and care for beautiful surroundings. Even though no one had told her, she knew it was Cole's room. She glanced toward the open window, saw a wrought-iron balcony lit by three brilliant moons.

The sounds of moving feet, of low-pitched voices drifted to her ears. Comforting signs that she wasn't alone, that life and business went on around her. She fantasized that Cole would have been with her but for the pressing needs of readying *No Bounds* for its grand opening. It was a beautiful place, she was sure, much like the one he'd talked about long ago, idle conversation then, something she never thought he'd do. But he'd done it, here on a planet far away from home.

Pain crept over Amber after she got up and took a shower, small twinges around the brand, moving outward, inward, seeping through her veins. She welcomed every twinge, each reminder she'd survived this latest assault on her body. Survived and won another round against the demon within her that wanted to die, wanted her to kill it and herself in retribution…

For what? For having lived when her parents and sister had died? For having been a constant reminder to her grandparents that they were gone? For the first time in her memory, Amber fought the pain, fought it with dreams not of death but of life… of a life shared with a master. Her master.

Cole Callender. A beautiful man, tall, rugged, strong enough to protect her against all comers. For years she'd watched him grow from a gangly boy who'd teased her and Ciel with cicadas and snakes to full, masterful manhood. Eyelids closed, she pictured his dark, wavy hair, his laughing blue-green eyes, sensual lips that smiled more than they frowned. The memory of his powerful muscles rippling against her softer flesh when he'd carried her from the transporter, of the gentle touch of his hands, of his deep voice full of concern, flooded her mind, blotting out the physical discomfort from the brand.

Amber didn't know where she'd ever found the courage to say she wanted him as her master, but she'd never take back the words. While he might hurt her -- which she surely would beg him to do while in the throes of passion -- the knowledge that he'd also protect her even from his own desires warmed her, calmed the constant fear in her that someday she'd let a Dom go too far, finish the job the plane crash that killed her family had left undone on her.

She crawled back into bed, settling on her side instead of her belly this time. Ouch! She winced at the sharp pain no amount of sublimating could suppress. When Cole strode in and sat beside her on the edge of the bed, she managed a ghost of a smile.

"Time for your medicine." Reaching into the drawer of the night stand, Cole fished out the bottle of pills and handed her one along with the glass of iced water he'd brought in. "Down the hatch."

"Yes, Master." Just having him here beside her chased away the pain. "I'm glad to be here. Anxious to see what Obsidion looks like."

Cole gestured toward the window. "Well, that's the most unnerving sight you're likely to see -- Obsidion's three multicolored moons. Otherwise, the planet reminds me a lot of a desert back on Earth, except that the sand's reddish-brown instead of white. Some people are experimenting with irrigating and fertilizing large blocks of land, enough for commercially growing familiar plants. When you're able to get up, I'll show you the garden I've started out in the courtyard."

His wistful expression reminded her he'd had to come here because of rescuing Ciel -- and her. "You know, I haven't told you how sorry I am about the fight that got you shipped here."

"It's nothing. At first I felt disoriented, away from everything I'd known, but now I'm looking forward to making *No Bounds* a success. To seeing Obsidion develop into a showplace pleasure planet that will attract the best elements from Earth. Already we're working on getting all the services -- hospitals, utilities, and so on, that will make it easier to attract immigrants." He paused, lifted a stray lock of hair off her brow and smoothed it back into place. "Having you here's the icing on the cake."

Amber couldn't help smiling. No one, not even Ciel, had ever made her feel as though she were the center of their world the way Cole did. She could hardly wait to serve him the way a slave should serve her master. "Thank you."

"It's true. I want to know all about you. Where you lived, what you did before you moved into our neighborhood."

Like all of Cole's orders, this one was couched as a request, but Amber knew he meant her to talk, to re-live that difficult time. "Before I came to live with my grandparents? My parents traveled. Most of the time I went with them, but they'd decided I needed formal education and left me at boarding school before they went on that last trip. Their plane crashed."

It still hurt to think about it, the sad face on the headmistress when she'd called Amber in to tell her the news, the reluctance of elderly grandparents to take in the child of their child whom they'd disowned because he'd chosen the BDSM lifestyle.

"So you came to Scarsdale?" Cole prompted.

"Yes. I'd never been so lonely. Never. Not that my grandparents didn't feed and clothe me, but they never *talked*. Until I met Ciel I had no one. No one at all." Older, street-smart Ciel had taken her under a well-manicured wing, introduced her to the world of bondage and domination. She'd called Amber the perfect submissive, one who found the ultimate pleasure in pleasing others. Perhaps she was. Back then she'd wanted nothing more than to make those around her happy, because evoking a smile, a snippet of praise, had meant everything to her.

Now all she wanted to do was please Cole in every way. Feel his punishment as well as his desire, so she could break past deep-seated feelings of guilt, unworthiness, and reach a sexual peak that never happened without the pain… the humiliation of being on public display for others' amusement… the adrenaline of fearing this time would be the last, that the Dom of the night would take her past the point of no return.

But she wasn't certain Cole wanted her. Wasn't at all confident she wouldn't become a liability to his political aspirations here on Obsidion, just as he'd been one to his father back on Earth.

"Please take me, Master," she said, needing reassurance. Needing him.

Cole could resist no longer. He didn't want to resist. Not when she begged him to take her, not when he sensed her lack of confidence, her fears.

He stood and looped his fingers in the waistband of his jeans, unbuttoning them and shoving them and his underwear down in one quick jerk. Taking his cock in one hand, he moved close enough to feel her warm, damp breath on its throbbing head, then put his knee on the bed and sat back down, his cock in easy reach of her soft, sweet lips.

"Kiss me," he growled. When she swirled her pink tongue around the slit at the tip of his cock, he skimmed his free hand over the rich pale fall of her hair, along the gentle curve of her spine, being careful as he did not to touch the healing but still tender brand. "I wish I'd killed him for hurting you." She sighed, then sucked his cock head into the wet cavern of her mouth, her teeth grazing him, making him want more. "Yes, baby. Like that. Take it all. Deep-throat me. Suck out my come."

God, yes. Because it was Amber sucking his cock, swallowing him, licking along the vein that pulsed along the underside, he felt stronger sensations than he'd experienced with any of the other subs who had pleasured him, whether here or back on Earth. "Take all of me. Swallow my come. Oh, yesss."

He'd never come so fast, so furious. Every constricting motion of her throat around his cock head triggered another burst, another wave of incredible pleasure. He grasped the headboard, steadying himself, determined not to move until she'd wrung him dry.

He rose, bent, licked his come off her swollen lips. "I owe you a climax now."

"Have I your permission, Master?"

Though he'd heard it hundreds of times from dozens of women, the title "Master" sounded strange coming from Amber's lips. Cole framed her cheeks between his palms, smiled into her eyes. "You may assume you have my leave to come anytime you like, unless I tell you otherwise."

"And you may use me in any way that gives you pleasure." When Amber laid a hand on his thigh, his cock sprang back to life. "Would you like to fuck me now?"

"Oh, yeah. I'm going to take you, ram my cock into your sweet pussy -- your ass too. But later. Today I want to eat your pussy. Make you feel good." For the first time in his life, Cole wanted to fasten his collar around a submissive's neck. Not just any submissive, but Amber. He wanted to tell the world she was his to protect, to love, to master. To him, that was what the collar meant, in addition to staking his claim of ownership for all other Doms to see and heed.

He bent his head, nipped her just below the pink shell of her ear. The light floral scent of her hair surrounded them, ensnaring him in her. He stroked along her flank, murmuring an apology when he came too close to her wound and felt her tremble.

"Roll onto your belly. Carefully. Lay your arms out over your head." When she complied, Cole cuffed her and secured her wrists to one of the rails in the headboard. "That's good. Now spread your legs and let me in." The sight of her face down, ass up, her legs apart in invitation humbled him. Such trust, so soon after Petrone had misused her...

But was it trust or just the hope she always seemed to harbor in her expression, the hope that a master would truly take care of her? Something she apparently wanted so desperately she was willing to be tortured, as if trying to prove she could endure anything for the promise of such care and love…

Cole was going to show her, starting right now, that she should expect her master to care for her always, never cause her the type of pain Dax had inflicted on her. And, if he wanted to be honest with himself, the sort of tortures Ciel had caused her too. "There, let me slide this pillow under your hips."

"Thank you, Master. Please…" Her voice trailed off, as though she was afraid to ask for what she wanted.

"Please, what? Do you want me to eat your pussy?" Cole ran a finger along her damp, warm slit, then cupped her plump mound in his hand. "I like that you've shaved like a good sub." Too many of the women he'd interviewed the past few days had shown off shaggy, hairy cunts, a sure sign they weren't really subs -- unless they had yet to shave or be shaved for a master's pleasure.

He dipped his head, found her quivering clit with his tongue. "Oh, yes, Master. I wish…"

"What?" He spoke softly, his breath making her clit harden further. "What do you wish?"

"That I could taste you again too."

Her wistful tone touched him deeply, made him realize Dax's abuse had scarred her inside as much as out. Maybe more. "Later, after I lap your pretty pussy to my heart's content and take you gently, not forcefully as I want to do -- as I will do once you're completely healed. As for tasting each other, that, too, can wait. The last thing I want to do is hurt you."

Amber shuddered, as though the mere mention of Dax's name terrified her. "What will happen to him?"

"The police came and hauled him away to the colonial clinic to get patched up. Afterward, they moved him to the jail. He won't be getting out any time soon." Cole intended to see to that.

The last thing this brand-new pleasure planet needed was a sadistic Dom like Petrone running around loose.

When Cole traced the length of her inner thigh from knees to crotch, Amber made a purring sound. He liked the way she responded to his touch, enjoyed the slow loving dictated by his care for her injury. "You like this, don't you?" he asked, running a finger along the crease between her thigh and pussy.

"Mmm. Yes, Master."

"Not Master but Cole. I want to hear you say my name."

When she turned her head, he saw her smiling profile. "Cole. Master Cole."

"Amber." It was as though they'd been lovers for years, yet Cole felt compelled to claim her fully. Rising to his knees, he positioned her, rubbed his cock along her wet, swollen slit. "Do I need to use a condom?"

"If you wish. I… Yes. I'm sorry."

Cole ground his teeth together, holding back a curse. Petrone had fucked her unprotected. Otherwise she wouldn't have hesitated. On Earth she'd have been tested weekly as all former pleasure-givers and seekers were -- as he and all of her partners had been. Of all the restrictive laws the Federation had enacted, that one made a certain amount of sense. So much sense that Cole had adopted it for all who wanted to work or play at *No Bounds*.

"I'll get one." He moved enough that he could reach the drawer of a bedside cabinet and selected a thin lubricated prophylactic. Settling again between her legs, he rolled it down over his erection. "You have nothing to be sorry for," he told her, settling a hand on her unhurt right hip and directing her to shift position just slightly so his cock would slide easily into her sweet pussy.

He sank into her slowly, savoring every contraction of her tight vaginal muscles, every moan he elicited by pulling back, then thrusting slowly, gently into her silken heat. Anger rose in him with every glance at her poor ass cheek, with regret he'd left

Petrone alive -- though hopefully not able to do this to some other unfortunate sub.

She was so wet, so hot, so perfectly submissive, with only her pussy moving, her lips emitting moans of ecstasy. Cole sped up the pace, felt his own climax coming on. He would not go alone. Slipping a hand between the pillow and her satin skin, he found her clit, stroked it, all the time fucking her slow and deep. His balls bounced against his knuckles, high and tight within their sac, ready…

"Oh, yesss, Master, I'm coming," Amber cried, her pussy muscles grabbing his cock in a stranglehold. "Oh… oh yesss."

If his life had depended on it, Cole couldn't have held back. One -- two -- three thrusts more, and he came as though he hadn't just come moments earlier. Her cunt felt like heaven -- it felt like home.

* * *

The next day Amber felt much better, except that when she thought about having promised herself to Cole, guilt nagged at her subconscious. After she showered and toweled her hair dry, she decided to stay up, escape these four walls that were beginning to close in on her.

She'd go find Ciel.

Ciel had been her anchor, the one constant she'd been able to count on. Amber couldn't count the number of times it had been Ciel shouting the safe word when she herself could not, jumping in and stopping the play before some Dom choked the last breath of life out of her… Amber owed Ciel a lot. Her life, if that was what she wanted.

She had to find Ciel. See for herself that Master Dax hadn't killed her. Biting her lip against the pain each movement caused her raw ass cheek, Amber managed to get up on unsteady feet before taking a crashing tumble onto the floor.

The next thing she knew, Cole had her in his arms, his touch as gentle as his words were fierce. "What the fuck did you think you were doing?" he spat out, bending and lowering her back onto the bed.

"Going to check on Ciel, Master." She didn't like the look on his face -- worry mixed with righteous anger. "I -- I can't believe he didn't kill her."

"You didn't believe me?"

"Y-yes. I believed you. I just needed to see for myself."

Cole swore softly, but he lifted her again, carried her across the hall, and kicked the door open. "There. Look all you want. Ciel is sleeping off an overdose, courtesy of your mutual friend Dax Petrone. As I told you before, she's not likely to regain consciousness anytime soon." Not giving Amber time for more than a cursory glance at the movement of the covers when Ciel breathed in and out, he turned and strode back to Amber's room.

"Thank you, Master," she said when he laid her on the bed again.

He shot her a questioning look. "Am I your master, Amber?"

"Y-yes, sir."

"Then you will obey me in all things," Cole said. "You will not risk yourself by leaving this room until Ulrica tells me you're completely healed. If you want to check on Ciel, you will let me know and I will take you to her. If you need a change of scenery, I will provide it. I was on my way here with some refreshments and your next dose of pain pills when I heard you fall. On your belly, now. I want to make sure you did no damage to my brand."

His brand. Given with consideration and affection, unlike the cruel brand it masked. Meant to adorn and not humiliate her. Amber turned gingerly, certain that if she winced, he would take it as an act of disobedience, yet equally sure her pain would hurt him too.

"You have a gorgeous ass," he commented, his breath bringing goosebumps up on the uninjured skin around the brand. "I'd hate to have to redden it with a flogger, but I will if you pull another trick like wandering around before you're strong enough." He bent, laid a kiss on the dimples just above the start of her crack, then licked his way down until he ringed her anus with his tongue. "When you've healed a bit more, I'm going to fuck you here."

When he worked first one finger, then two, beyond her anal sphincter, her cunt began to clench, anticipating..."Master, you don't need to wait." She trusted he'd be gentle, the way he'd been earlier when he'd claimed her pussy. She didn't care if he wasn't careful, wouldn't mind if he hurt her. She welcomed the pain, because without it, she'd never been able to reach the heights of pleasure before. "Please, fuck my ass now."

He raised his head, found her swollen clit with his other hand, stroked it. Pinched it sharply, making her bite her tongue to keep from crying out with the sudden wave of sexual awareness that made her lift her hips.

"Be still or I'll hogtie you." Cole freed his hand, gave her a sharp slap on her inner thigh. When she moved again in obvious defiance, he realized Amber hadn't been joking. She was a true submissive, able apparently to receive pleasure only with punishment. "But you'd like that, wouldn't you?"

"Oh, yesss, Master. Please."

Someday Cole would show her she could trust him to bring her pleasure without the trappings of Dominance and submission, convince her she deserved that pleasure, whether or not it was delivered with pain. Now, though, what he wanted most was to give her what she'd begged for so sweetly. He got up, shed the sweatpants he'd put on before going down to check on progress the workmen were making, putting the final touches on the private chambers at the club. Now he strode to the chest by the window. Once he'd opened it, he rifled through it until he found what he was looking for.

A linked pair of nipple clamps with a clit clip dangling from the center of the link. A brand-new eight-inch glass dildo to be filled with warm or icy water as was his preference of the moment. And finally, the restraint she was begging for, although Cole doubted she'd ever seen one exactly like this one he'd recently invented -- a braided silk four-point tie that would fasten left wrist to left ankle, right to right. The leash at the center of the

"H" would be fastened to a metal eye in the bed canopy, pulling her limbs together, keeping her pussy open for his pleasure.

It should give her a submissive's delight in helplessness without putting her in a position where the new brand would be irritated. Cole swore, realizing as he did at least one reason why he'd never gotten off on marking his subs. Doing so placed limits far stronger than safe words on what he might do to take a sub to the heights of sexual satisfaction. Limits that made him chafe as he rigged Amber in the device and secured the leash to the eye.

"You know, I've never claimed your pretty breasts," he said, raising her enough to slide the nipple clamps and clit clip under her. Lowering her again, he cupped the pale, firm flesh of her breasts with both his hands. "I see your nipples are pierced. Maybe I'll replace these curved barbells with gold rings to match the collar I'm having made for you."

Her breathing sped up as though the idea excited her. "Whatever gives you pleasure, Master."

"No. You have no idea what I might demand of you. I don't know for certain, myself. Your safe word will be 'boundary', and I promise I'll never ignore it." He pinched her nipples, hard, loving the way they tightened beneath his fingertips, as though they could barely wait for the bite of the clamps. "Like this, don't you?"

"Oh, yesss." She wriggled when he pulled harder on the rigid nubs.

"I'm going to clamp them now. Take a deep breath, then don't move a muscle."

Her nipples turned red, hardened further as he tightened the screws. Her breathing grew ragged. Cole's balls tightened, anticipating…

"Enjoy, my sweet slave. I will be back." She'd suffered too much of a shock already from the brandings to use ice water, he decided, turning on the hot water and waiting for it to get comfortably warm before filling the dildo. The sound of Amber's eager whimpers spurred him on, made him fight to retain the control he'd need to give her pleasure, not exacerbate her pain.

Anticipation built in Amber as the sound of running water echoed from the adjacent bathing room. She longed for Cole's touch, the heat of his big, muscular body. She loved the reassuring feeling of knowing he would take care of the burning need inside her -- the compulsion to be taken, swept out of the real world into a world where sensuality reigned. Where nothing else mattered but being mastered, taking her pleasure by answering her lover's sensual demands.

Her ass cheek still burned, but she hardly noticed it for the intense pleasure-pain radiating from her clamped nipples. Cool air tickled her exposed pussy, made her keenly aware of her helplessness, the soft bonds that held her open from clit to ass. Delightfully, totally unable to resist her master's will.

When she raised her head, she saw him, magnificently naked, his long, thick cock erect against washboard abs, his smoothly shaved ball sac framed by muscular thighs as he moved to the bed. In one hand he held a glass dildo, glistening with lubrication. Although not as large or beautiful as his own massive purple-veined tool, Amber found the clear dildo impressive as it caught the light from the recessed overhead lighting. She wanted it… and him, filling her, driving her to that place in her head where nothing existed but ecstasy.

"Please, Master," she whispered, meeting his gaze briefly before lowering her eyes, the way a good slave must.

He knelt between her splayed legs, ran the surprisingly warm dildo along her slit. "Good. You're already wet and swollen for me. I approve." Finding her cunt, he spread her outer lips and inserted the dildo. Slowly. In maddeningly slow motion when she needed hard and fast. Inch by inch he pushed the dildo inside her until she was stretched, filled. "When you are well, I will put this in a harness, use it here while I use my cock to fuck your pretty ass. Would it please you for others to watch us?"

"If it pleases you, Master. Oooh, that hurts so good." He'd found her clit and fastened a clamp to the tiny nub, the new pressure on its chain moving to her nipple clamps, tightening their hold on that tender flesh. His hot breath bathed her slit, followed by the touch of his slick tongue lapping, licking, swirling around the base of the dildo, burrowing its way into her stretched vagina. "Oh, yesss," she hissed when he took the tip of her already clipped clit and bit her. Not hard enough to damage her... but hard enough to take her over the edge.

The first waves of her orgasm swept her along, over the top. Nothing existed. Not pain, not embarrassment, not even fear when she felt him lubricate her asshole with something wet and cold and position his thick cock head against her tight rear entrance.

"I'm wearing a condom, baby. Let me in."

All she cared about now was having him fill her, take her ass the way he'd already claimed her cunt and her mouth. As another wave of ecstasy carried her along, she relaxed her sphincter muscles. The exquisite pain of him stretching her, of feeling his cock sliding slowly up her ass, colliding through the thin barrier of flesh with his dildo, making the water inside it undulate within her cunt had her panting, whining, screaming her master's name.

"That's right. Relax and let me in."

He thrust into her ass slowly, carefully, his hands on her hips controlling her movement, holding her still. His fingers dug in, increasing the sensation of being possessed. Mastered.

"Oh, yesss, Master," she moaned when he sped up the thrusting, sank his cock inside her to the balls, set the water in the dildo in motion, lapping to and fro inside her already wet and swollen cunt.

"Hold on. Don't move. I don't want you hurting my brand." Releasing her hips, he found the dildo and began to slide it slowly in and out, its movement an incredibly arousing counterpoint to the thrusting of his cock in her ass. When he caught the chain that connected the clamps on her nipples and clit and began to tug it rhythmically as he fucked her ass and cunt, she could only feel -- not think.

Felt so good. So full. His cock swelled inside her. Its heat seared her as wave after wave of delicious sensation began in her ass, her cunt… the tortured tips of her breasts and her hardened, swollen clit. Like wildfire, the waves undulated, spreading cell by cell throughout her body.

"Please Master, don't. Don't stop," she gasped, closing her eyes and concentrating on feeling him throbbing inside her. Growing harder and bigger with every thrust until she thought he'd burst.

"Squeeze my cock. Squeeze it now. Oh God in heaven, you're…" His words trailed off, replaced by a howl of completion that shook the bed, carried her along once more.

* * *

If it hadn't been daylight outside, Amber wouldn't have known whether they'd lain together for minutes or hours after Cole had removed the clamps, released her from her bonds, and tenderly bathed her bruised and swollen parts with something soothing. The drink he fed her along with the medication Ulrica had left made her sleepy -- so sleepy that as soon as he crawled into bed beside her and tossed an arm possessively over her shoulder, she drifted off into a haze of satisfaction.

Chapter Three

"Do you plan to keep me naked, Master?" Amber stood at the edge of the bed, still shaky on her feet but determined to get around under her own steam, at least as far as the bathing room. "Or might I go retrieve something from my trunks that you'd find enticing?"

Cole laced an arm under hers, supported her as she made her way to the bath. "Take care of the necessities. Call for me when you're finished. I will provide you with what I want you to wear."

It wouldn't be anything she'd brought with her, he thought as he pulled on sweatpants and a T-shirt, for he wanted no reminders that she'd dressed to please other masters before him.

Striding to the storeroom for *No Bounds,* he quickly located a woman's costume he'd ordered for a special scene. She'd been on his mind even then, he realized as he picked up the delicately embroidered brocade corset that featured a built-in slave collar and a matching silk skirt.

Good. The material was soft enough that it wouldn't irritate her brand much. He didn't trust her to tell him if she was uncomfortable, not yet. Everything he knew about her indicated there was a vulnerable area in her psyche, no less dangerous in its own way than Ciel's self-destructive nature, for Amber obviously harbored the belief that a good sex slave should suffer whatever her master chose to dish out. Cole would teach her, in time, that the slave of his fantasies would help her master bring her the greatest pleasure by facilitating his protecting her from harm and maximizing their mutual joy.

As he hurried back to his rooms, he imagined Amber suspended in the fucking swing, the skirt lifted to bare her firm ass cheeks and his brand, the corset cinching her narrow waist and pushing up full breasts tipped with rouged nipples that invited him to taste them. He'd never allow her to wear panties again, even when her brand healed.

He'd keep her cunt and ass easily accessible for his cock, his tongue, his hands... He'd hang her on the St. Andrew's cross and shave her pussy, then eat her until she begged for mercy. He'd come in her mouth and cunt and ass, then feast on her wet, swollen pussy and fuck her some more.

God but his cock ached even now. She had him crazy, thinking of nothing but her and him and the hot sex with his slave that he sensed he'd never get enough of.

"Master?" Her voice drifted to his ears from the bathing room, beckoning him, making him fantasize about fucking her in the big hot tub. Later. Like many other scenes he wanted to share with her, the tub would have to wait for her brand to heal. "Master?" He threw open the door and came inside.

She stood, her back to a floor-to-ceiling mirror, her head turned so she could see that brand. "It is beautiful already, Master, because it marks me as your own."

Turning, she presented her ass, the left cheek with its still-raw design of a lily -- his lily, the one he'd never look at and not grow angry knowing what lay beneath it. Her swollen pussy lips already glistened with her honey. "I found what I want you to wear. Come, I will dress you."

He'd been right. The pink brocade emphasized her delicate skin, made the pierced tips of her breasts seem redder, more inviting, as if he'd already reddened them with his teeth and tongue. A heavy pink leather collar ringed her slender neck, its metal loops positioned perfectly to anchor the slender straps that crossed from front to back of the corset. Hooked, the garment emphasized her tiny waist between fully exposed breasts and plump mound. Cole knelt and tongued her clit, then rubbed his chin against her glistening pussy lips before rising, motioning for her to step into the see-through skirt, and tackling the lacings.

Already his cock was hard as stone. His balls ached. She looked like a submissive angel -- his -- and he was of no mind to deny the silent demand she made on his sex. He buried his face between her breasts, squeezing them, taking both nipples in his mouth and suckling until they became rigid nubs. She grasped his head, holding him there, as though begging him for more. He obliged. His nose grazed the straps, tugged at her collar, a reminder to him that she was his slave… his responsibility to give the ultimate pleasure. A reminder to her that she'd given it all to him. Her body, her will, her very life if that was what he wanted.

Amber's heart overflowed as she watched Cole suckle her jutting nipples, felt the heat and warmth of his mouth as he flailed them with his tongue. Her breath caught in her chest, constricted not as much by the tightly laced corset as by the sheer joy of feeling his collar around her neck. Of realizing that, for better or worse, she was her master's to do with as he would.

She threaded her fingers through his dark, silky hair, then stroked the corded muscles of his neck, his broad shoulders. Every tug of his lips, each scrape of his teeth felt incredibly delicious, not just where he suckled her but deep in her belly, her swollen sex. If he didn't make love to her, she thought she'd die.

As though he'd understood her silent plea, he pushed down his sweatpants and sat on a chair by the window, pulling her down to sit astride him. Carefully she lifted her skirt, let it billow over his powerful thighs as she impaled herself on his cock inch by delicious inch until his balls rested between her cunt lips, warm and smooth and pressing against her throbbing clit.

"Fuck me, baby. Fuck me hard."

Hands steadied on his muscular shoulders, she raised up on her knees until his cock head was barely lodged inside her cunt, then slammed herself back down until he nudged the mouth of her womb. So long and thick. So hard. Her asshole clenched as though it wanted action too. Amber tightened her inner muscles around her master's cock, squeezing him, taunting him as she lifted her ass, relaxing as she slammed back down on him. Over and over. Again and again as the pressure built inside her, threatening to break free.

A moan escaped her lips. A moan that sounded a lot like his name. "Yeah, like this. Let go. I want to feel you coming for me."

Cole caught her nipples, elongated now from the attention he'd given them with his mouth, and used them like reins to direct her motion, down until he felt his ball sac pressing against her slit, then up until she held only his cock head within her cunt. Over and over she rode him as the pressure built, harder and faster until all the dammed up emotions inside her collided in a climax that seemed to go on forever as it bathed his cock in white-hot heat, as her cunt clenched his flesh as though it would never let him go.

He couldn't wait. Had to spurt out his come in her cunt, claim her once more as his own. "My God, baby, I'm coming."

Grasping her around her tightly laced waist, he slammed her down on him, hard, and held her there as he came in long, hard spurts. As she milked him of every last drop. As he collapsed against the chair back, spent, and she held his softening flesh deep within her cunt.

What a climax! It hadn't been just sex, wasn't only emotion. It wasn't only a sign of mutual acceptance, master and slave, but rather a combination… an erotic mix of feelings Cole vowed would never end.

* * *

As the days went by, Amber began to heal. So did Ciel, although Amber knew it worried Cole that his sister had not regained consciousness except for short periods when she moaned and whimpered but gave no indication she was aware of her surroundings. *No Bounds* was ready to open, its main dungeon and private rooms spit-shined and polished. The club Doms and Dommes had been outfitted with the tools of their trade, while the submissives awaited customers who would require their services.

Amber stood in the main dungeon, ready to play her part in the club's opening festivities. She fingered the fine gold collar Cole had locked around her neck just yesterday, replacing the one that matched the corset he had chosen especially for her. She now owned three more of the corsets in different colors and styles, acquired at a local shop with her master's tastes in mind.

Idly, she rubbed one of the lines left on her midriff by the corset stays, then ran the same finger across the still tender brand on her ass. Last night Cole had pronounced it healed. Tonight she expected -- hoped -- he'd use one of the fine floggers he'd bought to enhance his pleasure, and hers.

Maybe he'd ad-lib a flogging into the scene they'd planned for the club opening. She looked forward to kneeling at his feet, the matching leash attached to her collar and fastened to his belt, so all who looked would know she was his willing, devoted slave. She'd suck his cock, letting her juices flow yet refrain from coming as a good slave should, until her master granted his permission. Then he'd lead her into the dungeon's observation room to play out a scene they'd rehearsed every day for the past week, since Cole had changed the jewelry in her piercings, replacing them with small rings joined together with a length of slender gold link chain.

In the scene, he'd shave her cunt, lick her pussy, and make her suck his cock before looping her leash through the chain and pulling her to her feet. The part she liked best was when he'd kiss her afterward, licking the remnants of his come from her mouth while he jiggled the chains. In the finale, she'd go up on all fours, ass in the air, begging him to fuck her there.

The fact they'd be playing to a full gallery of customers gave her a wicked sense of arousal. Not that the idea of playing with her master wasn't erotic enough to keep her cunt wet twenty-four, seven.

Amber toyed with the end of her leash. Where was Cole? The doors of *No Bounds* were set to open in less than an hour now, and he'd surely want to be here overseeing the activity.

* * *

"But Amber is mine!" Ciel screeched. "Mine."

As glad as Cole was that his sister had finally awakened, he could have done without her screaming like a banshee less than a half-hour before *No Bounds* was set to open. "No, Ciel. She was -- is -- your friend. Never your slave or even your sub."

"Bastard. She's my slave. You can't take her."

"I have taken her. Collared her. Tonight I will claim her as mine for all my guests at the club opening to see." Cole spat the words out angrily, but then he looked at his sister's hollow cheeks, her sunken eyes. She was sick. Sicker than he'd realized. Damn it, he should have seen it, gotten her help long ago, intervened before she'd placed Amber's well-being at risk.

Still, as much as he loved his sister, part of him reacted to her claim to Amber as if Ciel had been another man. Amber was his. His to care for and protect, and Ciel was never going to get her back to use and expose to psychos like Dax again.

When Ciel trembled so much that the bed shook, Cole bent to embrace her. She turned in his grasp, clawing at him like a demon possessed. Blood ran down his cheek in the twin paths she'd gouged with talon-like nails as he held her wrists, restrained her from doing him or herself further harm.

"Calm down," he said, holding her wrists so she couldn't attack him again. "Nothing you do or say will change anything."

"Where is Dax?" she asked, suddenly still, apparently conceding she was no match for Cole's strength. "He swore he would brand her, make her so ugly no master would want her."

"He's in prison."

Ciel fought his hold, made Cole struggle to hold onto her. When she cried out, it was more a feral sound than words. Damn it, she'd completely lost touch with reality.

Cole pressed her back down on the bed and held her there. Then he looked her in the eye. "Believe me, Dax is in jail. And if there's a God, he'll be staying behind bars for a long, long time." Cole recalled Amber's theory that Ciel was a sub in Domme's clothing. She might have been right. "Tell me you don't think you want that sadistic bastard."

"I was about to subdue him. Amber was helping me." Ciel jerked loose from Cole's hold, practically leapt out of bed and went to stare out the window at the raw, red ground he'd had plowed to turn into a garden. "God, but Obsidion's a desolate looking place. Our father did me no favor, sending me here with Dax and Amber."

She'd get no argument from Cole about the latter. Many times when he'd tended Amber's brand, he'd wanted to kill Alan for having exiled the three together -- for having exiled Petrone, period, instead of imprisoning him for life back on Earth.

Ciel, always mercurial, seemed to have calmed down a bit. Cole managed to persuade her to take her medicine and crawl back into bed. "Give it time, Ciel. We will make Obsidion a paradise where Earthlings can come indulge their passions amongst all the luxuries of home. One step at a time. Meanwhile, I need to go. It's time we open our doors to our first customers.

"Rest now." Bending, Cole kissed Ciel's forehead. "I need you to get well, so you can show our club Dommes how we treat our subs at *No Bounds*." He had only a few minutes to tend his ravaged cheek and change into the black leather chaps, vest, and boots he was to wear in the scene with Amber.

* * *

"Ciel was awake just now," Cole whispered a few minutes later when he joined Amber and clipped her leash to the thick silver chain around his waist.

"I must go to her." Amber made a move toward the stairs but stopped cold when he didn't lead the way. "Master."

"Not now."

"But, Master…"

"I said not now. She took her medicine, and should be sleeping again. Besides, we have a club to open." If he could, he'd shield Amber forever from his sister's misplaced possessiveness. While he couldn't manage that with them both living in the quarters above *No Bounds*, he could and would postpone the inevitable confrontation as long as possible.

Amber reached a hand up to her throat, fingered his collar. "Does she know?"

"Yes. She knows. Did you think I'd keep this from my own sister?" Cole traced the path his collar took, feeling a burst of pride that Amber had chosen him to be her master. "I want the whole world to know you are my slave, that you love me and I love you."

Her eyes widened when she noticed the angry scratches along his cheek. "She… why did she do this to you?" Very gently she traced the lines of the wounds.

"Hush. It's nothing."

Tears filled her eyes, caught on the thick fringe of her eyelids. "We were friends. Never more. Oh God, Master, she must have thought --"

"That you were her slave. I assured her you were not and never had been, that you were and are her friend, even though the way she used you could easily have gotten you killed." Cole used his thumb to catch a tear on its way down Amber's cheek, then rubbed the moisture over her glistening lips. "Come now, we must greet our guests."

"She was to have been here, too, taking part in the opening ceremonies. Before we left Earth, she'd planned a scene…"

Amber's hesitation told Cole he didn't want to hear the details of what Ciel had planned. Not now, when all he wanted to do was concentrate on Amber, on showing the guests he'd invited to *No Bounds* on its opening night that he had taken a slave he loved dearly, one he would go to any length to bring to pleasure. "All that's in the past, sweetheart. Forget Ciel. That's an order." He shot her a smile, then tugged at her leash as though he had to coax her to do his bidding.

Chapter Four

Strobe lights played over the silver-flecked walls, the colors blue, purple, red and gold, moving in studied dissonance, focusing first on one piece of chrome equipment then another, showcasing the variety of devices a sexual Dominant might use in *No Bounds* to subdue or pleasure his or her slave. Muted exclamations from the observers in the glassed-in theatre above the dungeon floated like disembodied voices in a vacuum, reminding Amber that over a hundred pairs of eyes were looking down at them, even though the owners of those eyes were cloaked in darkness.

In the center of the room, she went down on her knees, head bent respectfully, hands locked behind her back in the classic pose of a submissive. Her master stood before her, his muscular legs braced slightly apart, a flogger gripped within one powerful fist. Music, muted until now, built to a crescendo, heightening her anticipation… her fear. Not true fear, for she trusted Cole with her life, but the pleasurable apprehension of the unknown, of how he would overpower her, the places he would take her, places far beyond her control. The fierce arousal that gripped her had begun the moment Cole had tugged on her leash. Even before that. Her pussy had been hot and swollen since Mistress Magda had laced her into this sparkling silver lamé corset so tightly she could barely breathe, secured her hair in a ponytail at the crown of her head, and rouged her exposed nipples.

"You may rise, slave. Have you prepared yourself for me?"

"Yes, Master." Amber made her voice quiver, in accordance with the script.

Cole reached out with his free hand, examined her swollen slit. "You are wet. But I believe you've forgotten at least one of my orders. Did you shave my pussy?"

"N-no, Master. I forgot. I am sorry."

He lifted the flogger, and she braced for the strike that never came. "I do not wish to mark my slave's tender skin. Not yet. Attendants! Prepare my slave for my attention."

Mistress Magda and a naked male sub moved out of the shadows, grasped Amber's outstretched arms, lifted her onto a chrome-plated table. They hadn't rehearsed this. At the sparkle in Cole's eyes, she knew he had planned it for her pleasure, thinking of her even on this night that was so important to him. It underscored to her what she was learning. That she was important to him. Perhaps, for once, she'd found a relationship where her master cared for her as much as she did for him. And it made her realize many things about herself, one of them being that she was worthy of being loved that way, for she loved with her whole heart as well.

A delicious frisson of anticipation shot through Amber as Magda clamped fur-lined handcuffs onto her wrists and stretched her arms back, high over her head, immobilizing them by hooking the cuffs over the pole at the end of the table. Her master arranged her legs in stirrups before ordering the sub to secure them with Velcro fasteners around each thigh, her knees, and her calves.

"Shave her cunt. Nick it and I will flay you within an inch of your life," Cole told the sub. "Slave, I order you not to come until I give permission," he said as he stepped up beside her and began to stroke her cheek, her earlobe, her throat. "So soft. So beautiful. So *mine*."

Her master's most innocent caress enflamed Amber more than the sensual scraping of the sub's razor over her mound, her pussy lips, around her ass. She closed her eyes, let the music and Cole's touch carry her somewhere safe, somewhere only the two of them existed, apart from the sub, Mistress Magda, and the unseen audience in the theatre above them.

By the time Cole found her nipples and began teasing them to tight, hard points Amber was squirming, needing to release the pressure building in her belly, her cunt, her ass. Yet she did not, would not disobey her master's order despite the burning need that intensified when he threaded a long gold chain through her nipple rings and arranged the ends over the lacings of her corset.

Bending, he kissed one taut nipple, then the other, before ordering the sub away and stroking her newly shaved mound below the pointed front of the corset. "Ah, that's the way I like my pussy." Bending, he tongued her where his hand had been, then moved lower to suck the rigid nub of her clit between his teeth.

When he raised his head and looked up at her, it was all she could do not to beg him to continue, to lick her pussy, suck her clit, and lap the honey from her pussy lips until she screamed for mercy. Instead, she managed a breathy "Thank you, Master," before he pinched her clit between his thumb and middle finger and inserted a gold ring -- larger than the one she'd had before, like the ones he'd just fit through the holes in her nipples -- through the already engorged flesh.

Her breathing grew ragged. Her pulse raced. Her cunt clenched and her juices flowed, turning her pussy lips wet and slippery to her master's touch. The weight of the two chains he'd attached to the ring before closing it with a captive bead sent incredible sensations throughout her body. "Please, Master, fuck me now," she begged, barely able to speak as she struggled to hold back her climax.

Cole tugged sharply on the chain that connected her nipple rings with the one in her clit. "Not yet." Bending, he brushed his lips across hers, at the same time laying a hand over the lacings of her corset, tilting the platform where she was bound until she lay upside-down, her face level with his crotch. The bindings on her legs held her firmly in place. "Suck my cock, my precious slave," he said, his breath tickling her freshly shaved cunt as he looked down between her widely-spread legs.

With her teeth, she greedily caught at the hidden snaps that closed the front seam of his leather jock and ripped it open. No longer tightly confined, his cock sprang through the opening. It didn't matter that the amphitheater was full, that hordes of guests were watching. She had to taste her master, show him... She reached out with her tongue, caught the creamy drop of pre-come that glistened in his slit, then opened her lips as he flexed his hips and claimed her mouth. She loved performing this service for him, swirling her tongue all around his massive cock head, taking him deep down her throat, swallowing convulsively around his rock-hard flesh. Most of all she loved hearing him groan when she sucked him this way, feeling his massive thighs tremble with the effort of holding back his climax.

Oh, God. He bent his head and licked her pussy, tugging with his teeth at the ring he'd put in her clit. His chest brushed against her nipples when he moved. When he sank two fingers into her pussy and another in her ass, she couldn't hold back any more. She took his cock deeper, sucked it, loved it. She loved him and the sensations he'd aroused until it felt…

"Now."

Incredible. Her cunt and ass clamped down on his fingers. It all felt so good she hurt, as wave after wave of ecstasy flowed through her. Limp, half-conscious now, she registered the fact he'd turned the platform only vaguely, until he flexed his knees and impaled her.

"I'm tired of gentle. I know you are too." His hands easily spanning her corseted waist, Cole steadied her. With every thrust of his hips, each hard stroke of his cock within her swollen cunt, she came again. And again. Finally, when she thought she could come no more, he came in her pussy, the hot bursts of life starting her to climaxing all over again.

Cole looked down at her, tenderness in his eyes. She raised his palm, kissed it, tasted the clean salty essence of his sweat. "Master, I…" A shout of warning and a shriek, the sound of a crash in the hallway outside the door, jerked his head around and stopped the words on her lips.

"Amber!" Ciel's voice was somewhere between a plaintive wail and a threatening roar, the Mistress warring with the pathetic soul she'd become. "You're mine. You're…"

Chapter Five

"No, Ms. Ciel, you can't go in there."

"Fuck you." A whip cracked. Somebody screamed. Another crack. Feet pounded on the marble floor as people got scared and started running. "My brother betrayed me, now I'm going to make both of them pay."

Quickly Cole loosened Amber's bonds, lifted her off the modified Cross. "Stay here," he ordered, shoving her into a darkened corner of the dungeon and striding to the door. He was going to have the head of the club employee he'd set to watching Ciel. Damn it, he'd personally given her enough medication that she should have slept through the night. She must have gotten hold of something from Ulrica's bag, something that had her wired up tighter than a guitar string.

It was clear his sister had completely lost it, but there was no way he was going to let her injure Amber. He opened the door to the dungeon and stepped out into the hall. "Ciel, put the whip down."

"You..." She lifted the whip, cracked it, flicked it with her wrist and wrapped the last three feet or so of its five-foot length around Cole's legs. While he struggled to get free, she dropped the whip and fled, her long black hair snarling around her like a medusa. The expression in her eyes in the split-second she looked at him would have curdled the blood of a zombie.

"Show's over," Cole shouted toward the audience. "Welcome to *No Bounds*. Follow the rules and have fun. Dungeon mistress tonight will be Mistress Magda."

He stepped back into the shadows, to Amber. "Ciel has lost it, sweetheart. We have to go find her."

* * *

Three moons shone in the night sky. Three.

Where the fuck am I? Ciel whirled first one way, then the other, disoriented. The neon lights of bars and clubs along the Street of Slaves blinked, blinding her to everything but her quest.

Kill. Kill Dax. Tricked me. Wanted Amber. Not me. Amber, my friend. Gone now. Gone. Cole's slave. Wrong. Ciel raised the dagger she'd taken from the equipment room, waved it at a couple of passers-by. *Yeah, right. I'm crazy. Crazy, you got it.*

"What's with you, lady?"

"Moons. Three of them."

The taller of the two men laughed. "Yeah, Obsidion's got three moons. Weird when you first go out at night, until you get used to it."

Ask him. "Jail. Looking for the jail."

"That way, lady. Take a right once you get past *Pierced Princes*, and you'll see it at the end of the street. Convenient, since half the Prince's customers end up there at one time or another."

Almost there. Tucking the dagger into the belt of her robe, she took off for the blinking *Pierced Princes* sign.

"You could have managed a 'thank you,' lady."

The man's sarcasm was lost on the wind.

Outside the jail, Ciel paused. *Have to collect myself. Can't rouse suspicion.* She paused, smoothed her hair. Straightened the folds of the white silk robe she'd snatched along with the dagger. And schooled her expression to one of sublime composure as she opened the jail door and stepped inside. "I want to visit Dax Petrone," she said, making sure she sounded not like a furious Domme, but like a sweet, compliant little sub. Like Amber.

* * *

They'd lost precious minutes, but they'd have been thrown in jail if they'd gone out in the street in the clothes they had on for their BDSM scene. Cole and Amber paused outside *No Bounds*, looked in both directions. A drunk stumbled out of one of the bars. A pair of tourists embraced outside a sex toy shop, their faces made surreal in the light of the neon signs.

Not a sign of Ciel. Anywhere. Amber tugged at Cole's sleeve. "Would she have gone to one of the other clubs, Master?"

"Not likely."

"Why don't you ask those guys if they saw her? They look as though they're still reasonably sober."

Cole followed Amber's gaze to the men outside the toy store. "All right. Let's do." Hurrying now, he dragged Amber along, stopping to scoop her up and toss her over one shoulder when he realized she couldn't handle his pace. "Sirs," he yelled as the two men started to amble toward *The Leather Gallery*.

They paused at the sound of Cole's voice. One of them turned "Yeah?"

"We're looking for a woman --"

"Wild black hair? A white dress? Actin' crazy?"

That sounded like Ciel, all right. "You seen her?"

"She wanted to know where the jail is. Took off that direction like a bat out of hell, didn't even say 'thanks.' Hey, don't anybody around here know how to say 'Thank you'?"

"Sorry, man," Cole yelled. "Got to hurry, try to prevent a murder."

A little winded after the three-block sprint, Cole set Amber on her feet outside the jail door. "Wait here," he ordered, but as he swung the door open, a body came through it, almost like a flying missile.

"My God, what's going on?"

Cole tore his gaze off the missile -- a cop from the look of his uniform -- and looked at Amber. "Ciel, I'm afraid."

He was more certain than ever that she'd taken something -- maybe more of the stims Ulrica had been giving her to break her out of the coma. Ordinarily Ciel would have been no match for a burly cop like the one who'd just flew out the door.

"I'm going in. She'll listen to me." Amber stepped through the door, certain Cole would stop her if she gave him half a chance.

"Damn you!" Ciel screamed, not at Amber but at the prone body on the floor.

The scene before Amber made her stagger back into the security of Cole's arms. Ciel, plunging a dagger over and over into the bloodied body of Dax Petrone, stabbing wildly at any cop who gathered the courage to try and stop her.

"Ciel," Amber said, keeping her tone mild, soothing, hoping her friend retained enough of her sanity to listen.

Ciel whirled, madness in her eyes, her hands bloody, fresh blood dripping down the white silk of her gown. "Kill you too," she rasped, lunging not toward Amber but around her, toward Cole.

"No, Ciel. You're sick. Give me the dagger." Cole looked desperate, sounded tortured, but he moved forward, caught Ciel's wrist that held the dagger. "Please."

Why were the two cops just standing there? Amber grabbed for Ciel's free hand, but found herself slammed against a wall as though she weighed no more than a baby.

Cole had Ciel pinned to the floor, but she was stabbing wildly at him.

"Help. Help Cole! Can't you see she's going to kill him?" Amber's pulse raced with fear as Cole continued to struggle for control of the dagger. "Shoot her!"

"The constable doesn't allow any weapons in the jail."

Amber moved in again, bent on getting the dagger, but she felt a cop's hands at her waist, setting her aside. "Stay out of the way. We'll deal with this."

One cop moved in, grabbing Ciel around the knees to stop her bucking. The other grabbed Ciel's arm and held it long enough for Cole to knock the dagger from her hand. Cole caught her shoulders then and wrenched her back to the floor.

"Quick. Cuff her before she gets away." The cop who had her legs was dodging vicious kicks, and Cole managed to hold her down only by pressing his substantial weight on her chest while keeping her arms pinned over her head. Even after the other cop put Ciel in handcuffs and shackles, she kept striking out, screaming obscenities, threatening to kill them all.

This blood-spattered woman who had lost a tenuous grip on reality wasn't the Ciel Amber knew, wasn't the friend who'd become her anchor after her world had fallen apart. Still Amber couldn't help seeing remnants of the friend she'd trusted. It was Ciel's high cheekbones, her regal looking nose, that dimpled chin and the slender neck Amber had always thought should wear the right Dom's collar. But the eyes... those wild eyes full of hate that watched every move as the guards zipped the man she'd killed into a body bag. They didn't belong to the Ciel she'd known.

Or maybe they did. Maybe this unfettered violence had been part of Ciel's nature for a long time, and it had worsened little by little, as an addict's need for drugs grew exponentially over time. Amber had been drawn into it, sucked in by her own vulnerability, the belief that she had to do something -- anything -- to deserve love.

She tore her gaze from Ciel to inspect Cole as he turned away from the jail's head guard. "Are you all right? Did she hurt you?"

"I'm fine. Come," Cole assured her. "There's no more we can do now. Ciel will have to stay."

Of course. Ciel had killed a man. Never mind that Amber couldn't think of one human being who'd more richly deserved to die. "What -- what will happen to her?" she asked, watching the guards pick her up and haul her away.

"An institution, I imagine. There's no way anyone could say she's sane. I'll send word to my father about what's happened and ask him to get a lawyer up here to defend her. Meanwhile, she's safer in jail where she can't harm herself than she would be back home."

They stepped outside into the eerie light of Obsidion's multicolored moons, and Amber took Cole's hand. "This wouldn't have happened if it hadn't have been for us."

"Don't say that. Don't even think it. I forbid it." Cole stopped, drew Amber into his arms, stroked her like a father might do to reassure a child.

"My sister has always had a tenuous hold on reality. We -- everyone in the family -- have always done our best to see that she didn't lose that hold. If what happened back there is anyone's fault, it's mine. I knew this afternoon when she finally woke that the news about us set her off -- I didn't realize how badly. She seemed to take it extremely well, for Ciel. Sweetheart, don't cry. I know Ciel's your friend. We'll get her the treatment she should have had years ago, and she'll be all right."

Amber looked up, saw the caring in Cole's dark eyes, eyes so much like Ciel's except, instead of hate, they held all the love she'd ever wanted -- love she'd found in his arms, his bed. "Won't she go to prison for killing Dax?"

"Not if there's a God. In her madness that was the one sane thing my sister did -- she got rid of the sadistic bastard who hurt you. Because of her madness, she'll be one of the few who gets away with murder."

Chapter Six

Cole quietly arranged for Petrone's remains to be disposed of once Obsidion's fledgling police department had collected the physical evidence they needed. He fought the guilt, but it wouldn't go away.

I should have killed the fucker myself. The memory of his sister confined in an eight-by-eight cell behind sturdy iron bars ate at him -- just as thinking of Ciel's tortured eyes, her madness, made Amber unnaturally quiet, reflective. For the first time since Amber had become his slave, he'd slept alone last night, unwilling to subject her to his nightmares, his own tenuous grip on sanity.

He stood in the main dungeon at *No Bounds*, looking at the shiny new equipment and wondering if his father had been right -- that this lifestyle he loved might have contributed to Ciel's final downfall. No. He wouldn't allow himself to go there. For whatever reasons, he got off on wielding sexual power -- using it to bring his lover pleasure. Ciel had chosen that way, too, though Cole now believed Amber was right -- that she'd cast herself into a Dominant role that didn't fit her and had lived her submissive fantasies vicariously, through Amber.

He'd talked with Alan, promised he'd help the lawyer and the shrink his father was sending get settled into what he imagined would become lucrative practices on Obsidion. He'd arranged with Ciel's jailers to treat her well. He never ceased to be amazed at how loudly money talked, particularly on a planet whose permanent inhabitants had almost all been transported because of some brush with Federation laws back home.

He had a business to run and a slave to tend. He'd done all he could for Ciel; she had to do the rest on her own. In retrospect, Cole decided, he and Alan had only delayed Ciel's breakdown. He knew now they'd been wrong, bailing her out of every scrape, every situation where she'd put herself and others in danger.

He'd never again believe he could save someone who didn't want to be saved. Not even the older sister he'd followed like a faithful puppy when they'd been children back on Earth.

* * *

They'd been children really. Teenagers trying their wings. Amber couldn't help remembering those first days after Ciel had taken her, welcomed her when all Amber had wanted to do was die -- join her family in that Great Beyond, wherever it might be. If not for Ciel, Amber might not have made it this far, might never have felt the loving sting of her master's domination.

Cole had arranged all he could for Ciel's care and comfort, Amber knew. He'd told her what he'd done, but he hadn't needed to, for she knew her master, trusted his wisdom, his kindness, his deep affection for the woman they both loved.

Last night Amber had dreamed. Jumbled, tumbled snippets, past and present scrambled. Horrific mind-photos of Ciel's hands dripping blood, of Master Dax's eyes glazed over in death and glowing as he stood over her with that red-hot branding tool, of him beating her with a cane… of Cole rushing in, turning the cane onto Dax himself.

She'd had sweet dreams too. Of Ciel taking her in hand, showing her the teenage haunts, introducing her to Cole who'd been in her grade in school. Of her first sub experience when she'd learned her pleasure came from believing a master cared enough to discipline her… and that sexual pleasure could arise from pain. Of Cole stopping her branding, making her his own…

Where was her master now? She never wanted to pass another night without him near her, bringing the security she needed, the sensual banquet she wanted. She needed the reassurance of his gentle touch, the sound of his voice in her ears, the smells of their mutual arousal… the slightly bitter, salty taste of him when he allowed her to suck his beautiful cock.

Hours ago Amber had readied herself for him. Her hair lay in riotous curls around her shoulders, the way he liked it. She'd shaved her pussy again, felt it to be sure it would feel smooth as silk beneath his fingers… his mouth. The chain that joined the rings in her nipples and clit swung back and forth when she moved, setting up a delicious tingling. Her bare pussy grew wetter and more swollen with every move she made, and when she heard his footsteps in the hall, she fairly gushed.

She longed for him to come, discipline her, show her once again that, as it had been when her parents had loved her enough to discipline her when she was a child, she could find the ultimate in pleasure from pain.

* * *

Fuck. What was a man to do? Cole tore off his clothes, his gaze never leaving his slave's plump, pale ass cheeks or the still-pink lily brand that adorned one side. He'd told her to wait in his room, but he hadn't fucking told her to bend herself nearly double over the pummel horse he used as part of his exercise routine, her position perfect for spanking…

His cock was about to burst. "Amber."

"Yes, Master?"

"Do you want me to spank you?"

"Oh, yes, Master."

He laid a hand over the brand, tracing its outline with one finger. "This is still too tender, sweetheart, for me to use the flogger on you the way I'd love to."

"I welcome the pain."

Amber deserved no punishment, though Cole imagined she was mentally flogging herself over the scene last night at the jail. "No. You deserve nothing but pleasure."

If it took him a lifetime with her, he'd show her she could experience sexual pleasure without pain -- without being restrained. He came up behind her, rubbed his rigid cock along her wet, swollen pussy, pushing lightly at her asshole, her cunt, then backing away and groping in a drawer for his stash of toys.

"Relax, my sweet slave. Grasp the horse's legs with your hands." Gently he worked lubricant up her ass, then smeared some on the butt plug and inserted it one bump at the time, watching her squirm at the invasion. "Easy. Does that feel good?"

"Oh, yesss. Please, Master, give me your cock."

He slapped her smartly on her unmarked ass cheek. "In good time. I want you to be quiet for me. If you can't, I'll have to gag you."

"Yes, Master. Oooh, that feels so good," she said when he slapped her again.

He moved away and rifled through the drawer. "Here, sweetheart, you asked for it." Kneeling beside her, he inserted a ball gag in her mouth and buckled it at the back of her head before slipping a folded silk scarf over her eyes and knotting it securely. "I want you to feel my every touch. Anticipate the next. You need neither to see nor speak. Concentrate on my hands, my mouth, my cock. Let me bring you pleasure."

She whimpered, a slight sound that escaped the ball gag. Cole skimmed his fingers through her hair, then rose, taking time to nuzzle the sensitive skin at the base of her skull, bare now below the hairline while she lay upside down. Another moan, this one barely audible.

The skin on her shoulders and back felt soft beneath his fingers, tasted slightly salty when he tongued her there. He kissed the indentation at the base of her spine, tracing each bony vertebra with searching fingers. When she let out a muffled cry, he gave in, found her breasts and explored them as thoroughly as he'd just done to her back, adding a gentle tug on the chain that led from her nipples to her clit. "Come now," he ordered. "I want your cunt hot and wet when I fuck you there."

A shudder tore through her, as though he'd wrenched the climax from her. Someday... someday she'd come without the stimulus of pain. Cole lifted her free while she still was in the throes of orgasm and carried her to the bed. "Now, my darling slave, I'm going to make love to you."

Amber had never felt such gentleness and caring as he'd shown in every touch -- as he showed her now with the sweep of his hands over her body as though exploring her for the first time. His kisses, soft as a butterfly on her eyelids, her cheeks, her swollen lips aroused her once more, as much as sharp slaps and cruel tugs on the rings he'd placed in her most tender flesh. "Yes," she whispered against his lips, "please love me."

"I do." Very gently, as though she were a fragile flower, he spread her legs and knelt between them, not entering her immediately but rubbing his hard cock along her wet, swollen slit. "This is how I'd have taken you your first time."

Her first time. Perhaps this was her first time, making love without shame, without the feeling she must be punished for wanting to be cared for by the person punishing her. Amber raised her arms, wrapped them around Cole's shoulders, held him close as she'd never done before. God but she felt free, wanted. "I love you too," she told him as he plunged inside her, joining their bodies as he'd joined their hearts when he fastened his collar around her neck.

This time they came together, great, shuddering bursts of ecstasy that caught her up, carried her over the top to a place only he could take her. A safe place where she needed to feel no fear, only the end of an erotic journey that wasn't really an end but a beginning.

More than she'd felt in ten long years, Amber felt secure as she lay afterward in Cole's arms, feeling the soft cadence of his breath against her hair. She'd found a home, where love could flourish with trust and caring. With *No Bounds* to the ways they could express it for one another.

Epilogue

The following summer

When Cole looked back on events of the past year, he couldn't help but feel complaisant. Yesterday he and Amber had re-enacted the scene they'd done a year ago, when *No Bounds* had first opened its doors. This time, thankfully, it had reached its intended conclusion, a mutual orgasm followed by Cole's speech of welcome to the ever growing number of upper income members coming for the first time to *No Bounds* to sample the forbidden world of BDSM.

Today, Amber joined him for a visit to Ciel at the institution where she'd been treated ever since the trial. Each visit, he noticed new improvements, beginning with a smile instead of the blank stare that had lasted from the day after she'd killed Dax until after she'd been found not guilty by reason of temporary insanity. Today she'd spoken a few words not only to Cole but to Amber. Those words made Cole believe for the first time that someday Ciel would recover and be able to join the kinder, gentler BDSM world she'd forced him to create on this planet so far from home.

Each week a transporter brought supplies, along with a few new colonists from the Federation. Most of them still came not of their own volition, and some brought serious problems for Obsidion -- the same problems that had precipitated their exile from Earth. But Cole saw hope in each brave soul who'd made a voluntary decision to come and make this a place law-abiding citizens could call home.

Cole fastened Amber's seat belt and gunned the engine of their hovercraft. It was time to go home. To *No Bounds*, where men and women could explore the farthest fantasies of BDSM, within the strictures of rules that ensured everyone's safety… where Doms sought to bring pleasure and subs sought to serve their masters.

Amber leaned over, touched his lips with her fingers, caressing him. "You're smiling, Master. What are you thinking?"

Cole kissed her hand. "That I've thought of a new safe word for you."

"I can never imagine needing one with you."

He'd sensed for a while that she'd gained more confidence in this area, but from the pensive look she had now, he knew he'd chosen the right phrase.

"It will be *No Bounds.*" He tipped up her chin, held her gaze. "When you use it, you'll be reminded that I will never stop loving you, that you will never be less than perfect to me, and that there is nothing I won't do to keep you safe and ensure your pleasure. You understand?"

Joy filled her gaze, and she nodded. "It also describes the way I feel about you, Master." A smile came into her own eyes. "I wish we could get home faster so I could prove it to you."

He gave her a wicked grin, put the craft on autopilot, and pulled her over to straddle his lap. "Why wait?"

Why, indeed? Their love indeed had *No Bounds. No Bounds* at all.

The End

Ann Jacobs

Ann Jacobs has lost track of how many books she's published. At least thirty at last count. That count includes several awards, including Eppies, Golden Quill awards, More Than Magic awards, and two Lories. Ann has multiple personalities -- she also writes as Sara Jarrod, Ann Josephson, and Shana Nichols.

Ann loves to hear from readers. You may contact her through her website, www.annjacobs.us, or visit her blogspot at http://annjacobs.blogspot.com

All Wrapped Up: Slave School Dropout
Dakota Cassidy

To all who indulge in the lifestyle of BDSM, please note that my slant on such is strictly humorous and never meant to insult or degrade anyone's sexual practices as long as no harm comes to the participants. I support and encourage all forms of sexual expression between safe, sane, consenting adults.

This book is for my kiwi, Jaynie. Smart, opinionated, loyal and supportive, she brings intelligence and fire to my cyber world. The love and friendship she shares with me each and every day are irreplaceable. I am awed by her strength, forever grateful for her in my life. This one's for you, m'love! Also, for a very special someone who began by giving me the gift of friendship in a decidedly uniquely wrapped package and then, turned into someone who brought me some much needed banter, ROFLMAO giggles, girlie sighs and a new perspective on what it is to be truly treasured.

Love Always,
Dakota

Prologue

I smelled him before I actually saw him.

Yeah, he was smokin', all right. He set my pert nose to twitching like no one before him. I honestly had a shiver from head to toe.

Full bodied tingle.

It was righteous, baby.

The shame in all this? This nose of mine can't smell the difference between high socie-tay and frickin' ASPCA.

But I digress.

So, like I said, I smelled Mr. Yummylicious from a hundred paces away in the kitty condo/collar and leash aisle. He's scopin' out kitty collars and I'm locked on his ass, all tight and pert in a pair of faded jeans like a laser scope sight. He was way big, not Arnold Schwarzenegger muscular, mind you, but big enough for this girl to contemplate climbing the mountain that is him and he had some killer hair. Sort of multi colored, with a million different highlights. The kind you can't get in a bottle or even at a fancy salon.

Meow.

I'm not ashamed to eyeball a guy. I'm all about gettin' mine and I wanted to get *his* while I was at the gettin'.

Okay, so, hot, fierce ass and shoulders the width of the River Nile.

Oh, yeah, did I mention I'm from Egypt?

Well, not like green card Egyptian. My *ancestors* are from Egypt. I've lived right here in New York all of my life.

My heritage has a great deal to do with this mess of shit I'm in right now, but again, I digress.

Ahem... Kitty condo aisle -- me -- Mr. Yummylicious -- a tight ass in faded jeans -- and a scent like Utopia in my nose. Better than tuna even...

I'm goin' in on a wing and a prayer. The prayer being that when his six-foot-four frame turned yonder -- he'd have all of his teeth.

Teeth become very important to a girl who's dated Bubba, trust me. He's alive and well and living in an apartment in Soho with his brother Cletus. I know because I've gone out with them. I think between them, they shared a tooth…

Anyway, I actually would have settled for even just the top row of teeth if he'd let me squeeze his rolls of Charmin right there in the kitty condo/collar and leash aisle.

He looked sort of familiar, but I didn't have my glasses on. Go figure, a feline who needs glasses? Absurd, I know. I'm nearsighted.

So anyway, he turns around.

Gimme a sec, because just remembering it makes me all breathless… well, horny too, if honesty is what you're looking for.

Okay, so it was kinda like in the old movies. All slow-mo and dream-like. He turned around and my heart did the flippy thing and my stomach followed suit so as not to be left out. I think I tripped on one of those squishy mice toys and fell into him.

I swear to Ra it wasn't on purpose. That sounds trite, doesn't it? Like I planned that stupidhead Amos wouldn't clean up the aisle or something. Plus, I was kinda standing on shaky ground and my knees became one with my neck. All at once, ya hear me knockin'?

I was totally verklempt when I finally saw his face and it wasn't just because he had teeth.

He was the shit.

You know who I thought of when I first saw him? Like really saw him? That Brawny paper towel guy. Rugged and craggy and some other bunch of adjectives I can't summon up now for the life of me because he's *that* hot.

And I'm *that* fucked because of it.

Know why?

Because he's my *friend.*

My friend, I tell you! Christ in a sidecar, I'm screwed and I need your help. He's not like me and my kind either, but he is *my friend.* How could I have not noticed my friend before this? I certainly never noticed him in a carnal manner. I mean, I always thought he was cute, but hot? Hot? As in so hot I want to throw down with you? *Never.*

It just happened, all at once -- like the proverbial ton of bricks and now, everything is SNAFU, baby. Yep, Situation Normal, All Fucked Up. Yet another frickin' problem in my already neatly compartmentalized problem department...

So, that's why I'm here.

Cuz I got a mac daddy of dilemmas to beat all dilemmas.

It has to do with *sex*...

Yes, that's what I said, s-e-x. Don't look so shocked.

So I'll tell you all about it and you can charge me the prerequisite two hundred greenbacks for me spilling my guts. Money is no object. I'm rich, well, I'm not rich, but my family is, so that makes me rich by proxy. Either way, it'll be taken care of.

Will lying on your couch make me feel better? I'll lie on the couch -- sit in the chair -- hold my breath and find my center -- visualize -- prioritize. I'm all yours -- do with me as you will.

I'll do whatever I have to in an effort to find my happy place. Do you have that test -- you know the one with the ink blots on it? The one where I tell you I see a butterfly, but I'm so completely full of crap because all I really see at this point is him?

How about you give me an IQ test? I'm pretty smart, ya know.

So smart I'm here in your office trying to figure out how the hell I'm going to figure this out.

Some serious shit has gone down and when all is said and done, I might not be as rich as I am right now.

So maybe paying the bill could turn into a problem... but I really need help. I'll charge it to my platinum Visa with the cute kitty emblem on it.

It's everywhere you want to be. I'm just going to hope it won't arrive at *everywhere* until next month when everywhere might be broke. So I won't have to worry until then.

I don't want to be *here*, per se, but I'm willing to give this a shot because I have to get my life back on track and find peace.

So I'll sit on the nice couch -- you break out the nice pad and paper to take notes and we'll get this show on the road.

Hang onto your degree because this is like Dr. Phil gone wild.

Like I said, I first *really* noticed him in that way when he came to the pet store I volunteer at three times a week…

Chapter One

"I'm so -- so..." Well, she didn't know what she was. She'd been on a mission to find the scent that made her nose feel like it'd exploded off her face and she was so enamored with the "scent's" ass she tripped on a stupid toy mouse and fell into him. As opposed to sauntering up to him like she was all va-va-voom or something.

That was how she'd planned it in her mind, anyway. She would follow the smell of this Utopia in a pair of faded jeans and saunter up to him like she was the Queen of Sheba.

Sometimes the road to hell and all that rigmarole...

So instead of sashaying like a supermodel on a runway, Nyla Jane Selim fell into yon hottie with not an ounce of sashay and a whole lot of Pee Wee Herman.

"I'm sorry. I didn't mean to -- I think I tripped --" Her nose was overwhelmed with the masculine scent of him. It made her heart skip and do a running vault over the parallel bars.

Strong arms held her for the briefest of moments before helping her to regain her footing and a deep voice, raspy and reassuring, interrupted her apology. "Tripped on a mouse," he finished her sentence. "Somebody needs to clean this place up."

Ohhhhhh, oooh, oh. A shiver of delight rippled along Nyla's spine and she arched into him, keeping her palms on his muscled forearms for a moment more. What a set of lungs... Nyla didn't know if she should silently curse or thank Amos personally for not cleaning up the kitty condo aisle. "It's been a bit crazy here and we're understaffed," she offered as she squinted, studying his face, angular and rugged.

Her eyebrows rose. No fucking way! *Lucas*? How could this be? Lucas never smelled like *this* before. Nyla struggled to find her glasses in the white coat she wore at the pet store. Slipping them on, she peered into her friend's face as if she were seeing it for the first time, not the like hundredth in a year.

He held a studded collar in his hand, rhinestones and black leather. It twinkled under the bright fluorescent lights of the store. His thumb ran over the studs, giving Nyla another carnal thought that had absolutely nothing to do with a collar and everything to do with slappin' this face jock down on the floor and slamming him one for Old Glory. Oh, my God! Had she really just thought that?

"I see that," Lucas commented, his tone rather blasé as he looked over the top of her head and gave a scathing scan of the store overall. "You talk about this place all the time. I thought I'd come check it out. You definitely could use one or two of those plastic Tupperware bins," he joked.

Nyla stuck her tongue out at him playfully. Okay, so it wasn't the most efficiently run place, but it had its advantages and a great volunteer program for adopting a pet, which Nyla ran. "Lucas, what the hell are you doing here? You need help with something in particular?"

His smile was cocky and glib, and his dark green eyes hinted that Nyla, for all of her ineptitude, couldn't possibly help him. "No. No. I don't need help at all, Nyla. I just thought I'd stop by and see if you wanted to catch a movie. You know that thing we do every Friday night? Me relegated to your fun date pile and all?"

At this particular nanosecond, despite the sharp stab of her nipples poking at her bra like a Dewalt drill bit, Nyla was tweaked. What the hell was going on? They'd been on two dates before she'd determined that they should just be friends. She and Lucas were so alike, ruining it with sex was something Nyla wasn't willing to do. Lucas was the only person in the world who understood her right down to her Prada heels, and she wasn't going to risk becoming his squeeze so he could dump her somewhere down the road. They were friends for life -- period.

And so now what? He was all of a sudden hot? She and Lucas had shared more than a dozen movies and he'd never smelled like *this* before. Fuck him for smelling better than tuna. Gathering her best disinterested attitude around her knees, Nyla gave him a narrowed glance before dismissing her moment of insanity and said, "Yeah, let's do a movie." *While I'm at it, could I do you too*?

Oh! Where had that come from?

"Nyla? You okay?" Lucas looked down at her from what seemed like way far up there all of a sudden… was he always this tall? Tall and luscious to boot?

"Yeah, I'm great. You?"

"I'm fine. So, the movie? Wanna go?"

Nyla's nose twitched again. Oh, my hell, he smelled soooo good. Nyla involuntarily sniffed his shoulder. "Are you wearing new cologne?"

"That's all me, baby. Nothing new," he teased. "You were the one who didn't want to sample it, remember?"

Oh, she remembered all right. As clearly as she now smelled him in a whole different way. "If I've told you once, I've told you a thousand times. We're friends and I won't risk having to dump your ass and take all of your toilet paper with me when I do, just so we can have sex. I can have that with anyone, but nobody does a good romantic comedy like you."

Lucas brushed a kiss over her suddenly heated forehead. "I know, I know. I'm the sexless friend." As he stood closer to her, Nyla fought the urge to lean into his hard frame and the bonfire that was him.

Lucas stiffened and backed away. "So, a movie? Popcorn, soda and your favorite 'no sex this lifetime' buddy -- friend."

Nyla cleared her throat. Yeah, no sex. She'd said that a dozen times or so too… what had she been thinking? Nyla put a hand on Lucas' chest. A chest that now, all of a sudden, out of the clear blue, felt… good.

With that, Nyla turned on her heel and stalked off toward the back room where she fully intended to cleanse her nostrils with sandpaper.

"Nyla?" Lucas called from behind her all smoky and brick shithouse like.

Nyla's feet stopped mid pissed off stomp as she turned back to Buns of Steel with a precise pivot, slow and lingering. "What?" she countered, sucking in her cheeks and giving him a smart ass grin.

Lucas cocked his head to the side, angling his square jaw upward, and smiled.

Nyla clamped her mouth shut and thwarted the gawk she knew wanted to take over her face when she saw him smile. As her eyes traveled the length of him, she glanced at his chest and stomach. His T-shirt pressed against his abdomen, hugging every defined ripple. When did Lucas get abs?

Fo shizzle…

Crap, abs were her weakness…

"Can you smell me, Nyla?" Lucas' voice sounded terse and laced with a shakiness she'd never heard before.

Nyla licked her now dry lips and cocked her head back at him. "I've always been able to smell *you,* Lucas. We're shifters. Remember we met at the Shifters' Single and Looking to Mingle? It's what we do. Why do you ask?" She raised an eyebrow at him with disdain and crossed her arms over her nipples, pointed and tight. What the hell was going on?

Lucas took two swift strides of his sneaker clad feet with a silent, almost prowl and stood in front of her. Smiling down at Nyla, his grin screamed confidence and arrogance when he answered, "Because you can smell me and I can smell you, and it's like nothing we've ever smelled before."

Nyla gulped before raising her eyes to fully meet his deep green ones. "Oh, really?"

"Yeah, really."

"And what do *you* smell?"

"Your desire."

Desire this, baby. "Maybe what you smell is the cat litter box in the back. It needs to be cleaned."

His chuckle rumbled in his chest, low, sinful, downright delish. "I smell your essence. That couldn't be cat litter, could it?"

"It's the multiple formula scoop away variety."

"I smell you and you smell me. It has nothing to do with cat litter and everything to do with our lust. The fact that you're a shifter means you know it too. You know what the lust means, Nyla."

Oy. When you're right, you're right. They were everywhere nowadays. Shifters, that was. Every walk of life, every profession, every freakin' pet store. It never surprised Nyla anymore. She'd met Lucas at a shifter function. They'd hit it off immediately and that was that. Shifters were fairly common and, for the most part, they acknowledged each other with a brief nod and went about their business.

Unless the business was *scent*. That held meaning where Nyla came from. It held meaning for any shifter of the feline variety. Sometimes the scent of another was merely lust and nothing more. Sometimes it was something far more significant. That meant they had to explore what the scent meant, and it meant them doing the mattress stomp.

Nyla was going to go with lust here. It had to be lust.

Unadulterated, sizzling hot lust. How could it be anything else? They'd been friends far too long for it to be anything else… right?

"So," she said with a cocky air of indifference and a roll of her tongue on the inside of her cheek. "I shift, you shift, we all shift. Big deal, Lucas."

He took a thick, long finger and ran it down the side of Nyla's face. She held her ground, but squirming might be open to supposition at this point. Her knees trembled as his stare held hers. "I guess it isn't a big deal for humans, but scent is a very big deal with cats, as you well know. So stop with the pretense, Xena and tell me how this happened all of a sudden?"

His words were a demand rather than a request. Very un-Lucas-like. It made Nyla's knees weaker still and the place between her legs not nearly as desert-like as she'd thought. He was right again. Scent was very important to a shifter and Lucas' was suddenly euphoric, divine, gloriously musky and male. Really making her nose shimmy like it never had before…

"Nothing happened, Lucas." *Ya cocky, over confident, tightly packed, friggin' hunk o' burnin' love.*

He tipped Nyla's chin upward with the finger that had trailed a path of heat along her cheek. "You're full of shit, Nyla. I know what you smell. It's the same thing I've been smelling for over a year."

Well, good on you. "Lucas? You're on crack. I'm Egyptian. We can't smell anything other than our own kind and you're not of my breed."

"Niiice bigotry there, Nyla. Egyptian breed, my ass." His breath fanned her face as he taunted the difference in their lineage.

"Yeah, Bast, you know?"

"Yeah, so what? Mongrel. Tomcat. Big ASPCA fan, ya know?"

"Oh, yes. I know."

"Doesn't matter. You *smell* me."

"I'm holding out for one of my own, Lucas, and you know it."

"Will it make a difference what breed I am when I'm between your legs, lapping at you?"

Lucas shot the arrow of words at her and it left Nyla stunned. Who the hell was this? This wasn't *her* Lucas. The Lucas who she'd hung out with everyday and treated like a brother. He sure as hell didn't feel much like family now. Lucas' thumb skirted Nyla's lower lip, the pad rough and sending out a clear message of feral desire.

Oh, fuck. Fucking liver treats and cat nip… Now here's where she should gather all her warning signals into one big damn pile of flashing neon lights and stop, but when had she ever backed down from a challenge? When had Lucas become Mr. Hot Pants? When had a dose of good common sense kept her from rushing headlong into a nice big pile of shit?

"That's debatable, I guess. *Cultured* tongues are always the best if you ask me," Nyla shot back. Yeah... take that, Nyla sort of teased him in the way they'd always best communicated. Via a little snappy repartee and a zinger or two.

Leaning forward, Lucas let his mongrel tongue graze the corner of her mouth in a delicious swipe that lingered near as her lips gaped open. Nyla fought a shiver, clenching her fists. "That's what my mongrel tongue can do, Nyla," he whispered.

Maybe shutting up and letting nature take its course would be what was best here. However, Nyla never did what was best. She abso-fucking-lutely was not going to risk her friendship with him because her nose was off kilter. Maybe she had allergies?

"I think you should keep your mongrel tongue to yourself, Lucas. It doesn't belong in my cultured mouth, nor does it belong anywhere near my finely cultured nether regions. Forget it. You're my friend and nothing more."

Lucas pressed his heated body closer to Nyla's, straddling her thighs with his own, powerful and sculpted. His looming frame gave off an oven of flames that set Nyla's own body to trembling. He seemed less than impressed with her efforts to piss him off, completely and totally unaffected.

Lucas' green eyes pierced hers, searing her flesh. "I think you lie and I also think you'd be a fool to pass me by because I'm not from the land of big pyramids, hieroglyphics and a river called Nile. But that's just me, Nyla. I've said it once or twice in this thing you call friendship. The beauty of this is that now you can smell it too. If you wanna pass up sex with me, that's *your* choice..." His words trailed off as the air between them pulsed, thickened with the scent of lust and sinful joining.

The spot he'd grazed with his tongue burned, and Nyla couldn't help but think he was right again. Why pass up a chance to boink? "Lucas? What the hell is going on here?" she asked out of the corner of her mouth that wasn't burning.

"I think you want me."

"I do not," Nyla said on a gulp.

"Do too."

"Not."

"Yep."

"Nope."

"You do too, and I'm going to run with it."

"No, Lucas. We're too different. You drink beer for crap's sake!"

"And you lap Dom from your diamond encrusted kitty bowl."

What of it? "I can afford the finer things in life and you knew that from the start, Lucas."

"But you won't find a mongrel tongue like mine this side of King Tut, Nyla."

Oh, fine, just fine. He might be right for the fourth time in less than ten minutes. Her sexual activity equaled zero as of late because she left an encounter feeling less than satisfied. She craved *more*. Hell, just last week she'd told Lucas the same thing. Nyla didn't know *what* more consisted of. It had been puzzling her for months now. "This is crazy, Lucas. Crazy. I refuse to risk a perfectly good friendship to get laid."

Nyla saw the flash of victory in his eyes, brief and flickering. "You've said that a hundred times before, Nyla. Now you can smell me. That makes things different."

Yeah, it made things different all right. So why hadn't she smelled him before this? "It's going to fuck everything up, Lucas. *Everything*. There won't be anymore movies. No more long nights on the phone talking about our dates."

"*Your dates*, Nyla. We talk about yours. I haven't had any."

"You have so. What about the chick with the hot ass?"

"What about her?" Lucas asked as he stared down at her. His eyes sharing something Nyla had never noticed before.

"Um, you talk about her all the time. You said her ass was like radiator fluid. Ya know, deadly to us kitty cats?"

"So?"

His tone was clipped and held answers Nyla suddenly wasn't sure she was ready to ask the questions to. "You just had a date with her last week, Lucas."

"It wasn't really a date, Nyla. Remember? She's still getting over the teenybopper boyfriend anyway. It was a 'Poor baby' date. Moral support."

Nyla poked his abs. "Yeah, the very date you were supposed to spend inching your way into her heart so you could have that ass that's as hot as a volcano!"

Lucas stared straight at her. "I'm not as interested in her as you'd like to believe or as interested as you'd like *me* to believe."

Nyla rolled her eyes at him. "Pluuease! All you talked about was her ass."

He shook his head. "No, Nyla. You talked about her ass and how great it would be if she noticed me. She has a nice ass, that's true, but with her it's work. We don't connect like you and I do, Nyla. I've said this over and over, haven't I? We get each other. We have from the moment you cracked wise about it over weenies in a blanket at the shifter meet and greet."

"Singles Mingle," Nyla corrected him.

Lucas held up a hand. "Whatever. Look it's just different with y --"

"Me…" Nyla interrupted as her voice trailed off and what was happening here became a realization. Yes, Lucas had said it a lot in the course of their friendship. There was no one like her. No one who understood him better than Nyla did. It was the same for her too.

"Yep, you."

"Oh, my God! You mean all the time you spent with the chick with the perky ass, you were thinking about me? *Me*!?" Her incredulous statement just flew out of her mouth before she had the opportunity to allow her brain to kick into overdrive and stop it.

Lucas cocked an eyebrow at her and sighed. "Maybe."

The light in his eyes shifted and Nyla had to look away, catching her breath, now ragged and shaky. What in Ra was happening here?

"I've tried to tell you, Nyla. I told you in the beginning that I thought you were shortchanging us because we get each other so well. We have chemistry, but you shut me out and I wasn't going to push my way in. I figured you'd come to see it someday, and I was right. You smell me. There's just no denying it, is there?"

Nyla snorted and leaned into him just an eighth of an inch closer. Totally against her will and completely in need of whatever he was offering. "I'd be crazy to do this. I can't believe I'm even acknowledging the idea!"

She'd spent some time in their friendship denying how she instinctively knew Lucas wanted her, but to have it laid out like this wasn't something she was ready for. But, fuck he smelled good. It was making her dizzy with lust, worry -- okay, lust.

"Well, my scent has definitely been acknowledged," he said, tweaking her nose with his fingers. His confidence and arrogance was hacking Nyla, yet, turning her on all at the same time.

Nyla's nipples again pressed painfully against her bra as she turned back to him and placed a finger between them, letting it rest on one rung in the ladder of his abs. *Oh, Lawd that was nice…* "This is crazy…"

"It won't be so crazy when you're in my bed, Nyla."

"Your bed? Hah! Shit on that. We'll use mine."

Lucas laughed. "Tough. I like *my* bed and I want you in it, on it, all over it."

Oh, good gravy… The visual of his bronzed body between her legs on some K-Mart blue light special sheets stole Nyla's breath away. For the first time in their friendship, Nyla had nothing to say. She was speechless and stopped resisting the urge to allow Lucas to take command.

How utterly unlike her to allow someone else to do the directing of a well orchestrated boink and she was enthralled, intrigued.

Horny.

Horny for *Lucas…*

Lucas, her fun date. Her friend. Her partner in crime. Her mental match.

"I suppose dirtying your sheets is better than messing up mine. Yours can probably be washed with *laundry soap*," she replied smartly.

"And yours have to be taken to the cleaners, right, Cleopatra?"

Nyla ignored his obvious scorn and focused on the friggin' flame between her thighs and finding the way to douse it without ruining the friendship she and Lucas shared.

Fuck, fuck, fuck.

"How about we skip the movie, Nyla and you think about it," Lucas commanded as he leaned into her, his lips hovering mere inches from hers. He hovered there, his breath fanning her face, warm and smelling of mint. His green eyes searched hers, demanding she look at him, and Nyla found her neck arching backward, her spine curling inward and her hips jutting forward. Lucas laid his lips over hers, unmoving, firm, full, hot as his big hands pulled her lower body to meet his.

Nyla's compulsion to stab her tongue into his mouth and clutch at his head was overwhelming, but she didn't, because somehow it seemed as though *he* should make the first move and she wasn't sure why.

Tilting his head, Lucas caressed her mouth with his, as though he were branding her with the lightest of touches. Lucas inhaled her flutter of a groan. "Good girl," he praised. "I'll *always* be the one on top." And with that, he let his hand find her ass, giving it a firm squeeze before moving out of her space and then turned to remind her, "Think about it, Nyla. Don't make me wait too long."

Nyla gulped as she watched his broad back exit the pet store and the warmth of his hand linger with a tingle on her ass.

Holy Fancy Feast…

Chapter Two

Two days later and on five hours of sleep, Nyla called Lucas on his cell phone out of utter frustration. She hadn't been able to stop thinking about him nearly every waking moment and it was eating its way though her intestines. When his lips had touched hers, Nyla had experienced a fire she'd never known before, and now she needed to find out why this was happening.

"Hey, Nyla. What's up?"

Hey, Lucas, you fricken' friend fucker upper. Not much new here other than if I don't do you instantly, I'm going to crawl out of my skin. Nyla bit the inside of her cheek and croaked into the phone, "What's up? What's up?" she squawked. "Well, Lucas, two days ago you were my damn friend. Two days later, I've slept like next to not at all. I even missed my cat nap, for fuck's sake. I'm tired and frustrated and pissed at you. However, I've come to a conclusion. That's what's up! We're going to get some shit straight right now, got that?" Nyla ran a hand over her hair and sighed the sigh of the utterly frustrated.

"Sure, Nyla." Oh, his voice was so damn relaxed and calm, thus fueling Nyla's pissed off further. "Bring it on. What do we need to get straight?"

My head, she wanted to scream. My hormones… "I'm coming over there, Lucas and we're going to figure this out. I don't know why I smelled you like I did in the pet store, but if I still smell you when I see you again? I'm going to nail you. Hear me? Nail your ass to whatever hard surface is available and kiss the living shit out of you, and if it isn't fricken' fab-u-lous, I'm going to kill you. I'd better see shooting stars and all that sappy crap or you die, kitty cat. Do you hear me, Lucas? I know we don't have a choice in this scent bullshit, but we could have resisted it and kept right on being friends, but nooooooo, you just had to go and tell me you were hot for me, didn't you? That was really in the spirit of friendship wasn't it? What a pal you turned out to be. So get your ass dressed or whatever and answer that door when I get there!" Nyla wiped spit from the corner of her mouth with her thumb and waved down a cab. She looked like shit. She felt like shit, but she was going to prove Lucas wrong. They were going to hump like the last two people on Earth and Nyla would come out on top. Lucas was *not* her lifemate. He was her friend.

"Okay, Nyla, but would it be okay if we ate after you see stars? I'm pretty hungry."

Food? Yeah, food would be peachy. Just what she needed for her topsy turvy stomach in her all of her fucked-up-ed-ness. "I don't care, Lucas. You can have a smorgasbord of mice if you want. I just need to get this over with. So shut up and put on your chap stick because you've fucked with my chi enough, thanks."

"You got it, babe."

Fuuuuuck him and his confidence, dammit! "I'll see you in a half an hour," Nyla barked into the phone.

"Don't be late…" Lucas chuckled into the phone.

Nyla clicked her phone off and stared out the window, her face flushed and her head fuzzy. She had no clear thoughts other than it would all be fine when she got this out of the way, and then she and Lucas could go back to being friends again.

She really wanted to see that new Adam Sandler movie.

Nyla rapped on Lucas' door exactly ten minutes later than she'd told him she would. Glancing down, Nyla smoothed a wrinkle in her filmy skirt as she waited for Mr. Self Assured to open the door.

As he popped the black, steel door open, he looked at his watch almost irritably. "You're ten minutes late, Nyla."

Fancy that… "I didn't know we had to synchronize our watches."

Lucas cupped the nape of Nyla's neck, grasping the long flow of her black curls in a loose grip and pulled her to him as he kicked the door shut with a foot. "You made me wait, Nyla. You're ten minutes late," he reminded her again. His voice was filled with an unmistakable command that left her speechless.

Words escaped her… *Okay, so hold the phone here.* Nyla's fist of reason knocked on the door to her common sense. She was about to consider having hot, screamin' sex with a guy she'd known like a year, that she'd met at a singles' mingle for shifters and had become the best friend she'd ever had. Not only did she want to have sex with him -- okay, she really dug him -- but she was all of a sudden envisioning him like he was the Captain of the *Starship Enterprise* and she was a wee Klingon.

Um, hellllloooo in there.

Are you rolling in reefer instead of catnip these days?

When had Lucas all of a sudden become this force to be reckoned with? Where had all this raw sexuality come from? When had he become the one on top? She'd always been in control of her portion of their friendship and of her emotions within the box she'd designated "friends only."

Lucas stepped away from her, allowing her the space he sensed she needed, and it made Nyla shake her head.

He smelled soooo good, she reasoned with herself. How could she deny that? He could be forceful if he wanted to…

Maybe.

Well, okay, Nyla had to admit, it was kinda floatin' her boat and she wasn't sure why. Maybe because she spent so much of her time keeping herself in check due to her stiff upbringing that it was a nice break to let go. But to let go to Lucas? Her movie buddy? The world as Nyla knew it was coming to a screeching halt. But, shit she wanted him…

Why bother to analyze it when sex was in the offing? It didn't have to be a production. It needed no therapy session at all.

As Nyla stared up at the man who'd been her friend for over a year, a whole new light was shed on him, standing there with his arms crossed over his chest and that fricken' superior look on his face.

Dipshit.

"Get over here, now, Lucas and let's do this." Nyla walked right up to him and slapped a palm on his chest, backing him up against the far wall. She looked up at him with tired, red eyes, blazing with fury over her pent up lust and the possible loss of a friendship.

"We can't go back to holding hands, Nyla."

"Now you balk? *Now*? You started this, Lucas!" Nyla accused on a shrill screech.

"No, your *nose* started this."

"Your nose started it first!"

"I never made that a secret."

"Well, ya know what? It was one of those better kept things."

"Are we gonna do this or not, Nyla?"

"Oh, yes, yes we are and if it isn't --"

"Fab-u-lous, you're going to kill me," he mocked her higher pitched voice.

"Yeeeeessss! I'm going to kill you. Got that?" Nyla asked as she grabbed hold of his shirt collar and Lucas bent his head close to hers.

And then, Nyla planted one on Lucas, full on lip press. Hard and with as much hope that it wouldn't work out as that -- just maybe -- it would.

The onslaught of flaming heat and rushing tidal wave in Nyla's ears threw her for a loop, and she clung to Lucas' strong arms that now came around her in a tight band of possession.

Lucas molded his body to hers, pressing a thigh between her own and rubbing seductively at the juncture between her legs. Her skirt, the material thin and filmy, allowed her to feel every slide of the rough fabric of his jeans. He nipped her jaw, moving her around, and now her back was pressed firmly to the wall behind her.

Grinding his hips into hers, Lucas whispered against her ear, "Can we conclude I've been right all along, Nyla?"

"Fuck you, Lucas," Nyla said on a half nervous giggle and half scolding him for being so damn right.

Whoda thunk this man packed such a powerful suck-face?

"Oh, I fully intend to do just that, Nyla. I've waited a long time for this," he whispered, low and sultry. When had his voice become like a 1-900-wanna-fuck-hotline?

There really wasn't a choice now. Nyla knew what had to happen. As shifters, they both knew they had to complete this cycle. But what if the end of the cycle meant they ended up hurting each other? Or worse, they were completely wrong about this and they had to sacrifice their friendship? How did you go back to "just friends" after you had your tongue down your buddy's throat?

Nyla's heart pumped hard in her chest as Lucas pulled her arms above her head, cuffing her wrists together, making her ribs press against his. It forced her body to bow into Lucas' steel length and her chest beat against his from the short, choppy breaths she took.

"A long time?" she managed to spit out as his other arm hoisted her up against the wall and required that she wrap her legs around his tapered waist. His silken tongue snaked out to strike at the soft shell of her ear.

His chuckle slid from the back of his throat, hot chocolate-like over warm pecan pie. "Stop worrying about it, Nyla. You can count on one thing I know for certain, something I've known since I met you. The completion of this cycle will be more than worth the worry you've suffered." Lucas punctuated his statement by gripping Nyla's ass hard with his hand, sending a wave of pulsating pleasure to her cunt. Nyla squirmed and bucked against him as the tight points of her nipples pushed at her thin cotton shirt, but he held her flush against him.

Nyla's breathing was ragged now and this -- simply from having his hard body press her against a wall? It was ludicrous, but that was okay by Nyla.

She wanted a piece of *this*.

"Then let's get on with the 'this,' could we, Lucas? So I can stop worrying about not having a movie buddy anymore." Nyla smiled with a teasing grin as he reared his head up and ground against her again, pinning her to the wall with his eyes as they flashed a darker green. It startled her as they glittered in the fading light.

"Believe me when I tell you, Nyla, *this* is something you'll want more of and the benefit is we can still see a movie when I don't have my head between your legs."

This was becoming less like the teasing banter they'd shared and more like making a point. Nyla was intrigued, a bit afraid. "Prove it, Neanderthal," she ground out between frustrated lips.

Lucas captured her lower lip in his teeth, taking a gentle nibble as he let her wrists go and moved both strong arms to surround her, carrying Nyla into what she assumed was his bedroom. She had no idea because she'd never been in it before.

Brief flashes of muted colors passed in a whir from her surroundings as he took the few strides necessary to get her to his bed. Lucas kept her body flush with his and Nyla ignored the view in favor of the reaction her length had to his. She wanted to rip his clothes off and drive her nakedness against his. Bore into him, burrow against the heat that emanated from him, but she waited with impatience. Under normal circumstances, Nyla would have stripped him by now and be riding the luscious cock she knew awaited her in his jeans to victory.

Yet, she hesitated. It seemed inappropriate to take control of this sexual rendezvous and she didn't quite know why. A shifter was keen to all senses, including the knuckle dragger kind. Somehow, waiting was the signal that called to her lust fuzzy brain.

Lucas lowered her to the bed with little effort and the grace of the cat he was. The cool cotton of his sheets soothed Nyla's back. He towered over her, the outline of his shaft evident, long and thick behind his zipper as he looked down at her.

Nyla's chest heaved and she licked her lips, dry with anticipation of release. Lucas tugged her shirt up with rough, hurried hands, pulling it over her head, making Nyla's nipples tight and hard, begging to be touched. His eyes, dark now, scanned her breasts, taking them into his heated gaze with apparent lust. Arching her back, encouraging Lucas to touch her,

Nyla waited as he trailed small circles over her ribs with a tapered finger, along her abdomen, under the soft curve of her full breasts. Yet, he didn't touch the neediest part of her body.

Nyla bit her lip in utter frustration and scrunched her eyes shut.

Yanking his shirt off, Lucas lowered himself over her, holding his torso up with his hands, bracketing either side of her body. His skin was smooth like marble, with a scar or two running in a jagged line just above his pecs. Nyla wanted to scream out in frustration for him to press himself against her. She wanted to wrap her arms around his neck and drag his smoothly muscled chest against hers, yet, she waited…

His stare, unseen but felt, made Nyla open her eyes and shiver. It was intense. The green of his eyes bore into hers as he assessed her, obviously gauging her desire. They grew dark as he held himself above her on solid arms. "Do you want me to touch you, Nyla?" he asked. Yet it was rather a demand for an answer than a question. His tone was hard in her ears, filled with something Nyla couldn't identify, but clearly controlled.

"Answer the question, Nyla. Do you want me to touch you? Do you want me to run my tongue over your breasts, lick you?"

Well, fuckin'-A. Yeah! However, Nyla held back, struggled with the words "Do it, already." She begged no one. Biting the inside of her cheek, Nyla refused to answer this alien man she'd once called friend.

Lucas sat up with a swift movement, leaving the heated air between them, cool and sharpening her nipples to tight points. He cupped her breasts, massaging them, avoiding her nipples and Nyla squirmed beneath him no matter how much she willed her body to be still. His hands were large, covering her small breasts, kneading the flesh of them with skill.

"Answer the question, Nyla. Do you want me to lick you?" His melodic baritone was gruff, thick with the honeyed request.

Nyla couldn't seem to stop herself. She nodded her head.

Lucas shook his. "I want to *hear* the word, Nyla."

Was this like payback for all the times she'd joked about Lucas' lust for her? She really hadn't meant it. Honest. It was just a joke. They joked about everything, but apparently Lucas took his sex way serious like.

Nyla grabbed his wrists, clamping her fingers around them, insisting that he touch her with silent force, but Lucas wouldn't be thwarted. She let her hands fall away and took fistfuls of the sheets instead.

"Do you want my tongue on you, Nyla?" he persisted as he shifted his hips and his rock-hard abs pushed against her groin.

She gulped. What was a "yes" in the scheme of having those yummy lips on her? It was pride and she had plenty of that. Yeah, like she'd had so much of that when she'd already fallen with the kiss of the gods from this man.

Leaning forward, his solid powerful hands still kneading her, Lucas ran his tongue over the hollow of her neck and along her collar bone. A trail of silken, wet fire ignited as he rounded the curve of the top half of her breast. He whispered, "There's no shame in asking for what you want, Nyla. I can wait. I've waited this long."

Nyla gripped the sheets beside her, refusing to touch him, as if not touching Lucas was payback for the complete agony he made her suffer.

Lucas seemed to sense her inner battle as he stroked the full underside of her breast with his fingers, but it wasn't stopping him from tormenting her further. "Let go, Nyla. It's one word and if you give me that *one word*, I'll lick you until you scream."

Nyla's eyes rolled to the back of her head, and Lucas' words became a jumbled, echo in her ears. She fought the wave of burning desire to feel him tongue her nipple and lost the war she waged with one word, drawn out and needy. "Y -- yesssssss," she hissed, unaware she had until her tongue touched the roof of her mouth.

Lucas chuckled again. That thick, warm river of sound caressed her ears as he leaned forward, gathering her breasts in his hands, and nudged her nipples with his nose. The slight contact made Nyla buck hard as the heat of Lucas' breath swept over the tight peak.

His tongue flicked it at first, rasping over the pebbled surface with a delicious slide, deliberate, circling the surface of it, skimming it with slow swipes before capturing it and inhaling deeply.

Nyla saw a multitude of colors, bright flashes of flickering light behind her eyes as he moved from one nipple to the other, thumbing them, rolling them between his roughly padded fingers, swirling his tongue over them, pulling them in and out of his mouth.

Well, he'd been right, she thought with vague remembrance of his promise to lick her until she screamed -- just as she screamed… low and long from the heat that pooled in her cunt and begged release.

He'd made her scream.

Now, she wanted this man in her, on her, absorbing her, and that wasn't something Nyla was used to. She only wanted the thick press of his cock, driving into her with steady, forceful thrusts.

Taken.

Nyla wanted to be taken, hard and fast with pounding thrusts of a cock she hadn't even seen.

Her hips, still clad in the thin skirt she'd worn, jutted upward, grinding as he slid his thigh between hers and let her ride it through the thin silk of her panties. Slick with desire, Nyla clenched her thighs around Lucas' strong one as he let his teeth skim her nipples. His golden head tilting and his tongue lapping at her made Nyla insane for more as she twisted beneath him, rubbing her throbbing clit frantically against him.

Nyla came with such force, from nothing more than what was essentially a "boob job" that it almost frightened her. It sucked the air from her lungs in a sharp gust. It stole every thought in her muddled head but that of release. It swept over her like a raging fire. It was sharp and raw and so real that now, as

Nyla lay heaving beneath Lucas, she could taste it in the back of her throat.

Lucas covered her body with his, both still dressed below the waist. It didn't prevent the burn of his cock through his jeans. The thick bulge pushed against Nyla's pelvic bone. "Open your eyes, Nyla, and put your arms around me."

Yes, Nyla, do as you're told. It's the least you can do seeing as this mongrel just gave you the best orgasm of your life and it didn't take much effort. Not to mention the fact that it took you an entire year to realize he was even capable of such acts of carnality.

Fuck you, she rebelled against the nagging voice. *I'll put my arms around him when and if I choose to, not before.*

"Put your arms around me, Nyla. Let yourself feel my skin against yours," his lips whispered over the line of her jaw and along the column of her neck.

Nyla would have liked to believe she heard him coaxing her, but somehow everything Lucas said sounded like an order and -- well -- it was turning her the hell on and scaring her at the same time. She'd never seen this side of Lucas…

Nyla's arms moved around his broad back in reluctance, knowing full well once she touched him it was all over. As she fitted herself to Lucas, Nyla melted against him, savoring the press of his flesh to hers.

Ooooohhh… Oh and oh again.

Lucas' smooth chest rubbed her nipples with tantalizing scrapes as his lips finally came to rest on her chin, inching his way toward her mouth. He reenacted the same move he'd made in the pet store, his mouth resting on hers, inhaling her breath, caressing her lips with his, absorbing the feel of them. Lucas' breathing was ragged now too. His chest beat against Nyla's as he held her to him with arms woven tightly around her shoulders and under her back.

Lucas dipped his tongue into her mouth with a purposeful plunge, stroking hers, suckling her lower lip. Nyla groaned with surprise at the silky invasion, hot and with the expertise of a skilled kisser.

Planting his lips firmly on Nyla's, Lucas devoured her mouth, pushing her against the bed with his weight and lapping at her lips. He pulled an arm from beneath her and stroked it along Nyla's ribs, splaying his fingers over her waist and finally coming to rest at the waistband of her skirt.

Nyla clung to Lucas' strong neck as she drove her tongue into his mouth, whimpering as he lingered near her cunt.

"Do you want me to touch you, Nyla?" he asked as he pulled back, leaving her moaning in aggravation. He rolled a bit to the left, keeping his powerful thigh over her legs.

No, I'm just squirming under you like a 'ho for lack of anything better to do with my day.

What did this man want? Was hearing the words what turned him on? How could she know? They'd talked sex, but certainly not in detail.

His finger trailed over the outline of the lips of her pussy, swollen and aching as he nipped at her mouth. Nyla's body screamed for his touch, but she wouldn't say so that easily.

Skimming the line of her panties, Lucas wove his fingers in and out, taunting her, teasing, stoking the fire that now raged. Kissing her one last time, he slid adown until he lay on her upper thigh. Nyla's legs spread involuntarily, but Lucas clamped them with his hands.

"Do you want me to touch you, Nyla?" she heard him ask again from somewhere parts south.

Nyla clenched her teeth as he moved to place himself between her thighs, tugging her ass to the edge of the bed. He slipped her panties off her hips and spread her thighs wide. With her heels resting on the bed, Nyla was vulnerable as Lucas stood between them. Vaguely, she heard the grumble in his chest, deep and, she hoped, approving.

Lucas placed the palm of his hand over her pussy, cupping it, moving his thumb back and forth. "You're shaven clean. I approve, Nyla. I love to lick a cleanly shaven pussy," Lucas commented as he spread her flesh with his thumbs.

Well, good on you. Could we do that now? The licking part? Because if he didn't get down to business soon Nyla's chest was going to burst from the anticipation. His gaze leveled on the most vulnerable part of her body was sinful and erotic and frightening, all rolled into one horny package. Not one of her lovers had ever looked much at that part of her anatomy. Not that she could recall.

"Open your eyes, Nyla. Look at me between your legs."

Nyla didn't even realize she'd shut them. She peeked out at him from beneath her lashes, his hard body taut and his stare transfixing her, rooting her to the bed. His thumbs massaged her, spreading her, but not touching what most needed attention. Lucas moved his hands to her thighs, gripping her flesh as he leaned forward, using her thighs to brace himself, hovering over her cunt.

Nyla could just see the top of his head and those piercing eyes of his over the flat plane of her abdomen. She wanted to clutch at his head, hold him down on her clit, force him to lick her senseless before she self combusted… but she didn't. She *wouldn't.* Instead, she gripped the edge of her skirt and held fast to prevent herself from ramming his face into her. Damn him…

"Do you want me to lick you, Nyla? Scrape my tongue over your pussy? Press it to your clit?"

Does a bear shit in the woods? Are Wheaties frosted? For fuck's sake, yes!

Yes!

Yes!

Yes!

But she'd be screwed blue and tattooed if she'd say it out loud.

Lucas bent his head to rest it on her thigh, inhaling her scent, grazing his lips over the tender skin. His breathing was as choppy as hers, almost whistling on the way out of his throat as his lips touched her skin, firm, hot, and moist. He trailed a hard finger over the outline of her cunt, distended with need, wet, hungry, flaming with wanton desire.

Nyla shifted in impatience as he skirted the crease between her thigh and the lips of her pussy. Her body begged him to snake his tongue outward and lick her swollen clit, but he didn't.

Again Lucas asked, "Do you want me to lick you, Nyla? Answer the question." The husky quality of his voice, the hitch in it as he lay on her thigh, caressing her with a stray finger, avoiding the needy center that had become all Nyla could focus on, was driving her mad. He wanted to lick her as much as she wanted him to, yet his refusal to do so made Nyla want it more than she'd wanted anything in a long time.

Screw it. Fuck this agony.

Nyla lifted herself on her elbows as Lucas raised his head and their eyes met -- his glazed and dark with obvious lust, hers furious with herself for what she was about to say, but it didn't stop her. "Lick me, damn you, Lucas!" Her words ripped from her throat, desperate, grating, tearing out of her mouth before she could stop them.

Lucas spread her thighs with a powerful hand on each leg and dipped his head toward her pussy, laying his mouth over her cunt, much like he'd done when he'd first kissed Nyla in the pet store. Nyla's hips bucked with a violent twist as the heat of his mouth enveloped her, damp and steaming hot. Lucas pressed his tongue flat to her outer lips, and then slithered between them, slick and rasping.

Nyla's knuckles whitened and she gripped the sheets beside her. She fought the urge to let go and come with a vengeance as Lucas stroked her clit with small, precise circles. Her stomach muscles clenched as he held her legs apart with big hands and lapped at her, laving the tender flesh, pink and heated to a level of intensity Nyla had never known. Stroking her with lips and tongue, Lucas moved to cup her ass, lifting her flush with his face, devouring her. His hands gripped her and the sting of them pinching her flesh made Nyla gasp and cry out between clenched teeth.

The pleasure, tinted with a thread of stinging pain, as Lucas licked her made Nyla writhe beneath his mouth and cling to the sheets until she finally gave up and clutched at his head. His tongue dipped into her in long plunges of searing, delicious strokes.

Lucas groaned deeply against her wet flesh, now taking long, sucking breaths as he let go of one leg and slid a finger into her, and then another, pressing upward and finding her G-spot.

Waves of fire engulfed her, screaming through her every nerve as Nyla thrust, seeking the pleasure that awaited her, the sweet release of orgasm. Lucas left her little mobility as he held her to his face, consuming her with each bold stroke of his tongue. She was trapped against him and completely vulnerable to his merciless ministrations.

Nyla blindly grabbed at his thick hair when the rise of electric pleasure engulfed her cunt. She let out a low howl as Lucas thrust into her with his tongue, fucked her with his fingers. The sound of slick flesh against flesh crashed in her ears as Nyla came.

The seductive sound of Lucas' tongue lashing out at her and his fingers driving into her wet, ready passage was more than Nyla could bear. She came with a crash of powerful, resonant heat that slammed into her cunt and clawed its way upward, touching every nerve ending she possessed with talons of sizzling heat. Nyla screamed Lucas' name in a long sob while she dug her fingers into his thick head of hair.

Thrashing against him, Nyla lost focus on anything but the harsh throb of her heart crashing against her ribs and the now more gentle tongue that continued to taste her.

Sliding his fingers from her body, Lucas caressed her thighs, before standing up and unzipping his jeans. The slide of his zipper brought Nyla back to semi-reality and she popped her eyes open as he let his jeans fall to the floor, positioning himself between her open legs.

Her eyes widened as she got her first glance at his cock, thick and hard. It bobbed between his legs as he wrapped a big hand around it and, once again, leaned over her. He allowed his shaft to slip between the sodden lips of her pussy, teasing her clit to yet another heightened state of awareness.

Lucas transfixed her with his stare, lingering near her lips. "Taste my lips, Nyla. Taste yourself on my tongue." Again, he demanded Nyla follow an order she was hardly in a position to decline and didn't want to anyway.

Nyla let her inhibition go and stroked his lower lip with a tentative tongue, savoring the firm yet silky flesh against her own.

Lucas moaned and whispered, "Can you taste your pussy on my lips, Nyla?"

Nyla's breathing stopped at his question. Instead, she closed her eyes and nodded, taking a dry gulp of air.

Lucas must have sensed that she had nothing left to offer in the way of words, so he lowered himself to her and her arms instantly wrapped around his strong, thickly muscled back. His tongue met hers stroke for stroke and her hips once again had a will of their own, pushing against his in a fevered heat.

"You're like the sweetest piece of candy I've ever tasted, Nyla. Remember your scent. Remember the flavor of your pussy on my tongue..."

Oh, Christ if he didn't enter Nyla soon, she was going to self combust. The head of Lucas' cock nudged her entrance and his words cut through the haze of piercing longing Nyla fought to control.

"Do you feel the head of my cock, Nyla? Do you want me in you, making you come again?"

Nyla whimpered, on the verge of begging, when Lucas drove into her with a thrust driven by such power, Nyla gasped sharply as the breath left her lungs and Lucas' mouth latched onto hers with fierce possession. His thick shaft stretched her deliciously, and her muscles convulsed around him as she greedily accepted the weight of him on her. Their tongues warred as each lift of Lucas' hips brought with it another slick stroke.

Lucas read her mind as he tore his mouth from her. The muscles in his chest tensed, flexing and rippling against Nyla's, crushing her breasts. "I won't last long, Nyla," was what he uttered as his pace picked up.

Nyla wrapped her legs around his lean waist, meeting him eagerly.

"Christ, Nyla, you're so wet and hot, so tight around my cock." His teeth were clenched and the hard line of his jaw was rigid with tension.

Nyla lost all coherence as Lucas gathered her wrists together above her head and plunged into her, shifting her body upward with each stroke, jolting her with the power of his hard frame.

Nyla's nails dug into his hands, pushing Lucas' cock into her more deeply as she met his hips, losing her battle with control as the thickness of him stretched her, plundering into her passage, pressing at her G-spot with maddening clarity.

In the moment they both became rigid with the final thrust and clap of flesh against flesh, Lucas' eyes met hers. The green of them seared her, pinning her own with the innate knowledge a shifter has for another.

As they drove the hard ball of orgasm home, rocking in a tight circle of rhythm and motion, cresting and then reaching a final plateau, Nyla sensed Lucas' awareness.

Crystal clear.

Finely honed.

Acute and powerful.

Complete in definition.

The awareness that you've found your mate.

Of the *life* like variety.

Chapter Three

Nyla rolled her head on her shoulders as she stared at her reflection in Lucas' bathroom mirror. Her face was flush with the fuck of a lifetime, and she couldn't help but grapple with the magnitude of what they'd both just discovered.

No *fucking* way.

How had her movie buddy of over a year ended up being her *lifemate*?

If this wasn't a double-u-tee-eff moment, like a total "what the fuck," then she couldn't fathom what was.

This meant that the gods intended them to mate for *life*. By discovering this, they'd opened up a world of shit. Oh, Jesus, her parents were going to freak. They had no control over who her lifemate was, but they sure as hell weren't going be happy that they didn't. Lucas was a tomcat, for crap's sake! Her snobby parents weren't going to like this one little, high-falutin' bit.

How had their friendship turned into *this*?

Well, that oughta teach her to keep her legs shut.

She knew rationally she couldn't do that. The call of your potential lifemate was heady indeed and not something that could be denied. Her and Lucas' mating had confirmed that.

Nyla took a lungful of air and stared at her image again, like she might find the answer in her kiss swollen lips and desire hazed eyes.

She needed to wash up and *think*. Turning, Nyla spotted a small door that she hoped would lead to a linen closet and a washcloth. On shaky legs, she let her feet absorb the cool of the tile beneath them as she opened the closet door and caught another gust of surprised air in her chest.

Jesus Christ in a mini skirt!

Why she'd thought someone as intense as Lucas had just been in that bedroom would have something as simple as washcloths in his bathroom pantry now escaped her. Where had her lighthearted friend gone and what the hell was that in the closet?

Nyla leaned against the hard frame of the door and plucked up what she could only be described as an ideal cobweb whacker. Picking up the item by what she figured was its handle, Nyla forgot about the washcloths and focused on this purple and black thing with long strips of leather hanging from the braided shaft.

Nyla swung it around, letting it dangle as the strips of what felt like leather clapped together. Surprise gave way to her endless curiosity and she couldn't help but wonder what it was. Tactile by nature, Nyla toyed with it.

Whatever the hell it was, it didn't look like something she could pick up at Walmart in the household products aisle, that's for sure.

Still naked, Nyla glanced inside the cupboard again to find more than one foreign object met her eyes. All sorts of paddles and things that involved leather lined the shelves.

A knock on the bathroom door startled her.

"Nyla? You okay in there?"

Okay? Sure, she was fabulous. How okay could she be when she'd just found some obviously very personal items of Lucas' that made absolutely no sense.

"I'm fine, just gimme a second," she called through the door. Guiltily, she placed the cobweb eliminator back in the so called linen closet and popped the door open. "Could you hand me my clothes please?"

"Sugarplum, are you sure you're all right?" Lucas' voice was tinged with genuine concern. Rather like the time Nyla thought she'd broken her paw after an eventful mouse hunt with Lucas. Damn her nearsightedness…

Lucas plopped her clothes in her hand, and Nyla put them on with hasty, trembling fingers and slipped past his yummy bulk, looking for her purse.

Lucas grabbed her hand and pulled her to him.

Oh, he *really* shouldn't do that. His body slapping up against hers was decadent.

"Nyla, talk to me. Tell me what's wrong. I'm still the same old Lucas who goes to the movies with you. I just have new privileges at the theater."

Nyla yanked her hand back and flicked his ear with her finger. "Whatever you say, Doctor Love. Right now, I want to go home. I have to think, Lucas. I mean really think about what just happened between us. We were friends and now…" *Now you have crazy serial killer shit in your bathroom.*

She needed to find her cell phone and call her best friend, Erin. Erin would know what to do. She had one of those lifemates -- not one with a cobweb whacker thingy, mind you, but a lifemate nonetheless.

Lucas grabbed her arm in a loose grip, his long fingers settling on her flesh with a possessive touch. The very same shiver that had set her ablaze at the pet store, ignited again in a swarm of heat across her skin. Dammit all! This was so out of the blue -- so left field.

"I understand, beautiful. You do that. Go home and think. I'll wait right here until you come back." Lucas tugged her toward him, pressing his lips to hers in a brief, yet scintillating kiss. "Later, lifemate," he said with smug satisfaction.

Nyla zipped out of Lucas' apartment like she was on her way to Macy's annual white sale.

Lifemate this, *baby…*

* * *

"Erin?" Nyla croaked into her cell phone on the way back to her apartment in a rickety cab.

"Hey, Nyla! How are ya?"

Peachy, fabulous, fucked up. "Well, I have some stuff I need to talk to you about."

"Shoot."

"I found my lifemate…"

"Oooooohhhh myyyyyyyyy Gooooooooddddddddd!! Who is he -- who are his people? What does he look like? Oh, please tell me he's not some dork who's balding and has a paunch in his human form. Or worse still, a guy who sells breast implants or something. Like Nia Schaffer. Remember her? Holy Hell, she ended up with the lifemate of the fricken' century. Know what her lifemate does?"

As Erin rambled, Nyla listened with half an ear. How could this be happening? She pinched the bridge of her nose with two fingers and screeched, "I don't care!" She well remembered Nia Schaffer, and right now she didn't need the very frightening comparisons. Her carefully balanced chi was teetering. "It's Lu..." Nyla coughed and cleared her throat. "It's *Lucas*." Nyla hissed the last letter of his name. She tried to be careful when in public, not to reveal her tendency to enunciate the letter s, but she couldn't help it today. She was a cat. Cats freakin' hissed.

The cab driver glanced back at her and Nyla averted her eyes.

A long pause ensued and Nyla took deep breaths. In with the good -- out with the bad.

"Lucas?"

"Lucas," Nyla confirmed.

"The Lucas that you go to the movies with and refuse to admit is hot for you?"

"Yes, Erin. That's the one. The one I go to the movies with and now have no choice but to admit that he's hot for me, okay? That's not the biggest issue I have right now. So could you shut up and help me?"

"Hey! Don't get pissy with me because your lifemate is exactly the guy I told you he should be, even if you didn't think he was."

"I'm sorry. I'm just fried. Whooped."

Erin whistled. "Was it the nasty that fried you? You know, lifemate sex is like no other. Is he good in bed? What's his lightening rod of love like? I bet it's huge! I can just tell, you know --"

"Erin! Listen to me, would you? How could I have possibly not smelled him before now?"

"I dunno. What difference does it make? He's perfect for you, Nyla. The two of you are like yin and yang. He's all yours and, I gotta tell ya, you didn't make out half bad. Don't make me remind you about Athena --"

"Erin! Shut up, please. I can't take anymore mindless babble!"

"Man, you suck today. Okay, I'm sorry. I tend to get excited when my best friend finds her lifemate and he's the caviar of lifemates," she said, her words dripping with sarcasm. "If you were here and you could see me, you'd see me zip my lip and throw away the key. This is me, shutting up."

For fuck's sake… "I'm sorry, Erin. I just can't believe this has all happened. I never smelled Lucas like that before, despite what he told me. Now I can't get his goddamned scent out of my nose, and that's not even the worst of it…"

Another silence at the other end of her cell phone.

Nyla laughed because if she didn't she'd cry. "You can ask why it's so bad, Erin."

"Why is it so bad, Nyla?"

"Because he's not a Bast descendant, Erin. You know what my parents are like. They're snotty, stuck up, pretentious know-it-alls. They will not be happy about Lucas being my lifemate. He's a tomcat."

"Well, there ain't shit they can do about it, now can they? Short of going to the lifemate council and we all know how that can go. I mean, remember Georgina and her arachnophobic lifemate? What cat is afraid of a spider, I ask you? Oops, sorry… Shutting up again."

Nyla sighed and rolled her eyes heavenward. "That's not even the half of it. He's into some weird sexual stuff I've even never heard of and can't begin to understand."

"Huh? Weird like how? Does he wear women's clothing? Oooohhhh," Erin said on a breathy, 'I know something you don't know' whisper. "Did he want to borrow your panties? God, that *is* freaky. I've heard about that, you know. There are all sorts of kinks and stuff. Women's clothing being one of them. I mean --"

"Erin! He didn't want to borrow my panties. He's very much the stud. It's something totally different than that."

"Well, for Christ sake, tell me! Otherwise, I'm off on a tangent again and you know how ugly that gets. I don't know how to shut up. It's like I have all this stuff going on in my head and I can't get it out quickly enough to --"

"Beatings."

"Who?"

"Not who. *What.* He had this thing in his linen closet and I can tell you right now, it wasn't a hand towel from Neiman Marcus." Nyla described what she'd seen in Lucas' pantry to Erin on a wing and a prayer that just saying it out loud would somehow help.

"It's called BDSM, Ny. What you just described is a flogger used in the lifestyle of BDSM."

"A what the fuck?"

"BDSM," Erin repeated. "I know a little about it. It has to do with some kind of control and whips and chains or something, right?"

BDSM? What the fuck kind of acronym was that? Beat Da Shit Outta Your Mate? No, that was too many letters…

Nyla blanched. "Well… I don't know. Oh, how the fuck am I supposed to know? I only know that this is bad, very bad, my friend. I know nothing about it and how can it be that we were meant to be lifemates if we don't share the same kink? That is some kind of kink, yes? I'm vanilla, or at least that's what I've heard from past sexual encounters. It sounds like ice cream. I always kinda liked chocolate, but --"

"Noooo, Nyla. Vanilla means you just like the sort of average, everyday sex. You know, missionary position, lights off stuff."

"I can do it with the lights on…" Nyla defended her newly acquired ice cream flavor.

"Aren't you all sexually enlightened then, miss? All it means is he likes to play with things in the bedroom, Nyla. There are all sorts of levels to it."

Nyla leaned her head back on the seat of the cab and closed her eyes. "He likes to play with *things* in the bedroom?"

"It would seem so."

Nyla groaned. "What the hell is a flogger anyway? How could I have not known this about Lucas and if I'm vanilla, what does that make him? Rocky road?"

"A flogger is used in a pleasure/pain thing, and I think it makes him a whole lot wilder than you, babe."

"Duh! So now what do I do?"

"Well, my first suggestion is the Internet. Just look up BDSM. There's plenty of stuff about it on the net."

Nyla ran a tired hand over her eyes. Eyes that might need glasses but still saw some freaky shit in Lucas' pantry. "What's your second suggestion?"

"Can I ask you something?"

"Oh, by all means."

"Was the sex good, Nyla? Lucas has always had a thing for you as far as everyone else could see, but is it possible you've always sort of had a thing for him and you just refused to acknowledge it?"

Nyla's heart jolted in her already tight chest. "It was the most incredible thing I've ever experienced, bar none," she whispered into the phone.

"Then, I do believe, you have your answer, toots. If I were you, I'd get a cute leather mini skirt and some thigh-high boots. Maybe a little latex or something."

Latex? Like the kind of stuff household gloves were made of?

Fricken' hell.

* * *

Lucas flipped the TV on as he paced the floor of his living room with impatient strides.

Well, he'd finally gotten what he wanted.

Nyla.

From the second he'd seen her at the shifters' singles thing, he'd known Nyla would be his. Shit, he'd have wanted her even if he didn't know she was his lifemate. She made his cock do things he didn't know were possible, and she'd never even had to do anything more than just breathe. Her beauty had stunned him -- rendered him downright speechless. The long curl of her inky black hair, the curve of her hip, the dip in her waist where she'd place her hand when she was giving him hell, the way she tipped her glasses up on her cute nose when she was trying to see something better, all made Lucas insane.

Thus far, he'd kept those desires to himself after Nyla had shut him down with the "let's be friends" thing. Now, the freedom of sharing that out in the open left him invigorated, excited by the possibilities of what was to come.

He'd always known Nyla was meant for him, despite their lineage. Trouble was, he didn't know when and he didn't know how. But he'd known, all the time they'd spent together, going to a movie, talking on the phone, whatever. It didn't matter, he'd always known someday, she'd want him right back.

Lucas just didn't know she'd be vanilla.

Her sexual preferences were pretty clear and now his task was at hand.

They'd talked about sex in a general way, and even if she had offered to give him details Lucas would have nipped that in the bud. Bullshit if he'd listen to her tell him some other guy had her in the way only he should. From the moment he'd met her, in his mind, Nyla was his. To hear anything different wasn't kosher.

Lucas cracked his knuckles and shook off the rage he was certain to inspire if he spent time dwelling on Nyla's prior sex life. Then he smiled. The only sex she was going to have now was the sex she had with *him.*

Then he frowned. How the hell were they going to do that if Nyla wasn't even a little submissive? Lucas didn't want her on her knees calling him Master, though that might not be the worst thing that could happen. Lucas grinned, then frowned once more. Her subservience wasn't something he wanted because he wished to humiliate her. However, he did like nothing more than to have control of the situation where bedroom play was concerned. And he enjoyed a toy or two.

Nyla wasn't terribly submissive. That was more than clear now that they'd done the lifemate dance of lust. She'd fought nearly every command he'd thrown at her. But in the end, he *had* won her over, hadn't he?

Maybe Nyla could learn to play...

And maybe she couldn't. No one could make Nyla do anything she didn't want to. She was as pig headed and difficult as they came. Lucas didn't want to make her do anything she didn't want to do, but he wouldn't mind seeing her tied to a bed, naked and writhing in utter compliance either.

His cock rose in agreement.

Could he live without that aspect to his life? He would if it meant Nyla was his for all of their nine lives. He was clear about that, now more than he'd ever been.

Shit, he needed to, like, go chase some pigeons or something and figure out how he was going to explain this to Nyla.

With the ease of much practice, he concentrated on bone and flesh and the transformation that would take him to his cat form. Lucas shifted and hopped up on his windowsill with a light thunk.

Think. He needed to think, and then he needed to have Nyla again.

And then again, and again.

He could do that now. She was, after all, *his* lifemate.

If he were in human form, he'd have grined again. But that would be smug and in essence, declaring he'd always been right about he and Nyla.

Okay, so it wasn't a bad thing to bask in his rightness, was it?

By, God, he'd been *right*.

Right.

Right.

Right.

Right wasn't going to make much of a difference when her parents got wind of the fact that her lifemate was a mongrel.

Lucas opted not to think about the ramifications of them calling the lifemate council to order.

Instead, Lucas swished his tail and set off to find a pigeon or two in Central Park.

Chapter Four

Nyla sat at her computer long after she'd finished her conversation with a nice man who called himself a *submissive* in a chat room for people who dug this thing called BDSM.

Nope. No fucking way was she going to be anyone's submissive. That implied Lucas was in charge and no one was in charge of her.

Yeah, you're not the boss of me… neener, neener, neener.

But did it really mean that? Not according to the nice man who liked to be called mean names after he washed your floor and licked your boots clean.

Oy.

This was insane. She wasn't going to clean anyone's floor while being called a shithead, nor was she going to have one of those cork things they called a butt plug rammed up her ass. Not a chance in hell. She had a maid to clean, and if she needed a little colonic cleansing, she'd get a damn enema, thank you.

Oh, God, she could feel a hairball form at the back of her throat, knotting her terror in a tight fist of panic.

According to *justasub* on BDSMandmore.com, it was a matter of allowing yourself the freedom to let go, which seemed peachily appealing if it didn't involve being tied to one of those damn racks of torture she'd seen in the pictures on the net.

Well, okay, it wasn't torture. For some, it was exceptionally pleasurable.

Not for this feline…

Nyla had seen some things on the Internet that alternately freaked her out and fascinated her. Other stuff just went too far. Who thought PVC pipe was a smokin' hot bedroom toy? There were extremes to this BDSM thing and if what Lucas had in his pantry was how he liked his sex, he had some splainin' to do.

Nyla couldn't remember seeing any clothespins in Lucas' closet of magic goodies. She'd have never believed it until she saw it with her own two nearsighted eyes.

Yep, clothespins. Used to arouse one in what was called a *scene* in BDSM. That wasn't even the half of what she'd witnessed.

They even had schools you could attend to become a submissive or a Dominant.

Jesus, she'd be some slave school dropout, now wouldn't she? Cuz she couldn't do some of that shit for all the tuna and caviar on the planet.

So was Lucas submissive or Dominant? Forget that question. Nyla knew the answer without hesitation.

He was Dominant.

Nyla gulped and closed her eyes, staving off the image of Lucas between her legs. She focused instead on the fringes of fear and worry that accosted her in waves of panic at the possibility he'd want to slap one of those ball gag things in her mouth. Like even that could shut up her screaming. They'd hear her in Idaho, for crap's sake.

Maybe he wasn't really into it, and she was jumping to huge conclusions and searching the Internet for things that didn't even apply to him.

That was sure a whole lot of leather stuff to not be into *something*.

She wasn't afraid of Lucas. Quite the contrary. Nyla was afraid that after chatting with some of the people who lived the BDSM lifestyle to one degree or another, that she and Lucas were somehow mismatched in the lifemate thing. If what she'd chatted with the submissive about was true, then you just *were* submissive or Dominant. There wasn't anything you could do to change that.

There was still no way in catnip she was going to allow anyone to tell her what to do on a daily basis. She wasn't wearing a collar and being dragged around by a leash. No damn way.

Nyla was always fighting the tide. She'd argued with her parents for one reason or another as a kitten, and she kept that up to this day. That couldn't possibly mean she was submissive. She was a kitty with a cause, not a stray with no rhyme or reason.

Yet, when she and Lucas had mated, it had been the most titillating experience of her life when he'd *demanded* she submit to him and answer him in the name of desire. It had made her insane with lust.

That's what he'd been doing and all while Nyla was completely unaware that he was. Lucas was a forceful presence, no doubt, but he never came off uber Alpha and pushy. Most of the time they spent together was spent laughing about one thing or another. Not demanding things, but now their dynamic had changed considerably.

They were lifemates.

Nyla shivered when she called to memory the slick plunge of his cock, the commanding way he'd insisted she own up to her needs verbally. They needed to talk. She just might be scaring herself over nothing.

Grabbing her phone, Nyla pressed speed dial and waited impatiently until Lucas picked up.

"Hey, lifemate."

"Funny. You're still just as funny as you were when you were my non-smell like Utopia friend."

Lucas sighed into the phone. Nyla could almost see the rise and fall of his broad chest. "So what's up? Have you been thinking?"

Oh, had she ever. "Oh, yes, and we have some stuff we need to discuss, buddy. Like right now. I need some clarification before I go any further in the lifemate thing with you."

"I'd say I have to agree, sugarplum." Lucas' voice slithered up her spine like a trickle of chocolate sprinkles on a hot fudge sundae.

"Yeah, Lucas. Like talk about the crazy shit you have in the bathroom at your apartment." There, it was out in the universe now. Deal with that, baby!

"So you've been in my linen closet then?" Lucas' words weren't at all astonished to her ears. Nor did he seem like he much cared she'd found those serial killer tools of the trade in there.

"Gee, go figure. I should have known you wouldn't have something as mundane as a damn hand towel. So you want to explain all that stuff or are we just going to pretend like I'm just so nearsighted I didn't see what I think I saw?"

"Why didn't you ask me what it was when you found it, Nyla? We've never had trouble talking before."

"Well, I was looking for a washcloth and I came up with that -- that cobweb thwacker," she said as she flung around in her office chair. "Forgive me for being freaked out about it. Care to explain the torture devices in the closet there, Mr. Nine Lives? Because if you're some freaky serial killer and you've been hiding it for a year now, I just have to warn you, I shift too and I'd be happy to give you a taste of this pussy cat in her finest form," Nyla threatened, but somehow the meat of her threat rang false, even to her own ears. She didn't fear Lucas, for whatever kooky reason, but she was definitely wary of the nutty shit he had in that closet.

Her lifemate could *not* be a serial killer. Well, wait, maybe that thought had merit, considering her overall luck amounted to nil most times when it came to men. It would be comical if it weren't mostly the case in point. Did anyone know John Wayne Gacy was a serial killer? People knew him for years and had no clue, all while he was busy hacking people up and stowing them away in his basement…

Okay, a grip was needed here. This was Lucas. Her not so friend-like lifemate/friend.

Lucas exhaled into the phone on a chuckle. "It's a flogger, Nyla. Ya know, like a sex toy?"

"Oh, yes, I know exactly what it is *now*, Lucas. I did some research and I've seen plenty, thank you. Besides who the hell uses *that* as a toy, you beer swilling Neanderthal? And how is it that I don't know about this side of you? What the hell is sexual about it anyway? It looks like something I'd use to snuff out cobwebs."

"It's a *flogger*, Nyla, and you didn't know because you weren't looking at me as anything more that your popcorn holder at the movies."

Nyla sighed with impatience. "I know what it is, Lucas!"

"A flogger is used in sexual foreplay in the BDSM lifestyle. It's used to arouse your partner. A pleasure/pain kind of thing."

Well, wasn't he like the king of BDSM factoids? Nyla shook her head. "I'm still not seeing the correlation here. How can pain be pleasurable?"

Lucas' laughter rumbled in his chest. "It sometimes can be, with the right person and done properly."

"So you *hit* your partner? What the hell is exciting about that, Lucas? If you hit me, I'm going to knock the snot out of you right back."

Lucas' sigh was getting louder. "I'm not going to hurt you, Nyla. I'd never hurt you. I'd learn your buttons and push them is all."

"Bondage-Domination-Sadism-Masochism," Nyla repeated what she'd read on the Internet. "How can it be that I just never knew this about you, Lucas?" She didn't think she'd ever get over the shock. They shared *everything*. He knew when she went into heat, for God's sake!

"Yep. That's what it means and it wasn't like we discussed things like that, Nyla. Not in detail, anyway."

"We did too. You know my favorite position, dammit!"

"Look, Nyla. I'm a Bedroom Dom. I'm not into some of the heavier aspects. I just enjoy some of the play. I would never hurt you. I would never humiliate you, and probably half of what you've seen and read on the Internet is stuff I haven't seen either, or have any wish to participate in."

Nyla gulped. "Domination? Okay, I need some explanation here. I mean, we are, after all, lifemates, *friend*. How that happened I'll never know, but there it is. You know exactly what that means for us -- there's no turning back. We can figure that out later. So gimme the scoop. Because all that shit in your closet looks like it should belong to Jeffrey Dahmer."

"Yes, Cleopatra, you *are* my lifemate. Funny how that works, huh? Funny how I've been telling you that for over a year. We have a lot to learn about one another, sugarplum, and parts of my sexual activity have to do with domination."

Nyla fought the rush of heat that inflamed her thighs at the sinful bliss Lucas' voice evoked when he said the word domination. "Sugarplum *this*, Lucas, and yeah, can we start with that flogger thing? I just can't get past it. Flogging would imply beating the shit out of me and that's just not going to happen. Not unless you want to find yourself minus a limb or two. Don't think I don't mean it either. Because I do." Her eyes narrowed as she threw out her empty threat into the phone.

"Oh, I've no doubt you can hold your own, Nyla. Now you'll just be holding mine while you do it. Flogging doesn't entail beating the shit out of you. It entails many things, but I would never hurt you. That's not what this Dom is about."

"I don't get it. How in all of Ra did I end up with you as a lifemate? We need to petition the lifemate council of adjustments for a variance or something." Nyla was only half joking about it, simply because the one sexual encounter they'd had wasn't something she wanted to give up on just yet. Why give up when she had no choice but to accept her destiny anyway?

"You don't mean that and you know it, Nyla. We're perfect for each other and we always have been," he chided her. "I don't live the lifestyle twenty-four seven, but I enjoy some aspects of it in the bedroom. That's why I have all of those toys in the pantry. It's that simple, honest."

"So you only enjoy flogging the snot out of someone *sometimes*?"

Lucas chuckled, "No, Nyla. I've said this already. I don't want to hurt you, and our bedroom time doesn't always have to involve a flogger or a paddle or anything else but us. Your ultimate pleasure is my goal. Like I said, this is something we have to discuss. Not only because BDSM is about trust and understanding, but because honestly, I'm a little puzzled as to how my lifemate would be someone who knows nothing about my sexual pleasures. I know we've talked about sex in a very general way, but somehow, I always thought my lifemate would share my kink."

Nyla snorted. "Oh, yeah? Well, that makes two of us. So get over here and let's get down to business. I want to know what the hell all that stuff is in your linen closet and I want to know what it means in my world. We both know the rules about lifemates and now we have to do the discovery thing. So why don't you tell me why the hell your lifemate was a year in the making and finally discovered you in a pet store and not at Phil's House of Bondage and Tattoos, a place I don't frequent and, I'd bet, you have a lifetime credit with? How could you have hidden that from me?" Nyla asked, still a bit hurt by Lucas not sharing something that seemed so important to him.

"We're doing the circle dance here, Nyla. I didn't hide it. I just didn't announce it by buying a T-shirt."

Nyla wondered if upon finding their lifemates all shifters just accepted it and their snotty upper class families did too. Cuz her family was not going to like Lucas. They knew of him. They knew Nyla and he went to the movies together. That was it. *Oh, and by the way, Mom? I found my lifemate today. He likes whips and chains. Can he come to dinner?*

"So, Cleopatra, you're my lifemate..." His tone was cocky and knowing.

"Yeah, that's me. Don't get too excited, huh?"

"Well, you have to admit, I have been telling you this forever. I mean, I knew you smelled different than anyone else I'd smelled before. I just had no idea it was *that* kind of smell, but I was pretty sure, babe."

The aroma of your lifemate.

There was nothing like it and only lifemates could identify it in one another. Sort of like when humans got that giddy, stupid feeling and had it in their heads that they'd found that perfect someone. It was just like that, minus the romance of it all.

"I think my nostrils are all messed up or something, because I didn't smell it until the pet store, Lucas. So what's next on our lifemate agenda? Do we ask each other stuff like what side of the bed do you prefer? Coke or Pepsi? Decaf or leaded? Liver and cheese bits or Chicken of the Sea? Oh, wait," Nyla slapped her forehead. "I already know about all that stuff, don't I, *friend*?"

"I'll always be your friend, Nyla. Now I'm a friend with a big, fat benefit," Lucas teased, a glint of the humor she knew and loved threading his tone.

"Does this mean we can't shift and hunt mice together anymore?" That would so suck. Lucas always found the plumpest of mice.

"Nope, sugarplum, you'll always be my favorite mice catching buddy. Besides, how will you see where the hell you're going without your glasses if not for me? We have a lot to talk about, Nyla. Don't sweat the small stuff right now."

Small? His kink was far from small. "Yeah, like the kinky stuff in your closet. Lucas? This is going to ruin everything. We were good friends. I loved hanging out with you. You're my favorite person in the whole world, and now I've had sex with you. Bonded for friggin' life with you. I don't get it, but I'm a little freaked out right now."

"I think it's going to take some time to get used to, Nyla, but for me, it's like the last piece of the puzzle that has always been us."

Nyla wrinkled her nose and fought the giddy rush of warmth she was feeling over Lucas' admission. "You're never going to let me forget you were right from the start, are you?"

Lucas laughed again. "Nope."

Laughing, Nyla nodded. "Somehow I knew that. So what's next, Lucas?" Lucas had an answer for everything, and this time he'd better have a good one because she just didn't know how the transition from friendship to relationship was going to work.

"Well, we have to go tell your parents."

Nyla gulped. That was going to suck big, fat weenies. "I think we both know how that's going to go."

Lucas blew out a breath added, "And we have to talk about my lifestyle and how we can make this work. We *will* make this work, Nyla."

"You know, maybe they made a mistake? The invisible lifemate people who determine this stuff?" Nyla said, dismissing Lucas' matter of fact statement. "We need to figure this out. Maybe someone made a colossal mistake in the lifemate department because I sure as hell don't want to be flogged with all of the crazy torture devices you have in that bathroom closet. At least I don't think I do." Nyla shifted to the end of her office chair and nervously played with the edge of her nightgown. "I think we have to think about this some more. I think we have to contact the lifemate people and lodge a complaint. Do you think they have a suggestion box?"

"It's a lot to take in, Nyla. We both know this means we're stuck with each other. I won't pretend I'm not happy about that, but in the end, there's no going back."

Oh, really? Christ, he made it sound as if it were a trip to the electric chair to be stuck with her. "You know, you should be doing the lifemate dance of the utterly euphoric. You just got what you claim you've always wanted."

"Oh, I am. Believe me, but I don't want you to feel like I'm being too smug about it. That would just be plain shitty of me, even if I was *right*."

Yes, Lucas had been right, and now he had what he wanted. Nyla discovered she had what she wanted and she didn't even know she'd wanted it until it'd happened. It could be much worse. Some shifters ended up with a mate who didn't satisfy them on any level.

Lucas had definitely satisfied her on so many levels she'd lost count. Which brought her back to the flogger thing.

Well, there was only one way to figure this out. "Lucas?"

"What, sugarplum?"

"Come over here, *now*, and bring that flogger."

Who's yer Dom?

Chapter Five

Nyla flung open her door when Lucas knocked, clad only in her briefest of nightwear. "Sorry, I didn't have anything leather handy." She snorted. "I guess this will just have to do." Nyla chuckled as she stuck her thumbs under the slender straps over her shoulder.

"It'll do just fine, Nyla. Now, come here." Lucas pointed to the spot between his feet as he closed her apartment door and leaned back on it with a slow smile. His jeans were snug and the evidence of his arousal, plain.

Christ, he was hot. Nyla's knees wobbled a little. Her bravado wasn't far behind…

"Ask nicely," Nyla countered.

Lucas gave her a cross-eyed smile. "Look, Cleopatra, I wasn't ordering you. I was letting you know that the very idea of your lips pressed against mine has my cock as hard as it's ever been and the need to kiss you is urgent. Not all of this BDSM thing has to be about a struggle, Nyla. You have nothing to prove when you show me how stubborn you are. I already know and breaking your will isn't what I want or need to do. Now, come here."

Oh. Well, put like that… okay, then. Nyla dutifully sauntered over to Lucas. He dropped the bag with what she assumed was the flogger and wrapped his hands around her waist, hauling her close to his thick frame. He lowered his lips to hers with slow precision, whispering his tongue over Nyla's lower lip.

She found herself clinging to his shirt front as her defenses melted and her nipples tightened.

"Now was that so hard?" Lucas said against her mouth.

Nyla sighed against him. "No, Lucas it wasn't hard at all." Oh, Ra, he was an amazing kisser… everything about him all slapped up against her felt right. Every single thing. Now, onto the business at hand. The flogger…

Nyla pulled away from Lucas' lips with reluctance and looked up at him. "So let's do this. Flog me or whatever it is we do with that," she said as she pointed to the bag on the floor.

Lucas rolled his eyes. "Honey, this isn't about doing things on command. We have to talk about what's expected, find a safe word, set the scene up."

A safe word. How did "What the fuck are you thinking?" grab him? No, that was a phrase. "I know, Lucas. I read about it on the Internet."

"Good, then you know I only want your pleasure and that doesn't involve making you uncomfortable. Trust is involved here, Nyla, so we'll take this slowly."

"Okay, so let's *slowly* flog me or whatever it is we have to do," Nyla said as she took Lucas by the hand and led him to her posh bedroom.

"Wow, you Ivana Trump wannabe. Nice digs," Lucas whistled as he assessed her bedroom and teasingly mocked her family's financial status. "I've never seen it before."

Nyla giggled, not at all nervous about Lucas' big, hulking presence in her decidedly girlie bedroom. "Thanks. I like it."

Lucas went to the big oak post on her bed and gripped it with a firm hand as he grinned. "Cool, four posters. Plenty of wood here to tie you up while I flog the hell out of you, just before I slam you with my mighty fuck stick."

Nyla flipped him the bird and stuck her tongue out at him. "You can shove that wood up your Dom ass."

Lucas sat at the edge of her bed with his sly grin and patted the space beside him. "C'mere, lifemate. Stop freaking out and being such a sissy."

Nyla rolled her eyes at him and then sauntered over to stand in front of him. "I'm no sissy. You're forgetting who you're talking to here. I mean, I was the one who caught the most mice last round, wasn't I?"

Lucas grabbed her ass and pulled her to him. His grip was firm and stung a bit with a sharp, but pleasurable sizzle. Christ, what the hell was going on with her body?

Lucas nuzzled the space between her breasts as he kneaded her ass, and Nyla found her hands threading through his hair with greed for what was to come.

"I haven't forgotten, Nyla. Now be quiet and let me ravish you. You talk too much sometimes."

"But don't we have to do the safe word thing and stuff?"

"Not right now, Nyla. Right now I just want to have you. We can talk about the other stuff when I'm done."

Nyla's head fell back as Lucas tugged her nightie off her shoulders and let it fall to her waist, capturing a nipple between his lips. His groan incited Nyla's senses and sent a pulsing heat to her pussy that made her squirm.

Hovering over her nipple, Lucas sipped it into his mouth with a twist of his tongue, rolling it over the now pebbled surface. "I've waited for this for a long time, Nyla," he murmured as he pulled her to straddle his lap, the rough texture of his jeans scraping her clit through her panties.

Lucas rose slightly and turned their bodies so that he was able to press Nyla into the cushiony mattress. Hot, strong hands shrugged her nightgown over her hips as he parted her thighs to lie between them.

Looking down at her, Lucas' eyes simmered. "I want to fuck you senseless, Nyla, but I don't want you to be frightened by me and my lust."

Nyla groaned, wrapping her legs around Lucas' waist. "I'm not afraid of you, Lucas." And she wasn't. She was, however, a little leery of that flogger thing.

"Roll over, Nyla. *Now.*"

Nyla's heart throbbed in her chest. The anticipation of Lucas taking her was thrilling, but tinged with the fear of what was next. Somehow, she no longer felt as if he were ordering her to do something because he liked the power play. His tone was too gruff and husky to be called arrogant. Nyla smelled his lust for her, but her delicate nostrils were also laced with something else. An emotion she was unable to decipher just yet.

Nyla rolled over to her belly and she heard the rustle of material as Lucas removed his clothing. Suddenly, his hands were on her, pulling her panties off with impatience, roaming over bare flesh, making her arch into his caress as he lifted her hips and placed himself between her thighs. Sliding a hand between their closely pressed flesh, Lucas leaned over her, pressing kisses to her spine as he opened her wet, aching flesh with deft fingers.

Nyla reared back against Lucas' abdomen, rippled and hard, encouraging him to touch her, but instead, Lucas skimmed the outer lips of her cunt, taunting her. Nyla bit the inside of her cheek and took a dizzying breath to steady the roar of lust.

"Do you want to fuck, Nyla?" Lucas asked as he allowed his cock to graze her pussy. Hot, thick and long, he moved in, only to pull out again.

Yes, she wanted to fuck. She wanted to bang him like a drum all damn night. Why was it so hard to say so? Her disjointed thoughts became more so as Lucas pushed her to answer him. "Do you want my cock in you, Nyla? Stroking you?"

Nyla nodded her head against the safety of the pillows that lined her bed.

"*Say it,* Nyla," Lucas demanded as he nipped the rounded flesh of her ass, removing the silken slide of his cock from the heated place between her legs.

Nyla clutched the pillows above her head with fevered hands, but still she was unable to let go.

The first sting of Lucas' hand on her ass took Nyla by surprise. It sent a shockwave of pleasure like she'd never known along every nerve in her body. The slap of flesh was sharp and clear as it rang throughout her bedroom. Palpable. She blushed because it felt so incredibly exciting. Lucas' hand smoothed over the now warm spot where he'd left his mark and Nyla arched against it, craving something she was too afraid to identify… too conflicted to ask for.

Lucas slid his cock between the lips of her pussy again with a swift, sure stroke and Nyla whimpered with a weak mewl. "Say it, Nyla." Lucas' words sang through her veins, thrumming and flagrant.

She cracked then, like a fine dish made of china. "Yes! Yes, dammit!" she yelped in frustration and need. Christ, he was killing her. She was as juiced as she'd ever been in her life and they were playing a friggin' game of mercy.

You win, she thought for the merest of moments. Nyla couldn't fight it anymore. The swollen lips of her cunt, the ache deep within her belly demanded satisfaction, leaving her without a qualm.

Lucas slapped the cheek of her ass again with a firm crack, but what followed wasn't painful, it was *exhilarating*. The heat that flooded every pore of her skin sizzled and Nyla throbbed with the need for him to plunge into her -- take her hard and without leniency.

"Say it nicely, Nyla," he demanded as he let his tongue glide over the spot he'd just warmed with his hand. The cool air he created made Nyla buck in agony for release.

Say it nicely, Nyla, she mocked in her head as she clenched her teeth together in a grip of death. *Here's the skinny, feline. You can give in and let that delicious cock drive into you, or you can struggle with the obvious power his charms have over you and go to bed frustrated. Your choice…* Fuck it. Hadn't she just been in this very same position the last mating of the millennium? It didn't kill her then and it wouldn't kill her now.

On a huge gust of air that burst from her lungs like a race horse just out of the gate, Nyla let go. "Please, please, Lucas." Her sob was audibly weak to her ears. "Pleeease put your cock in me." She almost said *now* to somehow retain some of her control, but she didn't have the time because Lucas thrust into her with the speed of a shooting bullet, hard, thick, silky hot.

Nyla gasped as he groaned low from behind her. A growl of fulfillment, final satisfaction. The force of his thrust made her entire body lurch forward, stretching her, filling her with the immediate need to orgasm.

"Dammit, Nyla," Lucas muttered and Nyla couldn't quite figure out why, but the words had a desperation to them that she didn't quite understand.

As his rhythm increased, Lucas again brought his hand down on her tender flesh and it drove Nyla right over the edge. The heat and slight sting of his hand overwhelmed her, flooded her pussy, tightening her nipples until Nyla screamed as her orgasm ripped through her.

Lucas came too, his seed spilling into her with heaving jolts of his cock.

Nyla collapsed on the bed and Lucas came to rest against her, his chest crashing against her back.

Nyla, in her distorted thoughts, remembered they hadn't even used the flogger. Lucas had used his hand and she'd liked it. Hell, she'd *loved it*. The sweet sting of his palm as he drove into her had successfully opened a door Nyla didn't know was in her *Let's Make a Deal* package and, as reality set in, it frightened her.

Aroused her.

Freaked her out.

And there it was again -- *aroused* her.

Holy hell, who was she and where had this come from? Who thought being hit was sexy? Did this make her some kind of freak? Did shifters around the globe like this kind of shit or was she some kind of weirdo pain seeker?

"Baby? Stop." Lucas warned. "Enjoying what just happened is okay, sugarplum. The only trouble is, I can't seem to control myself around you. I can't get into you fast enough. I can't get enough of you. I want to own your body, take it with abandon. I've never had that kind of trouble before. I'm always in control," he whispered as he nuzzled her shoulder with light kisses.

Nyla's belly flip-flopped. His words frightened her. She would not be owned like some damn slave. "Stop it, Lucas. Stop it now. No one owns me. *I* own me, dammit, and I-I… I'm… well, I don't know what I am, but I can't possibly want to be tied up and slapped around. I sure as hell don't want to hit Home Depot and troll the plumbing department for shit that you can use to torture me with!" Her panic could be heard in her voice and she knew it, but she couldn't keep the fear from spilling out of her big mouth and roaring into the space between them.

Lucas ran a gentle hand over Nyla's hair and slipped an arm under her from behind. "Baby, this doesn't mean you want to be tortured. It just means you like a little spice. Just because you enjoy some borderline pain, doesn't mean you want to be hurt. I promise you, Cleopatra, you're not a freak."

"Oh, really? What's next, Mr. Dom? Are we still going to be saying the same thing when I'm bound and gagged with duct tape and superglued to the fucking bed, with clothespins clamped over every available surface of my body and a plug in my ass?" Nyla struggled to breathe as she wormed her way out from under Lucas and scooted to the other end of the bed.

Lucas sat up, his naked body lean and honed in the dim light of her bedroom. "Nyla, I can help you understand. There's nothing wrong with it. C'mere and we'll talk."

His calm take on her spiral into leather and beatings only incited Nyla further into the tizzy she was creating with her fear. "No! No, I will not *c'mere, sugarplum*! I can't do this, Lucas. This is wrong. This isn't something I've enjoyed before, and all of a sudden I want to fuck like a rabid animal while you slap me around? Something is so wrong about that! The next thing you know you'll have a leash attached to me and I'll be licking your floors clean while you call me your bitch!"

"No!" Lucas said with a firm, sharp response. "No, babe, I do *not* want to slap you around. Did I hurt you in any way? No, Nyla, and I never would. I'm not into forcing anyone to do anything. Did I demand that you answer me? Did I demand that you ask for your pleasure? Yes, but would I ever hurt you? Never, Nyla. *Never*. That's the difference between 'slapping you around' and a Dominant male. I'm no lifemate beater and I resent that you could think that of me, even in your freaked out bullshit!" Now

Lucas' voice was raised and becoming louder, tight with indignation at her accusation.

Nyla scrunched her eyes shut and fought yet another wave of hysteria. "I don't know that I know the difference, Lucas, and what does that say about me? I pride myself on being in control of myself at all times. I come from a pretty classy family full of snobs who demand that I be just that, in control at all times. And now look at me! I'm writhing all over a bed, looking to be hit by a tomcat!"

Lucas' face distorted and he gave Nyla a pointed look as he slid from her bed and gathered his jeans. "You know, Nyla, I've wanted you for a long time, loved you for probably half of that, and never have I ever felt the differences in our lineage as much as I do right now. Maybe you're right. Maybe we should petition the lifemate council for that variance adjustment," Lucas said in a voice Nyla didn't recognize. Cold and distant. Not the Lucas she'd turned to for comfort and reassurance time and time again. He walked away from her to pull on his jeans and, with his broad back turned to her, Nyla wanted to crumble.

Stop him.

Hate him for making her discover this side to herself she didn't know existed.

Loved her? Lucas loved her?

She'd ignored it as if he'd told her something inconsequential. Then, to make it worse, she'd done the class thing like spending time with him was Paris Hilton at a hoedown. Somehow, she managed to end up insulting the barbecue. God, she was a snob, just like her parents. She'd never, ever had an argument with Lucas, and now adding all of this discovery crap into the mix was making her strike out in confusion and fear. "I'm sorry, Lucas. You know I didn't mean --"

"Forget it, Nyla. I'll contact the lifemate council myself," he said between clenched teeth as he cracked his knuckles and began to shift so he could avoid her big damn mouth, she figured.

She'd always loved Lucas in his cat form. No matter that he was what some considered a mongrel stray. He was beautifully marked and sinuously defined. Striking and lean, solid and secure.

Lucas took a last glance at her with a cocked head and ears that twitched before he headed out of her bedroom and to the living room window where the fire escape was.

Nyla followed him to the living room with sluggish feet and watched as Lucas slithered under the window, and then she let one lone tear streak her face. The salty bubble held all of her worries, encapsulated and coming to fruition. She and Lucas should have always been friends and damn the lifemate gods for saying otherwise.

Nyla went back to her bedroom and scooped up the shirt Lucas had left behind, throwing it over her shoulders and laying down on her bed. She curled into a ball, letting her mind race as she fought one of her biggest fears of all.

Who would be her friend, if not Lucas?

Who would make her laugh when she didn't want to? Who would have the missing pieces to her fucked up head's jigsaw puzzle, if not Lucas?

Who would hold her hand at the movies?

Chapter Six

"So do you see the problem here, Doc? I mean, I have a lifemate my parents don't know about and will hate -- and I do mean *hate* because he's not a damn purebred. And he likes some stuff, ya know, like sexually speaking that I don't know if I can participate in. Okay, so I admit, it turned me on when he spanked me, but the shit I saw on the Internet and the stuff I saw in his closet kinda freaked me out, ya know?

"The problem is, I love him. Like I couldn't imagine a day without him in it when we were just friends, but now? Now that we've done all this boinking and stuff, I dunno if I can part with him. Which brings me back to my original problem. My parents... they're going to go to the lifemate council to stick their noses in where they don't belong. That is, if Lucas doesn't get there first. He was so angry with me when he left my apartment, and that was three days ago. What the hell am I going to do? I'm blabbing like an idiot, I know, but I've got some real trouble here and I need help!"

The nice psychiatrist sat ever patiently as Nyla rambled on about her lifemate woes. His hands clamped lightly together in a steeple under his chin as he leaned forward over his desk to look at Nyla, pensively studying her when his lips began to move.

Oh, thank, Ra! He was going to help her. He would say something profound that would get her out of this fix. Some mumbo jumbo that would surely bring a ray of clarity to this fucked up mess.

The nice doctor's eyes were calming and very blue as he asked. "May I ask why it is that you chose to come see me, Nyla?"

Um, well, cuz you're a doctor of the mind, you hack and I've wandered around my apartment in Lucas' T-shirt for three days sniffing it like it was salmon? "Do you mean did I find you on the Internet or through an ad in the paper? Like the *Yellow Pages*?"

His blue eyes remained serene, still waters and all that bullshit. "No, Nyla. I meant, why did you choose to come see me? My area of expertise is very specialized, you know."

Duh! Of course it was, the quack. The ad was very clear. *Is your cat or dog experiencing difficulty adjusting? Do you sense emotional discord or an overall dissatisfaction in your cat or dog's personality? Do they seem depressed and lethargic? I can help...* Yes, that's what the ad had said.

"Yeah, you specialize in therapy," Nyla said with a wistful smile. Whoda thunk she'd be in *therapy*?

"Yes, yes, that's true, Nyla, but do you know *who* I counsel?"

Nyla nodded her head. *Dumb ass*. "Yeah, I know. Cats and dogs."

"That's right, Nyla," the doctor said in a soft, low, undertone almost as if he were afraid to startle her.

"Um, okay, so what's your point here?"

"Nyla," he said, all soothing and patronizing as he pulled out a hand mirror from his desk drawer. "Look at yourself in the mirror, Nyla. What do you see?'

Well, if her eyesight were better, she'd probably see a more clear version of herself. However, even fuzzy, she looked like something the cat just dragged in. Nyla'd laugh at her smart ass thought, if she could summon up even the hint of a giggle. "I see me and I'm a mess. My eyes are puffy and red, aren't they?"

"Nyla." Now his rippled, soothing tones held a warning. As if he might be preparing her for something dire. "I'm going to tell you something and I want you to hear me. Listen carefully to my words. You're a *human*." He sat back with a slow movement and waited but a moment, possibly because he thought she might lose her mind over her human status. "You're not a cat or a dog, Nyla, and I really believe you need something far more intensive in the way of help than I can offer."

Nyla caught sight of her face in the mirror again, just before the light of recognition dawned on her and she began to howl with laughter. "Ooohhhhhhhh -- I -- I'm soooooorrryyyy. I don't --

I don't know -- what I was thinnnkkkkking," Nyla sputtered in a fit of maniacal giggles.

"Nyla," the doctor said in a reassuring, non-threatening tone while he reached for the phone on his desk. "I'm going to call a colleague of mine and we're going to see that you get the best of everything modern medicine has to offer. How does that sound?"

Jesus Christ in a mini skirt! He thought she was a nut. Hell, she *was* a nut. He was a pet psychiatrist, for crap's sake, and she hadn't really been giving anything much thought other than finding a way to get rid of the gnawing ache of indecision over Lucas that sat in the pit of her belly.

Suddenly, her parents, her fears, seemed far away and clarity dawned on her. It was a simple answer. Nyla needed Lucas and she'd find a way to figure the rest out. Flogger or not, she couldn't live without Lucas in her life. He brought more than just the occasional movie and some giggles. He gave her complete understanding. The simpatico they'd shared had always been, from the very start.

It simply was, and Nyla just had to make it right and keep Lucas from petitioning the lifemate council.

As Nyla gasped for breath, she held up her hand to thwart his efforts to "save" her. "Doc?"

"Yes, Nyla."

She'd show him just who needed basket weaving one-o-one. "Watch this. Oh, and thanks for the help. You're da bomb. I think I know what I have to do now."

"You're very welcome and of course, Nyla. I can watch *and* call my colleague at the same ti --"

Nyla heard his intake of air, sharp and whistling like a tea kettle as she focused on calling up the visual of her feline form. Hopefully, the sometimes audible crunch of flesh and bone wouldn't freak him out too much.

The doc just might want to call in some of his connections for his own use when she was done.

Wide eyed and mouth gaping, the nice doctor fell back in his chair as Nyla scampered up on his desktop and peered at him through the eyes that brought her so much trouble when she hunted mice.

He wheezed as she rubbed against his arm, the arm that was now immobile and lying lifeless on his desk.

Nyla purred at him. Maybe he was allergic to cats? Wouldn't that suck as a pet psychiatrist? Nyla backed away and swished her tail in salute.

Just my way of saying thanks, doc.

Put *that* in your medical journals and smoke it.

* * *

"Hi, Daddy? Where's Mother?" Nyla shot the words into the cool air of his study as she stormed in to face her father in her parents' swanky Park Avenue apartment.

"Kitten? What's wrong?" Her father's weathered face held concern as he rose from behind his cluttered antique desk.

"I need to talk to you and Mom. It's important. No, it's critical. So buzz her on that fancy intercom, would ya? Or have Niles find her. Or I'll find her, but we need to talk."

"Nyla, sit down. You're flushed. Have you been spider chasing? Relax, honey. I'll find your mother."

Good, do that because she had some lifemate shit she had to work out before Lucas went and did something drastic, like petition the lifemate board of variances. That would be ugly. They had a waiting period and a rule of no contact. Nyla couldn't take the no contact rule. She needed contact with Lucas.

Forever.

Her mother entered her father's study with her usual grace and elegance. The stealthy fall of her feet carried with it her particular flair for fashion. Nyla's mother entered the room, a frown furrowing her smooth brow.

"Nyla! This is a wonderful surprise, darling. Come sit with me and we'll have some liver pate."

Nyla popped up from her chair and shook her head. "No. No, mother, I don't want liver pate or *fois gras* either. I need to tell you and Daddy something. Before I begin, I need to tell you that I don't give a hamster's cedar bedding what you have to say about it!" Nyla's voice bordered obnoxiously loud, but she didn't care. She was just going to spill it, and then she was going to go find Lucas and beg him to forgive her for being such a stuck up ass.

Nyla's mother held out her hand. "Sweetheart, there's no need to raise your voice. Come tell me what's troubling you and we'll figure it out. Did you go over your limit on your Visa? Nothing can be so bad that you need to be in such a dither, darling."

"Your mother is right, kitten. Calm down and talk to us." Her father's voice was balm to her ears, but he'd be screeching like a cat on a hot tin roof in no time when he found out *who* her lifemate was.

"No, Daddy. I can't calm down." Nyla paced in front of her father's desk as her mother's eyes followed her frantic movement. Frig it. No holds barred, all out war was going to happen, but frig it. Nyla wanted Lucas. "I found my lifemate."

Nyla let the words drop like a basketball in an empty gymnasium. The echo was resounding for a moment, and then her mother's squeal of delight was deafening. "Oh, Nyla! This is wonderful! It means we have to prepare, darling. We have much to do. There's the ritual, of course --"

"Mother!"

Nyla's mother stopped gushing and stared at her, smoothing a hand over her crisp linen skirt and composing herself. "What, honey? What is it?"

Nyla took a deep breath and, on one last gulp, she let it flow out of her mouth like the River Nile. "It's Lucas. Lucas is my lifemate. You know, the Lucas who goes to the movies with me? My friend. He's the best, mom. I didn't know it for over a year, and then one day I smelled him in the pet store and, well, you know, the scent thing and all. He smelled so good. How was I supposed to know he was my lifemate? He said he'd smelled me plenty before this, so I can't figure out why I didn't smell him. I don't care anymore why I couldn't smell him. I can now and, I mean, how perfect is it that he's my lifemate? I mean, really, we click, ya know? Lucas knows everything about me and he's still my friend. He didn't care that I have this fancy background or anything, and I want you two to know that I don't give a crap about my background either. Do you hear me?" Nyla said with a warning as she shook her finger at her parents. "I don't give a King Tut's tomb if you two don't approve because Lucas is a tomcat. I don't. I love Lucas and he's mine, even if he does have a kink that I just don't get right now. I'll learn to accept it as a part of me if it means Lucas and I are together. Do you hear me? I don't care one iota that he likes floggers…" Nyla slapped a hand over her mouth.

Holy, fucking maze full of mice. Oh, my God, she'd just told her parents that Lucas liked floggers, hadn't she? *Good, Ny. Fabulous.* That should make them far less likely to call the lifemate council on mental challenges, now shouldn't it?

The silence, thick and expectant, lay on Nyla's taste buds and she watched the faces of her parents. Oh, if she didn't have trouble before, she was now, officially calling the ASPCA her new Garden of Eden.

Nyla's mother was the first to speak. Her voice calm, rational, take charge. Just like the mother Nyla had always known. "Lucas, you say?"

"Yes, *Lucas,*" Nyla repeated. Damn them to the pyramids and back if they didn't like it.

"Precious? You have such a skewed view of us that if I didn't think I'd cultivated that over time, I'd almost be hurt." Nyla's mother held out her hand and Nyla offered hers. "Come with me, honey. We must talk."

Her mother's small hand in her own led her out of her father's study and down the long Persian carpeted hallway to her parents' bedroom. "Come look in here, Nyla, and when you do, please don't make too much noise. The servants will talk," her mother said with a low chuckle.

Nyla peeked around the corner of her parents' big walk-in closet and had to hold the door jamb with a shaky grip when her mother pushed a large oak panel. It swung open to reveal many, many things in… leather.

Nyla's mouth fell open and her mother put a gentle hand under her chin to close it. "I'd say you'll catch flies with your mouth open like that, but it looks like you could use the protein right about now."

Nyla blinked and looked into her mother's eyes, as green as her own, almond shaped and enjoying the shit out of Nyla's astonishment. "Um, care to explain? Do I want you to explain? Is there really any explanation?"

"Well, first, let me say this, Nyla. That Lucas is your lifemate and such a perfect fit for you makes both your father and I beyond thrilled. No, he's not of our lineage. We come from a long line of snobs, Nyla, but I've always cared little about that. I'm sorry I didn't spend more time proving that to you. As for the things here in our closet, well, as you can see, your father and I still enjoy a very healthy sex life and we enjoy a bit of spice. Nothing more, nothing blatantly frightening."

Oh, hell. Did someone have a butter knife she might gouge her mind's eye out with to cleanse herself of the visual she now had in her head?

Nyla's mother ran a soothing hand over her back. "Sweetheart, you mentioned a flogger?"

"Yeah… a flogger…"

"Does it frighten you? I'm assuming you and Lucas have mated. Of course you have. It's the only way to be certain you've found your lifemate. He likes a little kink, does he?" Her mother's laugh was throaty, secretive, freaking her the fuck out.

"I can't have this conversation with you, Mom. It's wrong on more levels than I have the wherewithal to count right now. I really don't want to know how you and Daddy get down, ya know?"

"Don't be silly, Nyla. A healthy sex life is so important. Who told you about your first heat? I did, of course. Which is why you finally smelled Lucas, by the way. You were in heat. The real kind. Not the kind that let's you know you're ready to embark on womanhood. You can talk to me about this because it's as much a part of my private world as it will be yours."

Nyla felt the heat of embarrassment singe her cheeks. "Okay, stop now. I don't think I can begin to think of you tied to that big bed out there with duct tape on your mouth while Daddy flogs you, okay? So please, stop before I hurl a hairball."

"Darling?" Her mother's face was that of the highly amused. "It isn't your *father* who wields the flogger…"

K, nuff said. No more. Nope. Not even a shifter needed to know *that* about their parents, and Nyla didn't care just how free thinking shifters were about their sexual encounters.

"Nyla, you're confused. I can see that. I'm the dominant force in the bedroom, not your dad, honey. There's nothing wrong with it."

"But Daddy's such a forceful presence. All quiet and solid and…" Her mother beat her father. How utterly absurd. She had this visual of her mother, standing over her father, dressed in some leather corset with fuck-me pumps and a whip, while her dad sat meekly in a corner, cowering as he awaited instructions and called her Mistress.

Ve have vays of makink you talk.

"Yes, honey, he is. That's probably the reason he's submissive in the bedroom. But submissive doesn't mean weak and it doesn't mean that your father can't take charge of things. It means little other than sexual preference, Nyla, and letting go of everything but your pleasures. I can see the idea frightens you. If you'll sit with me, I can explain some of it to you and it won't seem so frightening anymore, I promise, darling. Right now you're questioning your sexuality, but you shouldn't. Let's go talk, and then you can set about making things right with Lucas."

Nyla leaned her head against the cool oak panel of her parent's closet and giggled. Grabbing her mother's flogger, she snapped it. "Hey, Mom? Got some cobwebs you need taken care of?"

Nyla followed her mother out of the closet as her mother snatched the flogger away from her and pointed to her chair in the corner of the room.

Ooohhhh. Better sit and stay, Nyla before Mom whips you into submission. Nyla rolled her eyes and sat dutifully on the corner chair.

She and Mom were going to have a sex talk to rival even Doctor Ruth.

Hell's bells.

This was going to be a long afternoon, to say the least.

Chapter Seven

Lucas sat in silence, beer in hand as he thought about the lifemate council and petitioning them to release him from his obligations to Nyla. It was all he'd thought about for three days now.

Fuck.

This wasn't what he wanted.

He wanted Nyla. He'd always wanted her and he was willing to do nearly anything to have her.

Could he give up his kink for her?

Lucas' cock rose despite his heavy mood as he remembered Nyla spread before him, her ass still slightly pink from his hand. No one had ever turned him on more.

Stirring in his chair, he remembered their last conversation and his admission of love. Did he love Nyla?

Yeah, yeah he did. He'd loved her from the moment he'd laid eyes on her, before he'd known she was his lifemate. From almost the moment he'd seen her over that tuna on those pointed toast squares at the shifters' meet and greet.

Double fuck.

His stomach lurched at the thought of her parents razzing him because of his background. At the thought of them going to the lifemate council and telling them who they thought Lucas should end up with.

Bullshit.

Lucas slammed his beer down on the coffee table and stood. He'd go to Nyla's parents himself and, if he had to, he'd drag her out of there kicking and screaming because he knew she felt it too.

Beer swilling Neanderthal, he chided himself.

Nyla wanted him. He was sure of that. The rest would find a way to fall into place. Hell, he'd give his flogger away if it meant Nyla would make the final transition ritual to lifemates with him.

That settled, Lucas smiled.

Damn woman.

* * *

Armed with some kick ass information from her mother, Nyla had showered and changed, and now she was on her way to hunt Lucas' ass down and show him that she understood. She'd do what was within her boundaries to make him a happy lifemate camper.

Flying out of the cab, Nyla took the steps two at a time that led to Lucas' door.

Her palms were sweaty and her mouth was dry.

Oy.

Vay even.

Squaring her shoulders, Nyla took a deep breath and, with sure knuckles, rapped on his door.

Heart in her throat, Nyla peered at Lucas as he opened the door and cocked his head with a grin.

Nyla hurled herself at him, curling into his body and throwing her arms around his neck, grazing his head with the bag she held. "I'm sorry," she sobbed. "I really didn't mean what I said. I was afraid, but I'm not anymore," she whined on a hiccup of sobs. "I'm crazy about you and you can do what ever you want to me. Look." Nyla leaned back in his arms and held up the bag she had. She balanced it on his chest and rooted around in it, pulling out her purchase. "See?" She held it up just before she pushed it in her mouth.

"I bautthis. Niiiiccce, huh?" she grunted around the item as she looked him square in the eye.

Lucas threw his head back and laughed. "Sugarplum, why would I want to have one of those in your mouth? That would mean you wouldn't always be yapping, and I really kinda like the way you ramble." Lucas placed a thumb and forefinger around it and tried to pull it out.

Nyla shook her head vehemently. "Nooooo. Uh, uh," she grunted and shook her head again. "I cn doozis. Know whatit isss?"

Lucas tugged it out of her mouth with a pop. "Yes, baby. I know what it is."

Nyla smiled, totally relieved for the first time in three days. "It's a ball gag," she said proudly.

"That it is, but I don't want you gagged. At least not right now," he teased.

"Yes! A ball gag and I know all about it now. I have so much to tell you. My mom, well, she explained some stuff and now I think I understand. I knew you didn't want to hurt me, but what was happening to me physically kind of had me all weirded out. But I'm okay now and if you go to the lifemate council, I'll kill you. Do you hear me, Sir Pouncealot?"

Lucas' arms tightened around her waist and he laughed again. "Nah. I decided it was too much paperwork."

Nyla giggled, pressing into the bulk of Lucas' frame and clinging to his warmth.

"So, you're crazy about me, huh?"

"Yesss. Yes, I am," she declared openly, honestly.

"What about your parents, Nyla?"

"It's all okay. They're happy for us. I'll tell you all about it later. Now c'mon, let's go tie me up."

Lucas tensed. "No, Nyla. I'll throw away everything in that closet. It's not something we have to do to be together."

"Oh, stop being a pansy ass. You don't have to do that. I understand now. I was afraid because it excited me and I didn't understand it, but I do now. I might not always want to break out the handcuffs every time we hit the sack and some stuff is off limits, but I want to try."

Lucas' relief was evident and Nyla smiled again. He'd been willing to give up something very important to him. It must be love.

Nyla slid down his body and looped her arms around his neck. On tippy toes, she pressed her lips to his, experiencing the same thrill she had from the moment they'd kissed the first time. "C'mon, take me to your dungeon."

Lucas chuckled. "Nyla, we have to talk about what kind of play we'll indulge in."

"Oh, I already know some of the stuff that interests me. I want to try handcuffs today. Got some of those?"

"I do believe I do, Cleo."

"Good. I mean, even vanilla people like kink sometimes, so we don't have to have a safe word, right?"

"Vanilla, huh? Who've you been talking to?"

Nyla dragged Lucas to his bathroom and went straight for the linen closet, plucking up the fur-lined handcuffs. "I told you, it's a long story, but it was my mother."

Lucas began to open his mouth to speak, but Nyla stopped him with a reminder. "Later. For now, know that I'm willing to try some new stuff. Now, c'mon, Morris. Take me, I'm yours." Nyla was more sure than ever that she wanted this.

She handed him the cuffs and stripped off her clothes on her way into his bedroom. She lay on his bed, arms out and butt naked. Willing…

Lucas groaned and his face held obvious pleasure at her nudity. He pulled off his clothes too, and sprawled out over her, sighing when their flesh touched. His cock was hard, hot, pulsing against her thigh. "Woman, you've made me nuts these past three days. It's a wonder I didn't take up sniffing catnip."

Nyla wrapped her arms around his neck. "I love you. I'm a woman. It's my job to drive you bonkers. Adjust. Now, c'mon, tie me up."

"Who's the one in charge here?"

Nyla giggled against his neck. "Well, I am, but I'll leave you with the illusion that you're on top. How's that?"

Nyla grabbed the spindles of Lucas' brass bed and he clicked the cuffs into place with gentle hands. "Are you sure?" he asked one last time.

Heat flooded Nyla's cunt and her nipples tightened to stiff peaks. "Yes, Lucas. I'm sure."

Lucas parted her thighs, dragging his fingers along her skin. His voice was gruff as the half of him that demanded release took over. "Christ, Nyla. I've wanted you like this for what seems like forever. Do you want me too, Nyla?"

Bet yer bippy. "Yes, Lucas, I want you too." Her body shifted beneath his as she shivered to the tune of his touch.

His face was dark as he bent his head to her breast, laving the nipple, rolling it between his lips, tugging it. Lucas' tongue was rough and sandpapery as he whispered over her belly, toward her pussy, wet and slick with need. When he parted her flesh with an urgent swipe, Nyla bucked, but he held her thighs in place.

There were no demands as he brought Nyla to a climax that had her gasping for breath. It was hurried, but intense and sharp. Nyla wasn't sure she understood why Lucas didn't request anything of her. For now, their mating was enough, on any level.

Lucas towered over her, looking down at her as he brought his cock to her lips. "Lick me, Nyla."

Nyla opened her mouth to him, never wavering, allowing the glide of hot flesh between her lips, savoring the thrust of Lucas' hips and the groan that escaped his throat. She lifted her head, relishing the restraint the bonds around her wrists created as she took him deep within her, tonguing his cock as he plunged into her mouth.

Lucas gripped the edge of the headboard. Nyla felt the tension of his body as he pulled out of her and knelt between her legs to rain kisses over her arms. "Are you okay? Do they hurt you in anyway?" he asked with a husky voice.

"I'm fine, Lucas," she responded, breathy, crazed with need.

"Spread your legs wider, Nyla. If I don't take you now, I'll explode."

Nyla complied, greedily accepting the hard length of Lucas' cock at her entrance. She had no hesitation as he nudged her opening, then plunged into her.

Nyla writhed, accepting Lucas' cock with a moan of contentment, whimpering as he lifted her thigh high. His eyes glittered as he said, "Do you see that, Nyla? Can you see us joined?"

Nyla raised her head to see Lucas between her thighs, his grinding cock deeply imbedded in her. She heard the slap of his balls against her ass and the tidal wave of release flushed her veins drove her hips to crash against his.

Lucas bucked too, his shaft jerking within her, rock hard, thick and on fire.

As they came, Lucas ground out her name, rocking her into a manic frenzy of orgasm. Her chest heaved and Nyla let the wave of climax ease as Lucas ran his hands over her flushed, sensitive skin.

Lucas' hands went directly to the handcuffs, releasing her with a deft click. He rubbed her arms, now weak from tension. "Are you all right, baby?"

"I'm fine, Lucas, really. You didn't hurt me. The handcuffs didn't hurt me. What are you worried about?"

"I never want you to think I take pleasure from your pain, Nyla. That's not what this will ever be about between us."

Nyla ran a hand over his jaw in reassurance. "I know, Lucas. I understand it all now. I don't feel like some kind of freak because I dug a spanking anymore, but understand this wasn't something I knew about myself. I might never have known if not for you and your crazy closet in there."

Lucas laughed as he pulled her over on top of him. "Guess it's not so crazy now, huh? We'll take this slow, Nyla. We'll find out together what you like. I don't care about that as much as I care about you."

Laughing, Nyla teased him, "You're sooooo crazy about me."

Lucas nuzzled her neck. "Like you're not right there with me in the crazy aisle staring at the department of love, smart ass."

Nyla rolled her eyes. "Whatever. Admit it. You're nuts about me."

Lucas ran his hands over her spine. "This much is true. I can't deny it."

Nyla kissed him hard, full on his yummy lips. "We can't go back to holding hands, you know."

"That's okay. How about we just handcuff ourselves to each other?"

She giggled. "Fine. However, we do have some stuff to discuss."

Lucas tilted his head and looked her in the eye. "Now what?"

Smiling, Nyla said, "About that flogger..."

Dakota Cassidy

Dakota Cassidy found writing quite by accident and it's "been madness ever since." Who knew writing the grocery list would turn into this? Dakota loves anything funny and nothing pleases her more than to hear she's made someone laugh. She loves to write in many genres with a contemporary flair. Dakota lives with her two handsome sons, a dog and a cat. (None of them shape shift--that we know of.) She'd love to hear from you--she always answers her e-mail! Visit her at www.dakotacassidy.com or email her at dakota@dakotacassidy.com.

All Wrapped Up: Tainted Kisses
Kate Hill

Prologue

Land of the Scots, 797

Closing his eyes, Aru drew a deep breath, relishing the scent of death. Too long had he waited for this moment. In the beginning, there had been no worldly creature with the power to destroy him. Then *they* had arrived. Sent by the Spirit of Good, a new breed of blood drinker that hunted and killed his kind. One in particular had been thwarting him for centuries, following so close at his heels that he scarcely had time to indulge in destruction, but left the deadliest deeds to his offspring. Today's bloodbath had been his first real taste of utter violence in longer than he cared to remember. The excitement of crushing the life from hundreds of feeble mortals, feeling their tender flesh tear beneath his fangs and gulping their rich blood almost overwhelmed him.

What he couldn't drink, he and his army spilled, dousing the dry ground until it turned to burgundy mud beneath their boots. Their amusement was over now. The village lay in ruins. No man, woman, or child had survived his army's attack.

Already most of his men had ridden off. Only Kedar, his most favored son, remained with him among the rubble and broken bodies.

Then he heard it.

So faint it was almost indiscernible even to immortal ears.

A human heartbeat. But from where?

"I thought they were all dead," Aru growled.

"They are, Master."

"Listen! Can you not hear it?"

Kedar's brow furrowed as he strained to listen. Being only an offspring of a true blood drinker, his senses were not as sharp as his Creator's. Aru had been made by the Spirit of Evil itself, sent to walk the earth spreading horror and pain. Though his gift could be passed on to mortals through his bite, his offspring didn't possess all his otherworldly abilities.

Finally a faint smile touched Kedar's lips. "Yes. A heartbeat."

Grunting in reply, Aru strode among the bodies, seeking the mortal who dared live after such a marvelous attack. He paused beside a woman splattered with blood. Using his foot, he rolled her onto her back, revealing a very pregnant belly.

Aru drew a sharp breath, his own heartbeat quickening in time with that of the mortal. "Kedar. Come here. Quickly."

"Did you find the survivor, my Master?"

"Yes." Aru nodded toward the woman.

With a snarl, Kedar drew his sword and raised it for the death blow, but Aru caught his arm in a savage grip. "No. Carefully."

"But…"

"Do you not understand? *She* isn't alive. It's the creature in her womb."

"The child has survived?"

"You know what this means." Aru could scarcely contain his rapturous grin. Again he closed his eyes and spoke silently to the Evil One. *Thank you, Master of Wickedness. Since the beginning I have awaited this moment. It was not something I could take, but something that had to be given.* Opening his eyes, he continued, "The creature in her womb has been sent to me. Unlike the other blood drinkers I have created, he will be mine to shape from the beginning. A creature born in the midst of death. His life will be one of rage and torture. His heart will be cold and merciless. He will be flawlessly wicked, made in the image of the Evil One. Remove him from her womb. Be cautious. I don't want him harmed. Yet."

Kedar did as his Master bid, then placed the squalling, bloody infant in Aru's waiting hands. Staring at it, Aru murmured, "Excellent. A male child. We must find a woman to provide him with milk. It will be taken from her and fed through a bladder, for he must never know a mother's touch. The revolting emotions these mortals revel in will not taint him. No kindness, gentleness, and most important of all, no love. He must never, never be loved. When he is old enough, I will Change him and he will be the perfect living demon." Aru glanced at Kedar with a taunting look. "Yes, my son, even more perfect than you."

Kedar's jaw clenched visibly and he stared at the screaming infant with hatred.

Excellent. Let the rivalry start now. Kedar would no doubt make this child's life even more miserable than Aru had first imagined. Raised in fury. Born in death. He would become the most faithful of Aru's minions. "He will be called Etlu."

The warrior.

Chapter One

Mercia, 830 AD

Smoke from burning cottages stung Niabi's eyes, the scent of it burning her nostrils. Her arms, tightly bound behind her back, ached not only from their uncomfortable position, but from fighting the band of warriors that had attacked the village she had called home for the past five years.

Viking attacks had already destroyed more friends than she cared to remember. Mortal raiders were difficult enough to defend against, but this ruthless fellowship of warriors who had just destroyed her people were different. Even before they reached the village she had caught their scent on the wind -- the scent of blood drinkers. Unlike her and the blood drinker who had created her, this band of warriors used their otherworldly powers to terrorize mankind.

Though she had trained the villagers for battle, they were no match for these monsters, and she was but one against a small army. During the fight she had sought out the one who appeared to be their leader, hoping if she defeated him she might be able to take his army, or at least drive them off. With centuries of experience as a warrior, she had brought many men, both mortal and blood drinker, to their knees, but she hadn't been prepared for this chieftain's power, both in body and mind. By his adeptness at blocking his thoughts from her attempts at mind control, she assumed he must be quite old. He set a new standard for ferocity, even among their kind.

"Faster, boy!" growled the auburn-haired warrior walking behind her, shoving her hard in the back. She staggered, but remained standing.

His addressing her as "boy" didn't surprise her in the least. Much of her life had been spent in male dress, mimicking the voices and mannerisms of men since her femininity might discredit her considerable abilities in a male dominated world. Niabi had arrived in this village as a male warrior interested in helping them defend themselves and had remained as such. With her skill and courage, the people had unanimously decided to look upon her as their leader. She had never failed them -- until now.

After a grueling battle, the chieftain had disarmed her. Her heart still raced at the recent memory of the point of his bloodied sword hovering over her heart as she lay sprawled on the ground. All she could see of his face through his dome-shaped helmet was his eyes. Slanted and silver-gray, they stared at her with unfathomable coldness.

Moments after her defeat, the Viking chieftain claimed the village. He ordered his men to herd the few survivors to what was left of the village square and chain them up. He planned to take them to his homeland as slaves.

She overheard enough to know he had another plan for her. The Blood Eagle. While her people watched, he would execute her -- by ripping out her lungs.

Niabi approached the villagers who huddled together, mostly women and children, their bloodstained faces terrified. The Viking chieftain stood off to the side, flanked by several of his warriors. Tall and lean, he exuded evil like no one she had ever met. He removed his helmet and she stared at his face, wanting to see the bastard who caused so much destruction without the slightest remorse.

She found his rugged features -- a hawkish nose, strong chin, and those cruel gray eyes -- oddly captivating. His pale skin was smeared with dirt, blood, and sweat. A faded scar ran down the length of one sharp cheekbone. Tufts of unkempt black hair hung past his broad shoulders.

"On your knees, insolent whelp!" snarled the auburn-haired warrior, kicking Niabi in the back of her knee. She dropped to the ground in front of the chieftain, but lifted her chin so she met his gaze with all the rage burning inside her.

"There will one day be a price to pay for your evil," she warned.

A wicked smile twisted his slender lips. "There is nothing you can tell me about evil."

He motioned for the auburn-haired warrior to release her bonds. When her hands were free, she flexed her numb fingers but resisted the urge to rub her chafed wrists. The chieftain stepped behind her and in a swift motion tore off her armor and shirt beneath.

A collective gasp rose from the villagers and the Viking warriors at the sight of her sleekly muscled though undoubtedly female form.

Crossing her arms over her breasts, Niabi shivered with fury. Terror rippled down her spine. Glancing defiantly over her shoulder at the chieftain, she said, "Get on with it."

A slightly sick feeling rolled through her when she felt his gloved hand brush across her shoulder blades.

"Anxious to die, are you?" he asked, wrapping her hair around his hand until his fist pressed against the back of her neck. He stooped and spoke into her ear, his deep voice scarcely a whisper. "You realize the Blood Eagle destroys our kind as permanently as piercing the heart or burning to ashes."

"I have lived a long, fulfilling life and I don't fear death. Can you say the same?"

He laughed, a vicious, throaty sound. His hand still tight in her hair, he rose, taking her with him, and guided her through the village.

"Etlu, what are you doing?" called the auburn-haired warrior.

"Don't do anything until I return," the chieftain replied.

So, he was called Etlu. A Sumerian name. Apparently he must be as old as she had suspected.

"But --"

The chieftain stopped abruptly and turned to the man. Though Niabi wouldn't have thought it possible, his glacial eyes turned even colder. "Are you questioning my orders, Horik?"

"No."

"Good." Etlu continued walking out of the village to the nearby woods. There he released his hold on her hair. She spun, glaring at him.

"If you intend to rape me, wouldn't it have made more of an impact to do so in front of my people?"

"They are no longer your people, but my slaves."

Niabi's fists clenched and her teeth ground. She would fight this bastard to the last. He might kill her, but she would take a good chunk of his manhood in the process.

"What would you do to buy their freedom and their lives?" he asked.

"Excuse me?"

"What would you do?"

"This is a pointless discussion. You have no intention of freeing them."

"I didn't, until a few moments ago. You can give me something I want, but the only way I can think of to get it will be to set your mortals free."

"It seems you can take whatever you want without my approval." She hated to admit that fact, yet it was the undeniable truth.

"I want you to come to me freely."

"I don't understand. You want me to let you kill me and be happy about it?"

He shook his head slightly. "I want you to freely come to my bed."

This request stunned her so completely that for a moment she simply stared at him. A man like this took what he wanted without regard for the woman. Even if by the remote chance he didn't care for rape, there was a type of woman who would willingly go to his bed. He was rather handsome, undoubtedly powerful, and most likely rich from years of raiding.

"Do you mean for me to believe you cannot find a woman to come to your bed?" she sneered.

His lip curled and his silver-gray eyes flashed. “I won’t even dignify that with an answer. I am saying I want *you* to come to my bed without being forced. Agree to this, and I will free the villagers.”

“And leave them alive?”

“Yes.”

“And with the means to rebuild?”

He flung her a scathing look. “Do not press your luck.”

“Then no. I will not.”

“The Blood Eagle is excruciating,” he said, circling her like a wolf preparing for the kill.

“If you’re seeking a companion, this isn’t the best way to win one over.”

“I’m an impatient man,” he growled. “I’m also being more than fair by offering your life as well as the lives of your people.”

“What lives? You’ve destroyed their homes, their crops, and their livestock, not to mention killing members of their families. If you want me to willingly come to your bed, you had better provide more incentive than what you just offered.”

A slight smile touched his lips. “I like your spirit. Too bad you have to die. Now your people will, too.”

“What do you mean?” she snapped. “You said you were taking them as slaves?”

“I was, but you’ve annoyed me.”

“Loathsome bastard!” She spat at him, her hands clenched so tightly her knuckles threatened to tear through the flesh.

“You want to fight me again. I can feel it. Unfortunately you will lose.”

He was probably right. She was unarmed and half naked while he was still in full armor and carrying his sword.

“All right,” she said, the words leaving a bitter taste on her tongue. “I’ll bed you. Just release my people, if I can trust you to be true to your word.”

“My army is leaving for our homeland tonight. I will send them ahead while we remain with your people until the village is empty, then we will follow.”

"That is… acceptable," she said with as much dignity as she could muster for a woman who had just made a bargain with the devil.

"Good. Now come."

"Would you give me something to wear?"

His gaze swept her, lingering over the tops of her breasts. "No."

Nodding slightly, she began walking toward the village. One day she would make this bastard pay for what he'd done. For now she would simply play his game to gain freedom for her mortal companions.

* * *

No sooner had they reached the village than Etlu ordered his men to return to their ships, leaving the mortals behind.

Most of the warriors knew better than to question him. Only Horik approached and asked, "Why leave the slaves behind?"

"Because I said so," Etlu replied, leveling his fiercest look upon Horik who nodded curtly and walked away. Turning back to Niabi, the chieftain gestured toward a tree that had been knocked down during the attack. "Sit and watch me keep my word."

He knew by the anger flashing in her dark eyes that she wanted to tell him to burn in hell, yet she silently did as he ordered, still covering her bosom. He almost demanded that she drop her arms and provide a better view of the finest breasts he'd ever seen. Small yet firm and perfectly shaped, they were smooth as silk and tipped with reddish brown nipples.

Normally he didn't waste time ogling women. When the urge took him, he grabbed the nearest available female, flung up her skirt, and satisfied himself with a few swift thrusts. Blood taking was the same. When thirsty, he drank. It didn't matter when, where, or from whom. Mortals were made to serve his kind, and his kind were made to spread the power of evil.

His entire life had been one of pain, both giving and receiving. With his early years spent at the mercy of Kedar, his Creator's most favored son, he learned quickly to endure torture in all its most brutal forms. Master Aru told him many times that in order to fully appreciate pain, one had to know it intimately. Kedar and the other members of Master Aru's household had been more than willing to see that Etlu learned all the lessons pain had to offer.

A woman approached, her wary gaze fixed on Etlu. She clutched a ragged, filthy shirt that she offered to the warrior woman. Etlu growled, an animal sound that sent the villager scurrying off.

The warrior woman slipped on the shirt, providing another brief glimpse of her breasts. The nipples were hard from the cold, little bumps creating patterns on the tender skin.

"I didn't give you permission to dress," he said.

The woman stared hard at him, her square jaw visibly tight. "If you expect me to travel with you, I need clothing or else I'll freeze."

"It won't kill you. Or don't you realize our kind cannot freeze to death?"

"If comfort isn't a concern, why don't you undress and freeze along with me?"

He tossed her a leering grin. "Is that an offer, woman? It's good to see you're eager to fulfill your end of the bargain, but unfortunately you must wait for my convenience."

"You know that's not what I meant."

The spirited gleam in her dark eyes excited him more than he wanted to admit. Beneath the cover of his leather armor, his cock twitched and for the first time in his life he repressed the urge to take what he wanted.

It was only since leaving Master Aru that he had gained this strange fascination with a heretofore unknown reality called love. Aru had sheltered him from everything weak and gentle just as most mortal parents try to shelter their children from brutality.

Several years ago, on a rare night when he and his men were not engaged in battle, Etlu had taken a walk through a recently conquered village. Most of the mortals were asleep and the few who did see him paid little attention since he was dressed in everyday clothes, his face half hidden in the folds of his cloak. Glancing inside windows, he saw interactions between men, women, and children he had never noticed before. Parents had laughed with their children and touched them with gentleness Etlu had never imagined possible. He'd seen men and women wrapped naked in each other's arms, whispering endearments that he found both revolting and compelling. What did these strange words and actions mean and why did mortals seem to relish them? When he'd used his mind powers to touch their thoughts, he had felt their contentment that surpassed any pleasure he had ever experienced.

At first he'd tried to forget what he'd seen, bury it beneath bloodlust, but something compelled him to continue his secret observations. Something began to fester inside him, a sensation he didn't quite recognize. These people were *happy*. Without slaughter. Without torture.

Unfathomable.

Horik approached astride his shaggy gray war horse, leading Etlu's black mare behind him. "Everyone has cleared out."

Etlu nodded, grasped the warrior woman by her upper arm, and tugged her to her feet. He mounted his horse and offered her an arm up. The woman sat behind him on the saddle, but didn't so much as place a hand on his waist to steady herself. Still, he felt her body pressed close to his and another thrill of desire shot through him like a flaming arrow.

He kicked his horse forward. Several of the mortals watched as they rode out of the village. A couple even mustered the courage to wave goodbye to their fallen leader. Etlu reached out briefly with his mind, wondering how the woman felt about leaving these people she so foolishly tried to protect. He could sense nothing from her and this frustrated him. He had spent his life perfecting mind control, had surpassed much older and more experienced of his kind in the art of reading and blocking thoughts, but this woman was able to shut him out with shocking ease.

Everything about her intrigued him, which was why he had chosen her for this test of companionship.

The night grew colder and by the time they reached the shore where his fleet waited, the woman was shivering violently. Why did that bother him? Why did he have the urge to warm her? Many times in his life he had been cold and no one had cared.

Compassion is for the weak, Aru had told him, *and mercy useless.*

A short time later, they had boarded his ship and the fleet headed toward home.

The woman sat close to the side, her arms wrapped around her for warmth. Annoyed by his preoccupation with her, he tossed her his cloak then went about his business. The sun would be rising soon and he, along with several of his warriors, would wait out the day in a space sheltered by planks, designed specifically for that purpose. Other members of his band -- the ones with the ability to endure sunlight -- would keep the ship on course throughout the daylight hours.

His inability to endure sunlight frustrated Etlu, but no matter how he tried to condition himself to the day, his flesh continue to burn and his eyes went blind until moonrise.

Before retiring, he approached the woman and asked, "Can you face the daylight?"

"Yes."

He felt a twinge of envy at her ability to do what he could not.

"Come with me anyway," he stated. She had his cloak and he wasn't about to spend the day cold as well as bored, trapped beneath planks in a space scarcely large enough for him to move.

She followed him across the ship, past the men rowing, and crawled after him into the dim space. The other night creatures had already piled in, many of them sound asleep.

"Take off the cloak," he ordered.

"I'm not going to freeze --"

Growling, he began removing it himself, but she shoved his hands away, tore off the heavy wool garment and flung it in his face. The urge to toss her overboard almost overwhelmed him, but that would defeat the purpose of this test. Instead he grasped her by the wrist, tugged her beside him, and covered them both with the cloak. This seemed to please her because she edged a bit closer, her firm backside wiggling provocatively against him. His cock swelled, trapped between their bodies.

Perhaps asking her to sleep beside him was a bad idea. Even her slightest touch seemed to rob him of his self-control. Finally she found a comfortable position and lay motionless, except for each slow, steady breath. Etlu closed his eyes, though he doubted he would sleep. Not with this sleekly muscled goddess pressed so close, her thick, soft hair brushing his face and her wild yet feminine scent enfolding him in a silken embrace.

Daylight shone through several cracks in the planks and Etlu wondered what the world looked like bathed in sunlight. Though his Creator had waited until he reached manhood to make him a blood drinker, Etlu had been hidden from the day all his life. As a child, he recalled being locked in a dark, rat-infested hole below his Master's house.

We were made to rule the night, Aru had said. *Do not be tempted by the light. If you think you've endured pain, boy, it is nothing compared to the agonies suffered by those who bow to the Spirit of Good. Beware of blood drinkers who walk by day, unless they prove themselves loyal to darkness. Even then, trust no one of this world. Not offspring, brother, or servant. Believe only in the Evil One. He is the strongest power in existence. Hate. Vengeance. Pain. All else is useless.*

Etlu's experiences had taught him to believe his Master's words. Hate and pain had given him strength. They had earned him land, wealth, and the allegiance of the finest warriors to whom he had given the gift of immortality.

Still, he couldn't fathom why so many people hadn't learned this. Why did they waste their time with laughter and conversation unrelated to battle plans? How could they derive pleasure from a mere touch when there was so much blood to be shed?

Slowly his thoughts faded and sleep took its hold. His eyes slipped shut and unconsciously he let his arm drop over the woman. When his hand curved around her warm breast, he growled, a sound of arousal rather than warning. He squeezed the soft mound and ran his thumb over her nipple.

She grasped his wrist and pulled his hand away.

Again he growled, this time in annoyance. He pushed her onto her back and loomed above her. In the cramped space, they lay almost nose to nose.

We had a bargain, did we not? He spoke to her through pure thought, wondering if she would reply since she seemed bent on keeping him completely out of her mind.

Our bargain was that I would come to you willingly, she replied, her spirit voice like a caress on his mind. His stomach tightened at the sensation. *I am not willing to let you fondle me on a ship full of men.*

I could take what I want. He thrust his pelvis rather hard against her. She drew a sharp breath and he caught the scent of her fear, yet she continued holding his gaze steadily.

If rape is what you want, you wouldn't have wasted time bargaining and losing potential slaves. For some reason I have yet to fathom, you seek a willing partner. By the very little I know about you, I'm probably your only chance of getting one.

Etlu had slaughtered people for saying less, but for some reason she aroused him more than any woman he had ever encountered. Was this why Aru had warned him to beware of those who walked by day? Perhaps he should kill her and be done with it. He could find another woman to satisfy his nagging curiosity about love.

Chapter Two

Niabi stared into Etlu's eyes and for the first time noticed many heated emotions churning beneath their frigid surface. For a moment she thought he was going to change his mind about taking her to his homeland and kill her instead. Then with a flash of fangs, he rolled off her and positioned himself on his side again. Except for when his body brushed hers due to the limited space, he refrained from touching her.

Tugging the cloak a bit so that it covered her more completely, she released a pent-up breath and closed her eyes. Was it possible that there was more to this cold, cunning warrior than she had first suspected? Why had he struck such an odd bargain? Though she knew by his scent he was attracted to her, he must have a deeper reason for giving up control of a village he conquered than to have her in his bed. If it was simply her body he was after, he could have taken it, as she was certain he and the thieving pigs in his fellowship often did to women in the villages they raided.

Though she was tired, sleep eluded her. How could she possibly relax beside this beast who relished devastation?

Eventually she drifted off and awakened at dusk to a hand roughly shaking her shoulder.

"Up," Etlu said. She crawled out of the space, tugging the cloak around her, and drew a deep breath of fresh sea air.

Etlu and the day sleepers emerged behind her for shift change.

Niabi noted the men who had been rowing wore odd, trance-like expressions that slowly faded as the rested warriors took their place rowing. Reaching out with her mind, she felt nothing from them except the desire to reach their homeland.

Etlu approached with food to break their fast and she said, "Who is controlling their minds and why?"

"I am, and if the reason isn't obvious you're more of a fool than I thought."

"You are? Didn't you sleep?"

"I've mastered the fine art of light sleeping while at the same time keeping control of their thoughts."

"That's a rare talent."

"And a useful one."

"But being a fool, I still don't understand why." She wondered if he recognized the sarcasm in her voice.

His gray eyes swept her with a condescending look. "To avoid the possibility of mutiny. Because I do not walk by day, I am --"

"Vulnerable?" A smile flirted with her lips, achieving her desired reaction. Rage glistened in his eyes. She asked, "Don't you trust your own men?"

"Only a fool trusts anyone."

If she hadn't loathed him so much she might have pitied him. She couldn't imagine spending her entire life in such utter loneliness. She wondered why he'd chosen this path. "You can't have rested well if, even in sleep, your thoughts were guiding theirs."

He grasped a handful of hair at the back of her neck and leaned closer, his voice a husky whisper in her ear. "If you think the precautions I've taken have weakened me in any way, rest assured that I'm accustomed to surviving for months aboard ship. Except for my Master I have never met a blood drinker who can challenge my powers and skills."

"I believe you," she said. "I wonder why such a strong man isn't more comfortable with his own power."

"Complacency is the first step in a leader's decline and I intend to rule for many years to come." He nuzzled her neck and ran his tongue along the side of it.

Niabi tensed at the sensation of his fangs resting against her flesh. Her heartbeat quickened and she waited for his bite, but it never came.

Shoving her away, he turned and walked to the bow of the ship.

The days and nights fell into a familiar pattern. Other than brief orders, Etlu avoided speaking to Niabi. Several times she tried to initiate conversation with him and her other shipmates, but no one seemed interested in so much as knowing her name, let alone talking with her. Etlu had made it clear from the first that she was to be ignored and as she quickly learned, his word was always obeyed. Only Horik, on occasion, questioned him. The auburn-haired warrior seemed to be Etlu's second-in-command.

Many nights later, they docked on their home shore in the land of the Danes. Etlu left Horik in charge of unloading cargo, then he and Niabi mounted his horse and rode to his home deep in the frozen countryside.

Overhearing bits of conversation aboard the ship, she had learned that Etlu ruled a large portion of land on the coastline as well as farther inland. Feared by all except a few fools who had already lost their lives, Etlu had conquered many chieftains.

He dismounted outside a longhouse and strode in, leaving her to follow behind. Inside, a fire burned in the hearth and servants went about their work, cooking, cleaning, and making clothes. Several warriors sat at a wooden table, but their conversation ceased as Etlu approached and spoke to them briefly. Satisfied that nothing significant had occurred while he had been away, he summoned a young female slave and told her to provide Niabi with clothing more appropriate for the weather.

Niabi to follow her across the longhouse where she received a worn tunic-style dress of dark wool and a patched cloak. Though both were too short for her, at least they were warmer than the thin shirt she'd been wearing. After Niabi finished dressing, the woman brought her food. Several times Niabi tried to initiate conversation, but if possible the girl was even less talkative than the men aboard the ship had been.

While she ate, she observed the longhouse's inhabitants. The servants kept their gazes down and their lips silent. Some of the warriors spoke quietly among themselves, and no one so much as smiled, let alone laughed. From a couple of dark corners drifted the grunts and moans of men rutting slave women. Though the females revealed no signs of protest, Niabi wondered exactly how many of them were willing participants in the loveless, animal act.

In spite of Etlu's wealth and power, he and his people seemed miserable.

No sooner had she finished eating than the chieftain strode over, his intense gaze fixed on her. For the past several days she had been noting signs of fatigue on his face. She didn't doubt the cause was lack of restful sleep. So many weeks of controlling his warriors' minds, even during daylight hours, had begun to take its toll.

"Come with me," he ordered.

"Should I bother to ask where, or are you going to keep ignoring me."

"Dawn will break soon. I'm going to sleep and you're going to fulfill your end of the bargain."

Niabi's stomach clenched. The moment she had been dreading had finally arrived. This sullen, brutal warrior was going to claim her body.

He grasped her wrist and led her away from the others. Though a tall woman, she had to hurry to keep up with his long strides. Dozens of emotions churned inside her. It sickened her that she would soon mate with the man who had destroyed the lives of so many people she cared about. A hint of fear also haunted her. Most likely his lovemaking was as rough as his other actions. Worst of all, she felt a nagging curiosity about his physical attributes. Was the body beneath the armor and layered clothing as striking as it seemed to be? Was his flesh smooth or hair-roughened? What did his cock look like?

Strangely, instead of guiding her to a private corner of the longhouse, he left the structure and led the way over the frosty ground toward the forest. He paused before they reached the cluster of trees and removed a dark strip of cloth from the pouch at his waist. He lifted it to her face, but she backed away and demanded, "What are you doing?"

"I do not sleep in the village. My quarters are private and no one knows their location. You will not be an exception."

"I'm not going to allow you to blindfold me."

"You have no choice. Either you intend to fulfill your end of the bargain, or you will die where you stand."

She could try to fight him, but doubted she could best him in another physical brawl.

Sighing, she turned so he could fasten the blindfold over her eyes. Once it was in place, she felt herself being lifted off her feet and into his arms. Her pulse quickened and instinctively she clutched his neck.

"I don't have time to waste while you stumble blindly after me," he stated, already moving swiftly over the ground. Though she knew her weight was insignificant to such a powerful male blood drinker, she couldn't help but appreciate the solidity of his body. As with humans, body type fluctuated among their species and he was extremely well proportioned.

They seemed to travel for miles up a gradual incline. Even when they finally stopped Etlu's breathing was only slightly labored. He placed her rather abruptly on her feet, the ground beneath them hard and rocky. She unfastened the blindfold and glanced at her surroundings. Trees stood thick and tall around them. To her right a brook trickled down from higher country and to her left a cave mouth gaped in a craggy mountainside partially hidden by vegetation.

Etlu removed his sheathed sword and began undressing. First he shrugged off his cloak, then a shirt of mail and a woolen tunic followed, baring a torso as magnificent as she'd imagined. Powerfully muscled with broad shoulders, a lean waist, and flat belly, his body was enough to make a woman, even one as old and experienced as Niabi, lose her breath. A mat of black hair covered the upper part of his chest and tapered to a thin line down his stomach. For the first time since meeting him, she felt a stirring of desire and the sudden urge to run her fingers over that sinfully gorgeous chest. She noted many faded scars marked his flesh from shoulder to waist. Only silver caused lasting damage to a blood drinker -- not that the scars detracted from his stunning good looks.

The chieftain's gaze flickered in her direction and she knew he must have caught the scent of her lust. The self-satisfied look that passed over his face confirmed her assumption and vexed her even more. How could she possibly feel any kind of attraction to a man like him? Evil rolled off him in almost tangible waves. She was about to look away in sheer disgust when he bent and unfastened the strips of cloth wrapped below his knees. She couldn't resist watching as he pulled off his boots and woolen breeches, revealing long, hard-looking legs lightly dusted with dark hair and a perfectly-shaped ivory cock jutting from a nest of black pubic hair. In spite of the cold, his arousal was obvious.

Raising an eyebrow, Niabi asked, "You intend to mate in the middle of the forest?"

His lips curved into a malicious smile that exposed the glistening tips of his fangs. How would it feel when those fangs penetrated her flesh? A blood drinker's bite could bring either pain or pleasure, depending on the intent and emotions involved. She had made love with others of her kind before, had given and received their bite. This was the first time she would be bedding a man she didn't care about and knowing this disturbed her greatly. She could, of course, change her mind and either fight him or make a run for freedom. His sword was within her reach and if she lunged for it, there was a good chance she would reach it before he did. Even if she held up her end of the bargain, what was to prevent him from returning to her village and finishing what he started or sending his men to do so?

"Undress," he ordered.

"From what I've observed around here men are in the habit of merely hiking up a woman's skirt."

"If that's what you prefer, I'll be all too glad to accommodate you, but now I want to bathe. You will join me."

Niabi glanced toward the brook and nearly shivered. The weather was almost cold enough to snow and he wanted to go swimming?

His jaw set, he took a step closer and reached for her cloak, but she avoided his touch and undressed. Living a long life of training and hardship had stolen much of her modesty, still she resisted the urge to cover herself as she bared her body completely to his leering gaze.

Gooseflesh rose on her skin and she trembled, dreading the thought of wading into the undoubtedly cold water in spite of how much she needed a bath after weeks aboard ship. At the very least they would be clean when he took her.

"Come," he growled, grasping her upper arm and tugging her toward the brook.

At the first touch of cold water on her feet she began shivering harder and jerked away from him. "Let go of me."

Shrugging, he strode into the frigid brook and ducked his head under. He surfaced seconds later, his dark hair drenched and water streaming down his face and chest, making it glisten in the moonlight shining through the trees.

"You take too long," he said, advancing on her. She backed out of the water, but he caught her wrist and dragged her closer. Powerful from years spent as a warrior, she fought his hold, but his superior strength combined with the slippery stones beneath her feet overcame her and she slid into the brook, landing rather hard on her backside, frigid water up to her sternum. Her nipples tightened to hard pebbles and she shook with cold.

Though a wicked laugh escaped Etlu's lips, she took some comfort in seeing that he, too, was shivering, his nipples hard, and skin covered in gooseflesh.

Quickly, she began washing, even soaking her hair, glad to be rid of the stench of the ship.

Etlu waded out a bit deeper and ducked under again, then floated on his back.

"Don't tell me you're actually enjoying this," she said through chattering teeth.

"You learn to like it."

"Don't wager on that." She hurried out of the water, reaching for her cloak.

Etlu did the same. He slipped on his cloak, picked up his sword and the rest of his clothes, then headed into the cave.

"Come, woman," he said without so much as glancing over his shoulder.

"I have a name," she replied, following him into such darkness that even her superior vision took several moments to adjust. Around a sharp turn, the cave narrowed into a long corridor scarcely large enough to accommodate the span of Etlu's shoulders. Irritated by his lack of response to her statement, she continued, "It's Niabi."

"And that should be of interest to me?"

Just when she thought he could do nothing more to increase her anger, he said or did something to prove her wrong.

"If I interested you enough to bargain with me to come to your bed, I would think that you would like to at least know my name. Do you realize we've been traveling together for weeks and you never once asked?"

"Since you never once offered to tell me, I thought you agreed it was unimportant."

"If I mean so little to you, why do you want me?"

They reached the end of the corridor and stopped outside a steel door built into the cave wall. Etlu pushed it open and they stepped into another cave furnished with a trunk, table, chair, and a bed of blankets and furs. Two other steel doors were built into the wall directly across from where they stood. He turned and bolted the door. Even if someone did manage to find his daytime lair, they would not be able to enter.

"You live here?" she asked, glancing around.

"I spend my days here."

"Why don't you stay in the village?"

He glanced at her from the corner of his eye. "And leave myself vulnerable? One such as yourself who walks by day cannot comprehend the danger my kind faces."

"If you could trust your people, there would be no danger."

"Only a fool trusts anyone."

"You must be very lonely."

Curling his lip, he snapped, "You speak like a woman."

"I am a woman."

"You did your best to hide that fact from your people whom you claim to trust so much."

"That's different."

He snorted. "Is it?"

Sighing with frustration, she folded her arms beneath her breasts and studied him carefully. Other than the gleam in his eyes, he seemed almost inhuman. Regardless of what many of their kind might think, part of a blood drinker's soul would always remain human. His coldness and lack of interest in forming relationships, even among his own people, was unnatural and didn't agree with his apparent desire for her.

"Yes, it is different," she said. "I lied for their own good, because if they knew I was a woman they wouldn't have let me protect them."

One of his sleek black eyebrows arched in a most sarcastic gesture. "Is that what you were doing? Enough talk. I need to sleep."

He opened one of the doors, revealing a tiny hollow dug into the rock wall. When he took one of the furs and a blanket and shoved them into the hollow, Niabi realized his intent.

"You're not going to lock me in there."

"As if I would allow you to wander freely while I sleep."

"I thought you wanted to --"

"Later." He pushed her into the tiny room and shut the door. Niabi heard the bolt slide into place and started to panic. What if he left her in the cell forever? Etlu seemed crazy enough to do something like that if it struck his deranged fancy.

If he thought she would allow him to rest comfortably while she spent the day in a cell, he was sorely mistaken.

"Etlu!" She pounded on the door. "Release me! Open this door immediately!"

Niabi wasn't sure how much time passed with her shouting and pounding on the door before he finally succumbed to her racket and bellowed, "Silence, wench!"

"Not until you release me."

Moments later, the door opened and she stepped out. "It is about time -- what are those for?"

Silver manacles dangled in his gloved hand. He stared at her with a menacing expression and said, "If you won't stay in there quietly, then I will bind and gag you. Silver is quite painful, even to one who can walk by day."

Niabi stared at the manacles with loathing.

"What shall it be, the cell without the silver or the cell with it?"

"Fine," she said through clenched teeth and stepped back into the hollow. Before he closed the door, she extended her hand toward his chest and held his gaze. "I think I'm starting to understand you."

"How so?"

"I'm not stupid enough to anger you when you're locking me up. You might decide to let me rot here." Grinning, she dropped her hand and backed into the cell. "Have I raised your curiosity?"

"No." He slammed the door and bolted it.

This time Niabi sat quietly, pulling the blanket around her. After several moments, she tried reaching out with her mind, hoping to manipulate him into revealing more about himself. His mind was so exhausted from weeks without proper rest that it didn't respond to her guidance. All she could do was observe bits and pieces of his dreams -- horrible images of suffering and fear. She almost pitied a creature so twisted that even his sleep was poisoned by evil.

Tired of her efforts to learn more about the chieftain, she settled more deeply into the blanket and let her thoughts drift to happier times. At least she was warm, clean, and well fed. Slowly she drifted off, wondering what the night might bring. Her restless sleep included an all too vivid dream of the evil chieftain taking her in his powerful arms and kissing her breathless. Their naked bodies clung to one another and he murmured husky endearments in her ear.

Chapter Three

Niabi awoke several moments before Etlu opened the door. A fresh, outdoorsy scent clung to his nude body and his hair looked damp, as if he'd been swimming again.

"There's water for you to wash with in the basin and food in the bowl beside it." He pointed to the small wooden table on which rested the items he'd mentioned.

"You left me in there while you went out?"

"When I awoke, you were still sleeping. Having a rather *interesting* dream, actually."

Frustrated that he had penetrated her mind, she shoved past him, strode to the table, and began washing.

"Your dreams, or should I say nightmares, were interesting as well," she said, a sarcastic edge to her voice. "Repulsive, but interesting, particularly the image of you drowning in a vat of boiling blood."

His lip curled and he stared down his nose at her. "What are you talking about?"

"Don't tell me you can't remember --"

"I never recall my dreams. Not since I was a child."

"Really?" She held his gaze. Peculiar. "Surely some of the images stay with you once in a --"

"What does it matter? Discussing dreams is a waste of time. Foolishness. Another *woman's* trait." He sneered.

Studying him carefully, she reached for a chunk of bread from the soapstone bowl and began eating with enthusiasm.

"You have a healthy appetite," he observed after watching her devour first the bread, then salted meat, fruit, and nuts.

"It seems eating is my only pleasure around here." She paused, a wooden cup of mead lifted halfway to her lips. "Perhaps I shouldn't have said that. You're likely to starve me now."

By the contemplative look on his face, she knew her comment hadn't been far from the truth.

"No. I have other plans for you. I hope your appetite is strong in all directions."

She took a long sip of mead then said, "That depends."

"On?"

"The man." She flung him a teasing look meant as mild flirtation. After all, if she had to bed him, she could at least try to enjoy it.

Her attempt at playful seduction was lost on him. Picking up another wooden cup, this one filled with scented oil, he tore the mead from her hand and placed it aside, then dragged her toward the furs and blankets in the corner of the cave.

"Enough talk," he said. "I will have what was promised me."

He dipped his hand into the cup and rubbed the oil over his cock with a few rough strokes. His staff swelled, the ruddy flesh glistening. Pushing Niabi onto her back, he covered her body with his. A hand braced on either side of her head, he used his knee to nudge her legs apart.

The bulbous head of his cock prodded her pussy, then with a swift thrust, he pushed in to the hilt. Her entire body tensing, Niabi gasped in pain as he thrust, his motions short and much too fast.

"Please slow down," she said, bracing her hands against his shoulders.

Instantly he stopped moving and stared into her eyes. "Why?"

"Because you're hurting me. Not that you care, but unless you want me to start doing you bodily harm in return --"

"It might be amusing for you to try."

"Do you want me willing or not?"

He sighed in obvious annoyance, but resumed thrusting, slower and easier.

Niabi lay still while he plundered her body, noting that in spite of his apparent arousal, his expression revealed no pleasure or even raw desire. His eyes didn't close nor did the harsh lines of his face smooth in ecstasy.

After a moment, he stopped thrusting again, his brow furrowed. "You're not upholding your part of the bargain."

"Excuse me?" she demanded. She felt she was doing more than her fair share simply by enduring his primal touch.

"Why are you not willing?"

"I'm not fighting you."

"A corpse or a whore could lie here just as well as you are. I want a willing woman."

She sighed, exasperated. "I don't understand what you want from me."

"Cling to me. Cry out in pleasure."

Completely taken aback by his request, it took a moment for her to comprehend the true meaning of his words. Finally, she said, "Etlu, you mean you want me to make love to you."

"Yes. Come willingly. Make love. What is the difference?"

Could he possibly be serious? Was any man this ignorant?

"There is a great difference. Making love is what happens between two people who care about each other's happiness. A woman responds in the way you describe when she and a man give each other pleasure."

"It takes but a few thrusts to feel pleasure."

"If that's what you believe, then you have never made love properly."

He held her gaze, a contemplative expression in his silvery eyes. "Then tell me what must be done for it to be proper."

Niabi could scarcely believe what he was asking, not only because he seemed genuinely naïve in the art of lovemaking, but because he was interested in pleasing her and not simply having her lie "willingly" beneath him.

"First of all, women like to be touched," she said, brushing a hand over her breasts. "Here."

His eyes gleamed with interest as he glanced at her breasts and clamped a hand over one.

"Gently," Niabi snapped.

He loosened his grip and squeezed the plump mound almost tenderly. The tips of his fingers traced delicate circles over the flesh, edging closer and closer to the pert nipple. Finally he ran his thumb over the brownish bud, stroking in tiny, feather-light circles.

Niabi's breath caught, pleasure washing over her. His long, slender fingers continued stroking and teasing the nipple. It grew harder and more sensitive beneath his touch.

Resisting the urge to close her eyes, she looked at his face, noting that he was staring at her breast as he caressed it. Almost hesitantly, he bent his head and licked the nipple. Gasping, Niabi arched her back, pushing her breast closer to his face. He covered her nipple with his mouth, flicking his wet tongue over it then sucking deeply.

"Ah," she moaned softly, burying her fingers in his hair. Unable to keep her eyes open any longer, she allowed them to close so she could better enjoy the sensations breaking over her.

While sucking and licking her left breast, Etlu took the other in his hand and kneaded it, his thumb rubbing the nipple. His scent grew stronger, mingling with hers, as their desire increased.

The tips of his teeth worried her nipple and she cried out sharply, the pleasure almost too intense. Her clit ached with need, yet he seemed too preoccupied with her breasts to care about any other part of her at the moment.

He shifted position slightly and began licking and sucking her other nipple. Niabi ran her hands over his shoulders and back, relishing the feel of powerful muscles beneath warm skin. Her fingers traced the slight ridges of many old scars that roughened his otherwise smooth flesh. She threaded her fingers through his thick black hair and clutched handfuls of it when he sucked harder on her nipple, sending little ripples of delight through her entire body.

When he finally lifted his head, she lay panting with pleasure, her clit aching with need.

"You're enjoying this?" he asked.

"Heavens, yes," she breathed before she fully realized what she was saying. How could she possibly enjoy this brutal beast's hands and lips on her? Yet during these past moments he hadn't acted viciously. Quite the contrary.

"What else pleases you?"

Her eyes opened and she held his gaze. "Why is this so important to you?"

He took so long to reply that she thought he might simply ignore the question. "Because I never thought there could be pleasure without pain. I have seen people together and when I reached into their minds sensed indescribable things. Unknown things."

"Like what?"

"Sometimes what I felt from you just now. Other times different, though no less intense, emotions. I have taken pleasure with women, but it is not the same as what I felt from these people. It is not the same as what --"

"Go on."

"Tell me where else to touch you." He placed a hand on her belly and stroked the silken flesh. "Here?"

"That's nice, but --"

"Here." His deep voice just above a whisper, he swept his hand over her pelvis and hip, then gently grasped her inner thigh.

"Yes," she murmured. "That's nice."

His fingertips combed through her pubic hair then dipped between her legs again. Using one finger, he circled her pussy then eased the long, slender digit back inside her.

Niabi's legs fell apart, and she tilted her pelvis upward.

Completely focused between her legs, Etlu tenderly explored her slick passage, murmuring, "Wet. Very wet."

"Mmm," she purred, then stifled a sharp cry of lust when he withdrew his finger and touched her clit, so plump and sensitive from his carnal exploration. "Yes. Right there. That feels so -- ah!"

She gasped, her pulse leaping as he covered her clit with his mouth and ran his tongue over it, much like he'd done to her breasts. He lapped with upward strokes, varied at first, then settled into a steady rhythm that soon had her writhing so much he had to slide his hands under her bottom to keep her steady.

"Oh, yes," she breathed. "Please, please don't stop."

The pleasure was so keen that she scarcely knew what she was saying. She simply wanted his lips and tongue to stay with her until she burst in utter fulfillment. Several more long, upward flicks of his tongue against her clit and she came so hard she wondered for the first time if a blood drinker could die from too much pleasure. Throughout the extended climax Etlu continued gripping her bottom and licking her over-stimulated flesh until the last tiny ripple tore through her.

He slid up her body, his tongue leaving a warm, wet trail up her belly and between her breasts. This time when he mounted her, he eased his cock slowly into her drenched pussy.

Gazing at him, she saw his cold expression melt the slightest bit and heard his heartbeat quicken. Obviously he appreciated the difference between a "willing" woman and a lust-drenched one.

"How does it feel?" she whispered.

"Different."

"Good?"

He nodded slowly, his eyelashes lowering and the taut muscles of his shoulders and arms bunching as he thrust -- long, deep sweeps from head to hilt. The rhythm of his thick cock rubbing against her in all the right places rekindled her passion. Niabi slid the soles of her feet up and down his hair-roughened calves before locking her legs around his waist and her arms around his neck. She clung to him as his pace increased, edging closer and closer to fulfillment.

"Don't stop," she panted, her body once again catching fire. "Please don't stop, Etlu!"

He growled, his fangs grazing her neck and tongue lapping her flesh while he continued thrusting faster.

Closing her eyes, Niabi moaned with pleasure, her body straining against Etlu's until she burst in a climax even more intense than the last. With a ragged cry, he drove his fangs into her flesh and his cock deep into her pussy. Every muscle in his body taut, he surged into her, lapping her blood as he came long and hard.

When Niabi recovered enough to open her eyes, she found him stretched out beside her, staring intently at her face, his expression unfathomable. His fingertips absently stroked her hip and stomach.

"That was -- enjoyable," she said, surprised by how detached she was able to sound when the urge to melt into his arms almost overcame her.

"Apparently so," he said. "I didn't realize a woman could experience the same pleasure as a man."

"I'm starting to believe there is very little you know about pleasure of any kind."

"I have been with many women and fought in many battles. I have tasted all the pleasure in this world."

Niabi curled her lip. "How can you mention lovemaking and war in the same breath? Why is violence and pain your idea of happiness?"

"Our kind were made for pain. The world is for us to rule."

"Your Creator told you that?"

"Didn't yours?"

"No." She raised herself onto her elbow so she could face him more directly. "Even if she had, I wasn't raised to believe such nonsense. What about your family?"

"My Creator is my family."

"Your parents? Brothers and sisters?"

"If you mean a mortal family, I did not have one."

"Surely you were brought up some --"

"My Creator has always been with me. Plucked me from the battlefield and raised me to know the power of the Evil One."

A feeling of dread tightened her belly. Niabi's Creator had warned her about the Spirit of Evil and those who followed it, spreading agony and destruction throughout the world.

I cannot tell you how to live your life, Niabi, her Creator had said, *but I believe our duty is to fight the Evil One and those who serve him. We have been given the power to do this better than any other creature in the world.*

Niabi knew her Creator was right. She'd spent the first centuries of her life training and fighting beside her in that never ending battle against wickedness. Now, it seemed, Etlu had been fighting the same battle but on the opposite side. In spite of this, she sensed that somewhere deep inside he was not completely evil.

Chapter Four

Etlu noticed the fear cross Niabi's face at the mention of the Evil One.

"You are familiar with the Master of us all?" he asked.

Perhaps he had been right in choosing this woman. If she shared his belief in the Evil One, she was a more worthy mate than he had imagined. From the moment he had met her gaze in battle, even before realizing she was a woman, he had felt attraction to her. Something in her dark eyes revealed a depth of spirit rare among mortals and immortals alike.

Though she didn't have his strength, she exuded power. When they had fought, blade to blade, he remembered thinking she would have made a fine addition to his army had he not been so aroused by her. His desire had extended beyond the mere urge to claim her body and this worried him. For a member of his army to wield such power over him was far too dangerous, so he decided to put her to death.

When he'd ripped off her clothing to prepare for the Blood Eagle and discovered she was female, he realized he could possess her after all. She could become his concubine. Through her he could finally experience the pleasures he'd witnessed between men and women. Unlike slaves who feared his bed or other women he'd known who wanted part of his wealth and power, this female blood drinker was neither afraid nor lacking in strength of her own.

"Yes. The Spirit of Good whose strength flows through all things is our Master."

Her words sickened him. Gripping her throat snugly in one hand, he rasped, "How dare you speak the name of my Master's most hated rival?"

"Release me," she stated, her unwavering gaze fixed on his.

Slowly he eased his hold, which hadn't been particularly hard to begin with. For some reason he hadn't wanted to harm her, simply instill a little terror.

"Why is there such fear in you?" she murmured. "You trust no one and surround yourself with people who would as soon stake you while you sleep as look at you. All for what? Power? Wealth?"

"Destruction," he told her. "It's what we were made for. And I have no fear except for the Evil One. He has given me power and can take it away."

"He hasn't given you power, Etlu. Any that you have came from within you. And I disagree that we were made to bring destruction to this world. I know it's not my purpose."

"Then what is your purpose?"

"My Creator once told me we must use our power to fight evil."

"And my Creator told me that should I meet a blood drinker who spouts such nonsense, I should kill her."

"Because he wanted to control you."

"He made me in his image."

"What about your own image, Etlu? Do you want to be his puppet forever? Look around you. Think about what we've shared this night. You were gentle with me, and I with you. Tell me that didn't make you feel something."

"Weakness."

Her brow furrowed and she took his face in her hands, her thumbs stroking his cheeks. "How about joy? I felt it and I know you did, too."

"Joy is a form of weakness."

"No. You cannot believe that."

"It is the truth."

"Only because you've spent your life in the shadow of the Evil One. If you will not open your heart, then at least open your mind to other possibilities."

Drawing a deep breath, he studied her carefully. Everything he'd learned told him he should destroy her now that he'd taken what he wanted, yet something disturbing had happened to him. He had hoped that once he experienced a willing woman -- made love -- his curiosity would be satisfied. This newly found knowledge of the pleasures shared between men and women had increased rather than sated his desire. Already he wanted to claim her again, have her cling to him and wrap her warm, silken limbs around his body as he thrust into her until they both collapsed in delight.

Just as his Creator had warned, she was trying to manipulate him, use her feminine wiles to turn him from the Evil One. Steeling himself against her gentleness, he entered her mind swiftly, surprised by how easily she let him in. No longer did she toss up impenetrable barriers, but allowed him to roam freely through her thoughts.

He saw her life as a mortal thousands of years ago in a strange place as wild and untamed as the Northmen's land. Her people had lived by a river, fishing and hunting. The men were great warriors who defended their tribe against intruders.

A stranger came and with him a sickness that killed many members of the tribe, leaving them drained of blood. Believing the stranger somehow responsible, the warriors tried to drive him off, yet no matter how great the injury, he always returned as strong as before, like an evil spirit sent to crush their people. Then another stranger came, a beautiful dark-skinned woman called Adira. She fought and killed the evil spirit, and this time he did not return. The tribe accepted the woman, worshipped her as sent by the great spirit, yet she did not welcome such praise and soon left.

Niabi's family had been killed by the sickness and she thought her only means of survival would be to marry a man whom she did not love. Seeing the warrior woman had stirred her thoughts and she followed her into the wilderness. After hearing her story, Adira confided in Niabi about her true nature and offered to make her a blood drinker, her immortal daughter.

While exploring Niabi's memories of her first years as a blood drinker, Etlu sensed the love that had developed between

Creator and offspring and suddenly could bear no more. He withdrew from her thoughts, seething with jealousy and longing such as he'd never known.

"What's wrong?" she asked. "Why do you turn away?"

"Why did you show me those memories?"

"Because you were curious and I have nothing to hide." Sitting up, she reached for his arm, but he tugged away.

Her life, both as a mortal and a blood drinker, had been so unlike his. If he had known even a portion of such happiness existed --

"I have shown you my past. Will you share yours with me?" she asked, lifting a hand to his cheek. Her fingertips brushed across his skin with a feathery touch and he resisted the urge to close his eyes to better enjoy the sensation.

"You forget your place, woman."

"What are you hiding, Etlu?"

"Nothing," he seethed, his fangs bared. "You want to see my past? Maybe you should have a taste of it."

He advanced on her, pressing her onto her back. Fixing his unblinking gaze upon her, he opened his thoughts to her, forcing to the surface all the terrors of his mortal life -- days spent locked in darkness and physical torments he longed to forget but could not. He relived raids on villages. Forced, even as a child, to torment and slaughter mortals or else endure Aru's wrath. In his Creator's house, warriors ridiculed and beat him. Kedar in particular took pleasure in making his life miserable. His blood still pounded with rage when he recalled the sting of Kedar's whip and worse indignities no child should suffer.

Waves of horror and disgust rolled off Niabi, but to his surprise, sympathy did as well. He sensed that she wanted to tear herself away from his memories, but refused to leave him drowning in them alone.

Etlu broke their connection, but when he tried to pull away, she locked her arms around his neck.

"No wonder all you understand is hate," she murmured. "And I had no idea you are so young. Your power both of mind and body is that of a much older blood drinker."

"My Creator would not accept youth as an excuse for failure."

"I'm sorry."

"Why should you be sorry?" he snapped. "I possess more power than you, an ancient, yet *you* offer *me* pity?"

"It's not pity, but compassion."

"You're weak."

"Then let me be weak," she whispered, tightening her arms around him and pressing her face against his shoulder.

Gritting his teeth, he fought the urge to surrender completely to her embrace.

"What happened to that beast Kedar?" she asked.

"I killed him. I suppose I should have been grateful to him. He tested me like no other and made me strong. If not for him, I might not have known exactly how much I could endure."

"There's so much more to life than anger and pain, Etlu. You need not follow your Creator's twisted path."

"It's too late, Niabi," he said, her name shockingly sweet on his lips. "My fate was determined long ago, as was yours. You have fulfilled your end of our bargain, and now you must die."

Niabi froze, her heart pounding. In spite of his past, she sensed goodness buried deep in Etlu, if he would only give himself the chance to dig it out. She was beginning to understand him now and realized that in his mind, killing her was his only option if he wanted to remain true to the Master who had scarred his body and mind.

"You don't have to kill me, Etlu. You've only just begun to taste what has been denied you. Tonight was wonderful, but it can be so much better."

"I understand your fear of death makes you willing to continue as my slave."

"It's true I don't want to die, but as you recall from our battle in my village, I am willing. If I didn't feel for you, I would not offer myself, not even to save my own life."

"You can gain nothing from continuing this exploration."

"And you can gain nothing from putting me to death, unless you're afraid of me after all."

The look he gave her told her he wasn't about to dignify her comment with an answer.

He rolled onto his back and stared at the craggy ceiling. After a moment of silent contemplation, he said, "Very well. I will not kill you now, but I cannot promise I won't later."

Niabi resisted the urge to smile. That was all the reassurance she needed.

After they dressed, he blindfolded her again and toted her back to the village. Etlu placed Niabi in the company of several slave women working in his longhouse, then left to go about his business with his troops.

While helping two pale-haired mortal women mend clothes, Niabi noted their sullen expressions matched those of almost every other servant in the longhouse, both mortal and blood drinker.

"What are your names?" Niabi asked, hoping to initiate some conversation.

"I'm Freja. She's Helga," said the older of the two, not so much as glancing at Niabi.

"How long have you served Etlu?"

"Many years," Freja replied.

"Is he a fair master?"

"His punishments are harsh, but if you keep quiet and do your work, he usually ignores you."

"I see," Niabi murmured. "Does he --"

"If you're smart, you will keep silent and go about your work," said Helga.

"He frightens you, then?"

"Only a fool is not frightened by him," Helga continued. "And only a fool tries to make conversation when none is required."

Sighing, Niabi lowered her gaze to the shirt she was patching. It seemed she was destined for a long, boring night.

Etlu returned to the longhouse just before dawn to escort Niabi to his cave. Again she was blindfolded and toted in his arms. The latter part she didn't mind so much. It was rather nice being carried in his powerful arms, pressed close to his warm, hard body. Her thoughts drifted to the carnal pleasures they could explore. In spite of his rough, experienced nature, Etlu was innocent in the ways of love, yet by his superior performance the previous night, he was eager to learn.

When she had initially made the decision to bed him, the idea had disgusted her, but the longer she spent with him the more she believed he was not what he seemed. She had known many men in her lifetime, had seen those who took genuine pleasure in tormenting others. She didn't sense that pleasure in Etlu. He destroyed because he understood no other way.

Niabi knew by scent when they left the village far behind and entered the woods. Taking advantage of their privacy, she began kissing his face. She trailed her lips across his cheek and over his jawline. Blindfolded, she seemed even more aware of her other senses. Her lips detected the faint stubble from his night's growth of beard and felt the slender ridge of the scar along his cheek. Burying her face in his hair, she inhaled deeply, relishing its coarse texture and woodsy aroma.

Finally he stopped walking and placed her on her feet. He removed the blindfold and she saw they were standing in the cave, just outside the door to his secret chamber. He opened it and stood aside for her to pass.

Once he'd bolted the door behind them, he began undressing. She did the same, eager to make love with him again. Throughout the night her thoughts had often drifted to earlier when they'd taken such pleasure in each other's bodies. She'd known men in her long life, several she'd been quite fond of, but none had excited her like Etlu. His touch and scent made her pulse quicken. Caressing his well-muscled body aroused the passion of the primal female dwelling deep inside her.

"I want to taste you," he said once they were naked. Drawing her into his arms, he covered her mouth in a penetrating kiss. His tongue caressed hers, then thrust in and out with long, slow strokes.

Moaning softly, Niabi clung to him, rising onto her toes to better reach him.

He scraped his tongue against her fangs. The delectable flavor of his blood filled her mouth. She mimicked his action, piercing her tongue on his fangs, and enjoyed the taste of their mingling blood.

He broke the kiss and placed his hands on her hips, pushing her gently against the cave wall. The lust filled glint in his eyes made her quiver with unfulfilled need.

He smiled slightly and lowered his face to her neck, inhaling deeply. He kissed her throat, then her collarbone. Lowering himself to his knees, he licked his way down her torso, then pressed his face to her soft mound.

"The scent of your arousal stirs me," he murmured.

"Oh, Etlu." She entwined her fingers in his hair. "I love how you touch me. I -- oh!"

Her entire body tensed with pleasure as his tongue flicked over her clit. He traced the sensitive nub, first one side, then the other. Finally he licked its core in light upward strokes that soon had her trembling on the brink of climax.

Just before she came, he stood and turned her so that she was forced to brace her hands against the cave wall.

"What are you doing?" she panted, glancing over her shoulder. Placing a hand firmly on the back of her head, he made her face the wall. He brushed her hair aside, exposing the back of her neck to his lips.

Niabi moaned softly, her eyes slipping shut and her forehead pressed to the rock wall. He kissed her shoulders and the backs of her arms down to her elbows.

"Ah!" she gasped and arched her back as he trailed his tongue down her spine. Her nipples scraped against the craggy wall and a shiver ripped through her from head to toe.

Grasping her buttocks, he squeezed the taut orbs while running his tongue along the indentation between them. One hand dipped between her legs and he slid a finger into her wet sheath. Using the same finger, now slick with her essence, he rubbed her clit in small circles.

With a growl of animal desire, Etlu dragged her to the cave floor, positioning her on her hands and knees. Grasping her by the hips, he mounted her from behind.

Panting, Niabi clutched handfuls of dirt and rock, her bottom thrusting against Etlu who was driving into her with a fast, steady rhythm. Extending one long arm, he caressed her back and ribs, then grasped her breast. He kneaded the warm mound and gently pinched the nipple between his thumb and forefinger.

"Etlu, oh!" She moaned, bucking against him so he was forced to use both hands again to steady her hips. Niabi came so hard she might have collapsed had Etlu not continued supporting her. He withdrew from her and pulled her into his arms where she lay for several moments, catching her breath.

"You enjoy being possessed," he observed.

Tilting her face toward his, she smiled slightly. "By you, it seems."

He cupped her face in his hand, staring deeply into her eyes before abruptly disentangling himself from her and striding across the cave. Niabi's gaze followed him, roaming over his broad shoulders and powerful back that narrowed to a lean waist and prominent yet tightly muscled buttocks. Bending to open the trunk, he glanced over his shoulder at her, a wicked gleam in his narrowed eyes. He withdrew steel manacles from the trunk, thick enough to restrain even a blood drinker, at least for a short time.

As he approached, Niabi raised herself onto her elbows, watching him carefully. "If you intend to use those on me --"

"Don't even pretend to refuse. Already I can smell your desire, sense it. You have a measure of power for a female and are not accustomed to being claimed."

"Do you still not understand? I do not appreciate pain or --"

"Who mentioned pain?" He straddled her mid-section, though kept most of his weight on his knees and off her. "Besides, I'm starting to believe there are two different kinds of pain."

"What do you mean?" She studied his severe features from his penetrating eyes to his strong chin. Though good sense told her to fight him rather than submit to his whim, she remained still as he raised her hands above her head and snapped the manacles in place.

Leaning down, he spoke against her lips, "Keep your hands overhead or feel my wrath."

Her temper rose, yet at the same time a ripple of desire shot down her spine. Before she could consider the sort of reply she wanted to make, he moved swiftly down her body, knelt between her legs, lifted her buttocks, and covered her clit with his mouth. His moist lips and wet tongue tugged and stroked, instantly rekindling her passion. He traced the shape of her sensitive flesh then used the very tip of one fang to tease the plump nub. Niabi moaned, her body arching and hips wriggling against the pleasure. She instinctively brought her bound hands downward so she could grasp his hair, but the moment she touched his head, he dropped her bottom and sat up.

"Put your hands back where they should be," he growled.

"I want to touch you," she spoke through clenched teeth.

He pushed her hands over her head then bent and ran his tongue lingeringly over her clit. "This is what you want."

Niabi's leg jerked involuntarily and her eyes half closed. He was right. That was what she wanted. At the moment all she could think about was having him stimulate her with his shockingly talented tongue.

He glanced at her. Obviously satisfied with her surrender, he focused his complete attention between her legs. While he licked, sucked, and used his fine, sharp teeth to advantage, Niabi writhed with pleasure, her fingers twisting above her head as she fought the urge to touch him. When she was about to burst in rapture, he covered her body with his and shifted his thick erection into her well prepared pussy. He reached up with one hand and stroked her grasping fingers before bracing his hands on the sides of her head and pumping into her. A few swift thrusts hurled her over the edge, but he didn't stop there. Grunting, he continued surging into her, pushing her toward another peak.

Unable to control herself any longer, Niabi strained against her bonds, managing to snap the interlocking chain just before she soared again in ecstasy. Clinging to him, she sank her fangs into his shoulder at the same moment he bit her. The taste and scent of their blood sent new waves of passion washing over them, pushing them beneath its crimson surface until they lay sated and panting in each other's embrace. Finally Etlu stirred, though Niabi remained still, her eyes closed and a half smile on her lips. He removed the bonds and they clinked as he tossed them aside. Stretching out beside her, he again drew her into his arms.

After several moments of silence, he asked, "Tell me what love is."

Lifting her head from his chest, she stared at him. "Surely you must know. There must have been at least one person you…" Her voice faded when he shook his head, his silvery gaze fixed on her. She wondered how to explain to a grown man something he should have understood since childhood.

"Love is caring about a person's happiness. It's an incomparable feeling that has less to do with a meeting of bodies and more with a joining of souls. Do you understand?"

"No."

Sighing with exasperation, she tried another definition. "When you love someone, you want to protect them."

"I protect my people, but I do not love them."

"That's not what I mean."

"Did you love the people in your village?"

"I cared for them deeply and some of them were good friends, so yes, in a way I did love them."

His brow furrowed. "So you're here with me because of love."

"In a manner of speaking, but --"

"Love is a weakness."

"It's a strength, Etlu."

"It made you a prisoner."

"And your hate has made you a prisoner."

He stared at her, unblinking, as if trying to make sense of her words. Finally he shook his head and stood, tugging her to her feet and leading her to the cell.

"Why must I stay here?" she demanded. "Let me sleep beside you."

"You know that is not possible."

"How can you do this -- bed me then lock me away like a prisoner?"

"Must I remind you that is exactly what you are?"

"Someday you will have to trust someone, Etlu." She held his gaze but he remained immovable. The warm, breathing man who had pleasured her with his body had once again become the icy minion of evil.

Stepping into the cell, Niabi wondered if anyone could ever truly reach him. His Creator had made a chieftain, yet destroyed a man.

"Here." He offered her another blanket and caressed her cheek with the back of his hand. When he bent to kiss her, she turned away, closing the door behind her.

* * *

The following night, Etlu released Niabi from the cell and they returned to the village. Again she joined the women in the nightly tasks of cooking, sewing, and caring for the children. She noted how well the mortals had adapted to their chieftain's nocturnal way of life.

After several hours in the longhouse, Niabi stepped outside for some fresh air. Walking around the village, she sought out

Etlu but didn't find him among the warriors on the training field or with the guards stationed along the wall. Nor was he in the forge. Finally she asked one of the men his whereabouts and was directed to a clearing in the woods.

She found Etlu naked and knee-deep in a brook, a fishing spear in his hand.

More freezing water. How could he bear it?

Horik stood on the bank, his gaze fixed on Niabi with its usual hatred. For some reason her presence had angered the auburn-haired warrior from the first. Horik didn't interest her, however. Her attention focused on Etlu.

Though familiar with his body, she couldn't help admiring him. Tall and sleekly muscled, he exuded wild vampiric beauty like no man she had ever seen. His dark mane hung thick down his back. When he turned slightly, his silvery gaze following the movement of a fish beneath the dark water, his harsh yet captivating features came into her view.

The tips of his fangs glistened when his lips parted slightly just before he jabbed his spear into the water. He pulled it up, a large fish wriggling on the end. Grasping it in one hand, he pulled it off the point and tossed it to Horik. His gaze once again fixed on Niabi, the auburn-haired warrior bit off the fish's head, spat it on the ground, then devoured the rest of the scaly gray body raw.

Etlu glanced at Niabi before he resumed fishing.

"Return to the village, Horik," he said.

Horik's jaw tightened visibly, but he did as Etlu ordered, flashing his fangs at Niabi on his way by her.

Once Horik's scent faded, Etlu strode out of the water and picked up his cloak. He stood near enough for her to see him shivering slightly, rivulets of water streaking his flesh. Draping the cloak over his shoulders, he stepped even closer to her. The desire in his eyes revealed that he wanted her as much as she wanted him. What was it about the man that compelled her?

"Come." He opened his arms, inviting her into the warmth of his cloak. She obeyed, tilting her face up to his.

She was about to kiss him, but paused, her lip curling slightly. "You haven't been eating raw fish, have you?"

He chuckled. "No."

Nodding, she slid her arms around him and touched her lips to his. They felt cold from his swim but soon warmed against hers.

Their mouths still locked, he nudged her against a tree trunk and raised her dress to her waist. He prodded her sheath with his stiff cock while rolling his thumb over her clit.

Niabi's breath quickened and she grasped her dress, holding it so both his hands were free to caress her clit, buttocks, and thighs. By the time he fully eased into her, she was more than ready for him.

"Etlu!"

Biting her lower lip, he grasped her bottom and raised her off the ground. She wrapped her legs around his waist, allowing him to support her entirely. Grunting with pleasure, he used his arms to pump her on his cock.

"Ah!" she cried, clinging to him with all her considerable strength. At the same moment she came, he covered her lips in a crushing kiss. She cried out into his mouth, shaking and pulsing in ecstasy.

His breathing ragged, he released her, allowing her to lean against him until she recovered enough to stand on her own.

He left her leaning against the tree while he stooped by his pile of clothing and removed his belt. Tingling with desire, Niabi watched him approach, guessing what he had planned. Silently, he tied the end of the belt to first one wrist, then reached around the tree trunk and fastened her other hand with the opposite end.

Niabi's heart pounded, her chest rising and falling with excitement. He had been right when he'd guessed a part of her liked being controlled by him. When he took her in his arms and claimed her, when he growled possessively in her ear and used his fangs to pierce her flesh, she almost forgot she was his prisoner.

Etlu broke her thoughts by covering her mouth in a soul stealing kiss. He thrust his tongue between her lips while cupping her breasts and rolling his thumbs over the nipples that were already hard with desire.

"Oh please," she breathed when the kiss broke and he bent, taking one of her nipples between his lips and sucking hard. While he licked and tugged, worrying the taut flesh with his teeth, he reached between her legs and slid two fingers into her wet sheath. He explored with slow, tender strokes, then withdrew his fingers and teased her clit until her legs trembled.

Niabi's hands clenched into fists and she struggled to keep from breaking her bonds.

As if sensing her internal battle, he said, "Don't even think about breaking my belt."

"Then stop tormenting me," she groaned, arching her neck when he used the very tip of his tongue to rhythmically tap the most aching, sensitive part of her clit.

With a throaty, evil laugh, he licked her, then stood and entered her with a long, slow thrust. Flexing his knees, he drove into her, again pushing her over the edge. Panting and squirming against the rough tree trunk, Niabi came. As the marvelous pulsations ebbed, she was leaning hard against the tree while Etlu freed her from the bonds. When she opened her eyes, he stood in front of her, his handsome face tense with need, his cock hard and glistening with her wetness. The ruddy head looked ready to burst.

"I want to feel your mouth on my cock."

Niabi drew a sharp breath, her heart pounding. Oh, how she wanted to taste him, control his passion, and make him cry out as she did when he licked her.

She knelt in front of him and clasped his cock in her hands. Rubbing the staff, she leaned closer and took the head between her lips. Her tongue rolled over it, lapping and exploring, paying particular attention to the ridge along the underside.

Etlu wrapped his hands in her hair, his rock hard thighs tensing and his hips thrusting slightly as the pleasure grew.

The musky scent and the velvety texture of his skin raised her passion, making her clit ache with need. She reluctantly left the bulbous head and licked every inch of his staff, then worried the crown with her fangs.

He groaned, his hips thrusting faster. One hand clasping his staff and the other kneading his sac, she sucked his cock head. She swirled her tongue over it, then drew him so deeply into her mouth that he brushed the back of her throat.

Every muscle in his body tensed. His fingers tightened in her hair and with each ragged breath she felt his excitement building. Her mind reached out to his and she sensed him fighting his impending climax. Smiling around his cock, she sucked faster, squeezing his balls and rubbing his staff with her fist.

A hoarse cry escaped his lips at the same moment he pulled out of her mouth and came. Niabi watched, thoroughly aroused and fascinated by the sight of his essence shooting across the ground, every muscle in his magnificent body straining and his usually rough expression softened by pleasure.

Chapter Five

Several nights later, just before dawn, Niabi was in the longhouse helping Freja grind flour for baking. Though still not the friendliest person, Freja had warmed to Niabi the slightest bit and occasionally engaged in conversation with her. Perhaps because Niabi had proved herself a good and willing worker, or maybe because the villagers were overcoming their initial wariness of her, some of the other women had welcomed her attempt at friendship.

She and Freja had just started discussing plans for making new dresses when Horik burst into the house. "We're under attack!"

Warriors who had been eating at the table or lounging by the fire sprang to their feet and followed Horik outside. While the women rushed to collect their children, Niabi went to join the warriors. Her keen hearing detected the distant sounds of battle on the outskirts of the village -- the clash of steel and men shouting and screaming in death.

No sooner had she stepped out the door than Etlu's horse blocked her path.

"Get back in the house," he ordered.

"Give me a weapon. I can fight!"

"I said get back in the house. If I find you have disobeyed, you will feel my wrath."

"Etlu, listen to me. It's nearly dawn. You and several of your men cannot endure sunlight. I can be of help."

"I don't need a woman to fight for me! Get back inside," he said in a low, dangerous tone, his gaze meeting hers with such ire that she knew protesting would be fruitless.

As she reentered the longhouse, she glanced over her shoulder and saw Etlu and his horse cantering out of the village.

A short time later, she and Freja sat in a corner, preparing herbs to treat the warriors' injuries. "I wonder what's happening out there," Niabi fretted.

"Don't concern yourself. Etlu has never been defeated. He is a harsh master, but our people here are well protected and none of us starve, which is more than I can say for this place before he overthrew our former chieftain."

Freja's words surprised Niabi. This was the first time anyone had spoken well of Etlu. Not that anyone spoke badly of him, either, though his people's fear of him was obvious and justifiable.

"I wonder who is behind the attack," Niabi continued.

"Most likely Harald, a chieftain from across the ridge. He and Etlu rule most of the land in these parts. It was only a matter of time before one provoked the other, as both are ruthless and hungry for power."

The women continued mixing herbs in silence until the first casualties arrived, then they busied themselves tending the wounded.

Hours later, several uninjured warriors whom Niabi knew had positions of power stepped inside. Sunlight shone through the open door and Niabi's belly clenched. Where was Etlu and how had he survived the daylight?

Overhearing bits of conversation among the newly arrived warriors, Niabi learned that Harald had been behind the attack. Etlu's army had crushed their enemies and pressed on to Harald's land where, after another bloody battle, Etlu claimed it as his own. Relieved to finally know Etlu had survived, Niabi continued her work.

It was late afternoon when Etlu returned, covered from head to toe in heavy leather and mail armor that left no bit of skin exposed. Even his eyes were hidden behind a metal grate built into his dome-shaped helmet.

He turned in her direction, and though she tried to sense something -- anything -- from him, his mind remained closed to her. After exchanging a few words with one of his most favored warriors, he approached Niabi and said, "Come."

Nearly bursting with curiosity, she followed him outside where he placed the customary blindfold on her and lifted her onto his horse. He mounted behind her, his arms winding snugly around her as the horse lurched forward.

Once they reached their destination, he removed the blindfold and told her to await him in the cave. A short time later, he joined her.

"What happened today?" she demanded, watching him remove his helmet.

His dark hair clung wetly to his head and neck, a stark contrast to his corpse-pale face. Blood red eyes, darkly shadowed beneath, stared blankly across the room.

"How did you manage the sunlight?" she asked softly, stepping closer and touching a hand to his cheek. If his severely irritated eyes were almost painful to look at, she could scarcely imagine how they must feel. "Daylight renders you blind, does it not?"

"Obviously." His voice dripped sarcasm. "By now you should know the power of my mind. I have learned to fight by sensing my enemies' plans. I see through their thoughts. As for sunlight, this armor protects me from its deadly rays."

"It must still cause you pain," she said, her deft fingers loosening ties and buckles in an attempt to help him remove the armor. He brushed her hands away and lifted off the leather and mail. Beneath, his shirt clung to his sweat soaked body, the powerful muscles and lean lines sending a thrill of desire through her. Even weakened by sunlight and battle, he was the most stunning man she had ever seen.

"I can smell what you want," he said. "But later. I must rest first."

It was odd having him speak to her without focusing his gaze upon her. Even in the darkness of the cave it would take time for his vision to return after prolonged exposure to sunlight.

"Of course. Are you hungry?"

"Thirsty," he said, removing the remainder of his clothes.

A new wave of desire broke over her. He was thirsty for blood. *Her* blood. She sensed that he needed it quite desperately.

Quickly she undressed and grasped his hands, tugging him toward the bed of furs and blankets.

Stretching out on her back, she welcomed him into her arms. Though she expected him to bite quickly in his hunger, he surprised her by gently licking and kissing her neck. The tips of his fangs grazed her flesh then pierced it.

Niabi gasped at the pleasure of his bite and tightened her arms around him. His hot, damp body felt so good. Her breasts crushed against his hard chest and her legs entwined with his, she felt his cock swell. "Etlu."

Niabi, his thoughts touched hers. *So much for resting.*

Using his knee to nudge her legs apart, he shifted position so the tip of his cock slid into her pussy.

"Yes, oh, yes," she panted, longing to feel him deep inside her. Drenched with passion her body easily accepted his length and girth.

Groaning with need, he continued lapping her blood while pumping into her. Niabi quivered, her internal muscles clamping around his cock. She locked her legs around him and wove her fingers through his hair.

"Etlu," she breathed, splaying her palms across his back, relishing the feel of his straining muscles. He was so powerful, such a raw, lustful, untamed beast, yet for her he had tempered his savage appetite and learned to touch her with love. His scent filled her and somehow every thrust of his cock seemed connected to her heart.

His groans deepened to a thoroughly animal sound and he thrust faster, his heart pounding in time with hers.

Niabi came quickly, clinging hard to his neck, her legs wrapped around him, riding out each spectacular burst of passion.

Lunging into her, he tore his mouth from her neck and drew several ragged breaths. "Niabi! Damn you, woman!" With a final thrust he came. Collapsing atop her, he gasped, his body quivering in the aftermath. "Destructive, beautiful wench."

As sleep claimed him, she sensed his thoughts. *You're killing me, Niabi, and I almost don't care if I die.*

* * *

Etlu awoke in comfortable darkness, refreshed by sleep and Niabi's blood after the strength-sapping daylight battle.

Harald had been a more worthy opponent than he'd imagined, managing to discover Etlu's aversion to daylight. The man had planned his attack well, but Etlu had long ago prepared himself to fight on any ground, at any time. Daylight could destroy him, but he had found ways of outsmarting it.

A soft moan and the sensation of a warm body nearby drew Etlu's attention. He turned sharply, staring at Niabi curled up beside him, her lovely face softened by sleep.

What was wrong with him? He had fallen asleep in her presence, leaving himself vulnerable.

"Good evening," she purred, her eyes opening halfway. Smiling, she rested her hand against his neck. "You look better. Rested."

He nodded curtly, still irritated by his negligence.

"It was nice sleeping beside you," she said. "And you see, you can trust me."

"I can trust no one."

"Didn't you enjoy sleeping with me?" She edged closer and draped one of her long, smooth legs over his. "You seemed to. I never would have guessed you'd like to cuddle so much, oh fierce chieftain."

The teasing expression in her eyes annoyed him, mostly because he found it bewitching. "I do not cuddle," he said stiffly.

"You held me so close it felt like we shared a single body."

He stared at her, his eyes narrowed. The image she described was almost too appealing. He stood and reached for his clothes. "I must return to the village. Enough time has already been wasted here. There is much work to do."

"If you weren't so quick tempered and unduly harsh, you would be a good chieftain. Your people are well fed and protected. I believe some of them even admire you, in their own way. You --"

"I *am* a good chieftain," he interrupted. "More important, I am true to my nature as a blood drinker."

"You know my feelings on that matter."

He grunted, not wishing to begin that conversation. The woman had already corrupted him enough, making him feel for her. A leader, especially of immortals, could not allow emotion to influence his decisions. What she called harsh, he called survival. "Dress quickly unless you want to stay locked in the cell all night. I do not intend to wait while you dawdle."

A slight smile touched her lips, but she pulled on her tunic. Standing in front of him, she held his gaze, then kissed him -- a tender brush of her lips that sent an odd tingling sensation throughout his body.

Growling, he turned and led the way out of the cave.

Chapter Six

Days turned to weeks during which Niabi and Etlu spent much of the day making love while at night she worked at the longhouse and he trained and hunted with his men. Though sullen and hot-tempered, Etlu usually allowed his people to go about their lives without unwarranted punishment. He had even learned to hold rather long conversations with her without resorting to threats when she disagreed with him or asked a question about his past that he preferred not to answer.

If he needed prodding to converse, he needed none to make love. During those hours wrapped naked in each other's arms, he opened himself to her in a way she had never imagined possible. He perfected kissing to an art, pouring his every emotion into each brush of lips and sweep of tongue. No longer was he simply claiming her body, but possessing a part of her soul. Though he continued blindfolding her on their way to and from the cave, he no longer made her sleep in the cell, but kept her possessively in his arms throughout the day.

Niabi was starting to think of him as a fair leader until one dusk after a particularly heavy snowstorm two men were caught attempting to steal a few strips of salted meat.

Horik and several other warriors awaited Etlu outside the longhouse, the two men chained, shivering, on their knees in the snow. The men had been beaten, and by the chalky look of their faces, Niabi immediately knew Horik and the others had quenched their blood thirst upon them. "We waited for you to give word for them to be executed," Horik said.

"Please," one of the men said, swaying slightly, his voice weak. "Since your attack on our village several weeks ago, many of our people have died. Our families are starving. We needed just enough to feed our children --"

"Silence!" Horik's gloved hand lashed across the man's face, knocking him into the snow. "Your groveling makes me sick."

Niabi stooped to help the man sit up, but Horik grasped her roughly by the arm and pushed her away.

Growling, Etlu advanced on Horik. "Who gave you permission to touch what's mine?"

The auburn-haired warrior looked surprised. "But she has no business aiding a prisoner."

"Etlu, it's the middle of winter. Their families are starving," Niabi said in a calm, steady voice, careful to control the rage simmering inside her. "I'm sure these men would be willing to work for the food --"

"We're not here to give charity," Horik said, holding Etlu's gaze. "Shall it be the Blood Eagle?"

At Horik's words, both men paled even more, their eyes glittering with terror.

"Etlu, don't do this," she whispered. "Punish them if you must, but to kill them over a few pieces of meat is --"

"Our law states they must be executed," Horik continued, then lifted a taunting eyebrow in Etlu's direction. "Unless you are no longer making the laws here."

"Insolence on top of touching my property?" Etlu glared at Horik. "I know there will be at least one man punished this night."

"Etlu --"

"I have heard enough out of you as well." Etlu glowered at Niabi. "You will go to the longhouse and join the other women until I tell you otherwise."

"I will not go anywhere until I know the fate of these men."

Several of the warriors exchanged glances, before their anxious gazes fixed on Etlu, waiting for his reaction to her impertinence. Too late Niabi realized her mistake. Now he might kill the thieves just to prove that he, not a woman, made the decisions here.

"You will go where I tell you," Etlu said, his tone and expression leaving no room for argument.

Her belly taut with rage, Niabi decided it best to do what he asked, simply for the sake of the two mortals.

Etlu, please, she spoke in a spiritual voice, hoping he would not block her out. *At least consider hiring them. That would mean two more loyal workers rather than two lives sacrificed for a bit of food. You have so much --*

He cut off her thoughts and thrust her out of his mind. Trembling with fury, she stepped into the longhouse and silently joined the women in preparing food for later that night.

Etlu returned for her within the hour. "Come with me," he stated in a curt tone.

Flecks of blood marked his shirt and his eyes glistened with malice. Drawing a deep breath, Niabi tried to penetrate his thoughts to discover if he had killed the men after all, but she met an impenetrable barrier.

She followed him out of the longhouse to where his horse waited. They rode to a clearing in the woods.

After they dismounted, he approached, using his height advantage to glare down at her. "Never question my authority again in front of my people."

"Did you kill those men?"

"That is not your concern."

"You did, didn't you?" She ground her teeth in anger.

"If someone steals from me, they will be punished."

"Is death the only acceptable form of punishment to you?"

"You fight like a man but think like a woman," he scoffed. "Unless you want punishment as well, you will heed my words. I am the chieftain and I make all decisions here. Not you. Not Horik. And certainly not a couple of pathetic thieves."

Nearly blinded by rage, Niabi yanked the silver dagger from the sheath about Etlu's waist. She pressed the tip of it to his throat.

"You want to kill me," he stated calmly, not so much as flinching though she knew the silver against his skin must already be burning. Rather than back away and attempt to disarm her, he stepped nearer, the blade pressing harder to his throat. "Go ahead. Do it, Niabi. Pierce my throat. Or better yet, here."

With a savage jerk, he tore open his shirt, exposing the pale flesh of his powerfully muscled chest. Grasping her wrist, he placed the point of the blade over his heart and applied enough pressure to break the skin. The scent of his blood filled the air. Crimson rivulets trickled down his pale flesh to stain the waist of his breeches. His expression remained hard and unreadable, as if the pain meant nothing.

Niabi stared at him, torn between rage and pity.

"Do it, Niabi," he said in a low, dangerous voice. "Do it."

She should kill him and rid the world of another monster, a blood drinker unworthy of his power, yet something stopped her.

"No?" His lips turned upward in an evil grin and he twisted her arm, forcing her to drop the blade. He shoved her so hard she landed on her knees. Bending, he picked up the dagger, wiped the blood on his thigh, and sheathed the weapon while Niabi rose to her feet. Striding toward her, he backed her against a tree and spoke against her lips. "Don't ever threaten me again."

His mouth covered hers in a crushing kiss. Thrusting his tongue into her mouth, he explored with long, rough strokes, wrapping her hair around his hand until his fist pressed against the back of her head.

When the kiss broke, both were panting. Disgusted that she could still feel lust for such a brutal bastard, Niabi brought her knee up fiercely between his legs.

Grunting in pain, he pushed her harder against the tree trunk.

"Release me," she said. "Or why don't you kill me, like you did those men? You're good at bullying anyone weaker than yourself. Does it feel good, after so many years at the mercy of men like Kedar and your Creator?"

Without another word, he tugged her toward the horse where they mounted and rode back to the village. When she entered the longhouse, Niabi was stunned to find the thieves kneeling in a corner while Freja and Helga tended their backs that bore evidence of a flogging.

Etlu hadn't killed them after all. Why hadn't he told her?

Niabi approached the men.

One of them looked up at her and said, "Thank you. If not for your intervention, I'm certain he would have killed us."

"Our families are being brought here for the winter. We'll be allowed to work for our keep," said the other man.

"I wonder what's gotten into him," Helga said under her breath.

Freja glanced in Niabi's direction, the slightest smile on her lips. "I have a good guess."

Niabi's stomach fluttered and her heart soared. It seemed she was making progress with Etlu after all. As if sensing her thoughts, he stepped into the longhouse, his shirt once again buttoned but stained with blood where he'd pressed the blade to his chest. Even from a distance she noticed the bright red burn mark on his throat. Dampening a bit of cloth with water from a basin, she approached him.

"I'm sorry for the way I acted," she said, gently pressing the cloth to his throat. "Why didn't you tell me what you decided to do about the men?"

"It was not your concern."

Using her spirit voice, she said, *Tonight I will give you a proper apology.*

Though he didn't reply, his eyes shone with desire and his scent grew stronger, more aroused.

A young, dark-haired warrior stepped into the house and strode to Etlu, who turned away from Niabi. "Horik has left," the warrior said. "After he recovered enough from the flogging you gave him, he took his belongings and rode off. Several other men went with him."

"Take what men you need and bring them back."

The warrior nodded curtly and left.

"Why did you flog Horik?" she asked, though she suspected the answer.

"For insolence. And for touching you."

"Your property?" she said, an annoyed edge to her voice.

"Yes."

I belong to myself, Etlu, she spoke in his mind.

Cupping the back of her head snugly yet without causing pain, he told her, *You belong to me, Niabi. You are mine, do you understand? Mine.*

She stared into his eyes, sensing a desperation in him she had never felt before. Was Etlu, the savage chieftain, falling in love with her? Even more important, had she fallen in love with him?

* * *

The following evening when they arrived at the village, the young warrior whom Etlu had sent after Horik and the others approached with news. Due to their head start and the heavy snowstorm, the deserters had avoided capture. Etlu ordered the search to continue, though he didn't seem terribly concerned about their escape. Most likely they would ally themselves with another chieftain and no doubt face Etlu in battle where he would take his revenge.

He had no idea how soon that reckoning would take place, or the outcome it would have.

Chapter Seven

Etlu was on the training field practicing swordplay with several of his men while Niabi stood nearby when he caught Aru's scent. It filled him with a feeling of dread, stirring all sorts of terrible memories. In spite of his thick gloves, Etlu's hands grew cold and his heart pounded.

Horses galloped over the snowy ground -- Aru's white stallion followed by an army of chestnuts and bays.

Dressed in black and silver armor and a dome-shaped helmet, Aru motioned for his men to stop a fair distance from the village. Flanked by two mounted warriors, he urged his horse toward Etlu.

It had been so long since Etlu had seen his Creator that he had almost forgotten the ruthlessness in his expression. Aru exuded power like no blood drinker Etlu had ever known. His physical strength was incomparable and his mind impenetrable.

In spite of the shiver that ran down his spine as his Creator approached, Etlu stood his ground.

Aru's pale eyes swept Niabi, then fixed on Etlu with loathing. "I have heard disturbing rumors, Etlu. It is said you've abandoned me and the Evil One, that you've become soft and weak. That a woman is the true chieftain here." Again Aru glanced in Niabi's direction.

"Then you have heard wrong," Etlu stated. "Tell me who has carried these lies and I will destroy him." He knew full well who had done it. The scent of Horik and the other deserters mingled with the blood drinkers of Aru's army.

"I would rather see you destroy her." Aru pointed at Niabi. "Unless she is, after all, your master now."

"I have but one Master."

"Then prove it. Destroy her or I will."

Etlu turned to Niabi who met his gaze, unflinching, though he sensed she understood as well as he did the implication of Aru's words. If Etlu did not kill her, Aru would take both their lives.

After a lifetime of pain and hatred, his self-preservation instinct was powerful, yet his newfound love for her rivaled it in strength. The thought of resuming his lonely existence before meeting Niabi was unbearable, as was the thought of her dying.

"Well?" Aru demanded, baring his fangs, his eyes gleaming with bloodlust.

Grasping Niabi's upper arms harshly, Etlu dragged her toward him.

"Etlu," she whispered, though her voice carried no plea, only sadness. He knew that even when facing death his Niabi was too strong to beg.

"Silence, woman," he growled, hauling her toward his horse. In a swift motion, he threw her belly down across the saddle and slapped the mare's rump hard. It bolted.

Aru looked momentarily surprised, then grasped a silver dagger from the sheath about his waist.

Etlu leapt at his Creator at the same moment Aru raised the dagger in Niabi's direction and knocked him to the ground. She had managed to right herself in the saddle and was headed toward the woods. At least now she had the chance to escape.

"Traitor," Aru snarled, shoving Etlu off him.

He landed hard on his back, his head striking a rock. Knowing he wasn't a match for Aru's strength, which came directly from the Evil One, Etlu realized he would not survive this battle. If he was to die, it seemed only fitting that the man to end his wretched life be the one who had created it.

"Bring her back!" Aru roared. His men and several of Etlu's mounted their horses and chased after Niabi.

Simultaneously, Creator and offspring leapt at each other. Their bodies locked in a writhing mass of straining muscle and ripping teeth. Etlu didn't care if he lived or died. All he knew was that he could no longer exist, unquestioning, by his Creator's ways. Niabi had exposed him to a world he had never imagined and he needed it as he required air to breathe and blood to drink.

Using every bit of skill and strength, he fought Aru, but his Creator's superior powers overtook him. The ancient blood drinker drove his fangs deep into Etlu's shoulder. He gulped his offspring's blood until the world faded to black.

* * *

Etlu awakened on his back in a hole in the earth. Bound by barbed silver chains that cut into his wrists, torso, and legs, he gritted his teeth against burning waves of agony. Silver was the least of his concern. The rising sun shone in the pit, blistering his skin and robbing him of his vision. Grunting in agony, he rolled to the edge of the pit, the barbs driving deeper into his flesh. He stopped, panting, his eyes tightly closed. At least here an overhanging rock provided enough shade to keep him from roasting like a pig on a spit.

The day passed far too slowly, yet even the darkness of night brought little relief to Etlu's battered body.

When the moon rose to its highest, Aru came to stand over the pit. "You have disappointed me, my son. Did I not raise you from a field of death and teach you to wield the Evil One's power? You've wasted your strength. Become weak as a mortal. You've been tainted by that woman's kisses and trapped by her illusion of happiness."

"You lied to me, Aru. You told me there was no pleasure outside of pain. You stole my life just as you stole my mother's and my people's."

"I am your people. I am your Creator and the Evil One is your source. I could have killed you quickly, Etlu. Drained you to death. But that would be too simple. Your demise will be slow so that you may think about what you have relinquished for a mere woman -- a dead woman."

"She's not dead."

"My men captured her in the woods. She is dead, as you will be when I'm finished torturing you as you've never been tortured before. You think you understand pain? Your childish experiences are nothing to what you are about to learn."

Aru's scent faded and Etlu sat alone, his head resting against the rock, his flesh stinging and limbs aching. The need for blood was almost overwhelming. If he didn't get some soon, madness would claim him and death would follow swiftly. Unless Aru intended to feed him just enough to keep him alive until he grew bored with these savage games.

In spite of Aru's taunts, Etlu did not believe Niabi had been killed. If she had died, he would have sensed it. Her strong, living presence still existed in his heart and mind. She had escaped from both Aru and Etlu's evil. She was free, just as she should have been from the first.

"I think I finally understand," he whispered to the night. "I know what love is, Niabi."

Chapter Eight

"Etlu, can you hear me?"

A soft, familiar voice whispered so close to Etlu's face that the speaker's breath gently fanned his cheek. Around him floated muffled sounds of men and women talking softly as they went about their nightly chores. The scent of cooking food made his empty stomach grumble. Such comfortable, familiar sounds and aromas seemed like a dream.

A hand caressed his face. With each breath Niabi's beautiful scent filled him.

"Etlu."

He forced his heavy eyelids open and gazed at her beloved face, not truly believing she was there. After so many weeks trapped in Aru's pit, fed just enough blood to survive while enduring his Creator's torments, the presence of the only person he'd ever loved was unfathomable.

Growing up with Aru, he believed he'd suffered every possible agony and indignity, but during these past weeks he'd discovered his Creator had invented even more. No part of Etlu had escaped unscathed. So many times he'd longed for death. Only thoughts of Niabi offered any comfort. In the scorching light of day when he cringed, blinded and engulfed in pain in a dark corner of the pit, he would remember the times they had slept peacefully in each other's arms.

"It can't be you," he murmured, his eyes fluttering shut.

She kissed his eyelids and said, "It is me. I'm here. You're safe in the main house in your village. Aru and his followers are gone."

The wild scent of a powerful blood drinker wafted on the air, making Etlu's heart pound in terror. Only Aru had ever exuded such a scent, yet this aroma was not his Creator's. Etlu opened his eyes again, willing them to focus.

"It's all right." Niabi smiled slightly, smoothing hair from his forehead. Her hand felt wonderfully cool against his feverish skin.

"Who else is here?" he asked. "That scent --"

"After you helped me escape, I eluded Aru's minions and sought out my Creator. She and her traveling companion, Ariel, returned here with me and helped me reclaim your land. Ariel destroyed Aru. Afterward we found you in the pit. That was almost two days ago."

"Is he awake?" asked a deep male voice.

"He's starting to come around," Niabi said.

"Aru is dead?" Etlu could scarcely believe it.

"Yes," she replied.

"But he could not be killed. I have seen him survive fire, silver, heart injury. He told me the Evil One himself had made him indestructible."

"That is true," the male voice spoke again. This time a shadow fell over Etlu's bed. He turned his gaze from Niabi to a tall, pale man with piercing gray eyes. "I am Ariel. As your Creator was sent by the Evil One, I was sent by the Spirit of Good to whom all other spirits bow. I, and those few like me, possess the power to destroy all blood drinkers, even those empowered by the Evil One. We exist to punish the wicked."

"And me?" Etlu moistened his lips, cracked and blistered from exposure to daylight and weeks without enough water. "Will you punish me?"

"Ariel," Niabi said to the man, her eyes glistening. For the first time Etlu heard a plea in her voice. She had never begged for herself, but now she pleaded for him. This touched him profoundly. He reached for her hand, squeezing it gently, ignoring the way his fingers ached from the simple movement.

"By freeing Niabi and denying your Creator you've shown that you're capable of change. The question is, do you want it? If you prove yourself worthy of life, you need not fear my wrath. A man of your power can do far more good for our cause, alive and well, than punished for an unfortunate past. Remember my words, for your life shall depend on them." Ariel stared hard at Etlu for a telling moment before he turned and left.

"Do you want a new life?" Niabi moved closer to Etlu and placed her hands on his shoulders, her warm gaze fixed on him. "Do you want me?"

"I have never wanted anyone the way I want you. The only real happiness I have ever known was the time I spent with you."

"Etlu." She brushed his mouth with a tender kiss.

Folding his arms around her, he tugged her onto the blanket beside him, relishing the warmth and solidity of her body against his. "I vowed if I ever saw you again, I would tell you how much I love you," he said, stroking her hair. "I do love you, Niabi."

"I love you, Etlu."

"I don't deserve you and I have no right to ask, but will you be my wife?"

"Yes. Oh yes." She grinned, kissing him again, more deeply this time.

"From now until the end of time I will love you and only you, Niabi. You've freed my heart and I will dedicate my life to proving myself worthy of your love."

"You are." She leaned her head against his chest, one hand resting lightly on his bandaged side. "Now rest. Heal. We have centuries ahead of us to make plans."

Closing his eyes, Etlu drifted back to sleep, Niabi in his arms.

Epilogue

After Etlu recovered, he resumed his position as chieftain with Niabi ruling at his side. The effort he had once devoted to conquering and killing, he now turned to providing for the protection and happiness of his people. Eventually he turned leadership over to a worthy warrior so he and Niabi could move on to other lands.

The evil reputation of his youth faded as if it had never been. Like Niabi, he became known as a blood drinker of integrity and power. Together they upheld the spirit of good and every passing age strengthened their love and devotion.

Each dawn, when Etlu and Niabi settled to sleep in protective darkness, he held her close and whispered, "I love you, my heart. I am forever yours."

The End

Kate Hill

Kate Hill is a thirty-something vegetarian New Englander who likes heroes with a touch of something wicked and wild. Her short fiction and poetry have appeared in dozens of publications both on and off the Internet.

When she's not spending time with her family or working on her books, Kate enjoys reading, working out, and researching vampires and Viking history. Feel free to drop her a note at katehill@sprintmail.com or visit her website to learn more about her current releases and upcoming projects. You can find Kate online at http://www.kate-hill.com.

Changeling Press E-Books
Quality Erotic Adventures Designed For Today's Media

More Sci-Fi, Fantasy, Paranormal, and BDSM adventures available in E-Book format for immediate download at www.ChangelingPress.com - Werewolves, Vampires, Dragons, Shapeshifters and more - Erotic Tales from the edge of your imagination.

What are E-Books?

E-Books, or Electronic Books, are books designed to be read in digital format – on your computer or PDA device.

What do I need to read an E-Book?

If you've got a computer and Internet access, you've got it already!

Your web browser, such as Internet Explorer or Netscape, will read any HTML E-Book. You can also read E-Books in Adobe Acrobat format and Microsoft Reader, either on your computer or on most PDAs. Visit our Web site to learn about other options.

What reviewers are saying about Changeling Press E-Books

Dakota Cassidy -- Wolf Mates: An American Werewolf in Hoboken

"Ms. Cassidy's blend of humor and lust make for a marvelous read… [This] is a terrific book and I'm looking forward to more sinful humor from Ms. Cassidy."

-- Romance Junkies

Marilyn Lee -- Daughters of Takira

"A thrilling read from the first page, Daughters of Takira will bring a blush to the cheeks. A story that packs a powerful punch, it weaves vampires and science fiction into a short but satisfying plot. Daughters of Takira will blow your mind!"

--Romance Reviews Today

Eve Vaughn -- Agency of Extraordinary Mates: 4 Play

"The sex is hot, hot, hot, but how could it be anything else considering this is a ménage or should I say 4 Play romance! Eve Vaughn's Agency of Extraordinary Mates: 4 Play is one book you don't want to miss."

-- Lady Amethyst, Fallen Angel Reviews

Elizabeth Jewell -- Dark Callings I: Bloodlines

"...an unforgettably, blisteringly hot romp through the world of vampires, hunger and sex. This isn't one of those eroticas where sex is the main element; there is emotion, excitement, danger and, did I mention vampires? *g* This reader fervently hopes Dark Callings: Bloodlines is the first of many male/male erotic romances Elizabeth Jewell pens. Don't miss! "

-- Ayden Delacroix, In the Library Reviews

Camille Anthony -- Women of Steel 1: Marti Gets Her M.A.N.

"Ms. Anthony combines talented story telling and a humorous twist of stereotype to create this must-read tale! I loved this launch to the Women of Steel series and have read it more than once. If you like it hot, funny and positively addicting, then this is for you!"

-- Niniri Theriault, The Road to Romance

Willa Okati -- Freedom Rising

"The love scenes are passionate, erotic and tastefully written, with a plotline that keeps you turning the pages. I'm hoping Ms. Okati will write more stories about this fascinating paranormal world she has created. A keeper that I will be re-reading again."

-- Luisa, Cupid's Library Reviews

Ann Jacobs -- Luna Ten Chronicles

"Luna Ten is a hot, steamy, turn up the air conditioner to super high, have plenty of cold water on hand, type of read. You will do yourself an injustice if you do not add Luna Ten to your reading collection."

-- 5 cups from Coffee Time Romance

Michele Bardsley -- The Pleasure Seekers 1: Dake

"This book had that little something extra to keep me on my toes while reading it. The hero, in particular, was a pleasure and I found the sex scenes very erotic. Short and oh, so sweet, this yummy vampire tale has it all."

-- Johnna Flores, Coffee Time Romance

Rachel Bo -- Guardians 1: Heart of Stone

"Utterly amazing and completely unforgettable…every moment of this novella left me begging for more…wonderful depth not often found in a tale of this length…destined for my keeper shelf, where (it) will receive many rereads as I await the second book in the Guardians series."

-- In the Library Reviews

Kate Hill -- Dangerous Cravings: Disdain

Rated Five Angels - "Dangerous Cravings: Disdain by Kate Hill was another excellent example of skillful writing by a consistently fabulous author. I thoroughly enjoyed this book."

-- Serena, Fallen Angel Reviews

www.ChangelingPress.com

Printed in the United States
54060LVS00001B/86

9 781595 962843